BLACK TIDE

BLACK TIDE

KC JONES

NIGHTFIRE
A TOM DOHERTY ASSOCIATES BOOK
NEW YORK

This is a work of fiction. All of the characters, organizations, and events portrayed in this novel are either products of the author's imagination or are used fictitiously.

BLACK TIDE

A Nightfire Book
Published by Tom Doherty Associates
120 Broadway
New York, NY 10271

tornightfire.com

Nightfire™ is a trademark of Macmillan Publishing Group, LLC.

The Library of Congress Cataloging-in-Publication Data is available upon request.

ISBN 978-1-250-79269-3 (trade paperback)
ISBN 978-1-250-79270-9 (ebook)

Our books may be purchased in bulk for promotional, educational, or business use. Please contact your local bookseller or the Macmillan Corporate and Premium Sales Department at 1-800-221-7945, extension 5442, or by email at MacmillanSpecialMarkets@macmillan.com.

First Edition: 2022

Printed in the United States of America

0 9 8 7 6 5 4 3 2 1

For Kendra

for sticking with me that day on the beach,
and all the days since

BLACK TIDE

BEFORE

My mom once accused me of being a human car wreck. I laughed in her face when she said it. I was so covered in emotional scars by that point, her words could no longer draw blood. Also, it was kind of a funny picture. Go ahead, try to imagine it: You're at home. It's a quiet evening. Everything's fine, you're kicking back, jaw slack, entering the third hour of your current Netflix binge.

Then, a sound from outside: the screech of tires, an engine screaming into the red. You turn from the TV in time for headlights to blind you through your living room window. You might have a beat to register that something very bad is about to happen, to try to dive for safety, to get the hell out of there. But it's too late, and suddenly you're staggering through the smoking wreckage of your home.

And there I am, in the middle of it all—sprawled across your splintered coffee table, leaking out onto that expensive area rug, motor still humming along, feet thrashing stupidly—wondering what happened to the road. Eventually, I'm hauled off on a greasy flatbed, never to be seen again, leaving you with broken bits and bad memories and a burn or two.

Here's the part that isn't so funny: she wasn't wrong.

I've been like this for as long as I can remember—a driverless car perpetually careening toward my next big crash. I don't have friends, no besties or lovers, only victims who couldn't get out of the way in time. And I know one of these days, there won't be anything the body shop and wrench heads can do to get me back on the road. One of these times, they'll give my burnt-out, twisted self a scornful once-over and say, "Totaled." That'll be it. That'll be how I end. A hunk of rust in a forgotten, weedy lot off the interstate. A three-sentence blurb on page five. A nightmare that wakes you in a cold sweat, before you breathe a sigh of relief, comfortable in the knowledge that your world is safer without me in it.

I don't want that, despite what might look like a mountain of evidence to the contrary. I'm a liar, but I'm telling you the truth about this: I want to stay on the road. I want to go as far as these wheels and gears can take me.

The problem is, sometimes you don't know you're losing control until it's too late to correct. And it's hard to stick to the road when you don't even know where it is you're supposed to be going. I try, I really do. I tell myself to stay focused, to pay attention to the signs showing me I'm headed the right way. But eventually, the horizon begins to blur. I drift across the line. Before I know it, I've veered off at high speed and I'm barreling straight toward the next living room window or telephone pole—or cliff.

This time was different, though. This time, the car came through *my* window. It came through *everybody's* window.

This time, the world ended.

1

BETH

This time, the road took me to the edge of the Pacific Ocean, to a sprawling Northwest-style Craftsman, all cedar and stone, nestled along a lonesome stretch of Oregon coast called Neacoxie Beach.

It's not *my* house. God no. I could barely afford the gas it took to get me here from Portland. The driveway is made of wood pavers—like, *real* wood, I'm not even joking—and my shitty Toyota is parked on it like a giant turd dropped by some colossal, prehistoric horror. I keep waiting for somebody to call the police, to report a squatter in the house, except there's nobody else around.

Well, almost nobody.

The beach house is in a very private, very gated community called Strawberry Dunes. I don't know why—there aren't strawberries, and the dunes are the same muddy sand color as every other dune on the Oregon coast, blanketed in waist-high, pale-green beach grass I've come to learn is actually a non-native, invasive species. The upper crust has to gild everything, I guess. Where's the prestige in Weedy Lots off the 101 with Ocean View? Strawberry Dunes—whatever.

Most of the places in this development are for sale too. Transplants from Seattle or California or wherever who wanted a little slice of heaven, but aren't willing to stick around for the hell the winters can bring. Almost everybody who owns here is a strictly seasonal resident. By the time I arrived, they'd all hightailed it off to wherever rich people go at the first sign of bad weather. The couple who hired me are in Vietnam for three weeks. He's a veteran, wanted to go back and see how it all looks now, or something.

That's what I'm doing these days. Professional house-sitting. Thirty-three years old and spending my time sampling other people's lives, like an interloper at a gathering of socialites, stealing tastes of fine cheese and expensive wine from roving silver trays. Better than smashing through their living room windows, I suppose. The money isn't spectacular, but I like the variety. The constant change of scenery keeps me on the road—literally and metaphorically. Since starting this gig, I haven't been in one place long enough to get bored, space out, drift. Wreck. So that's good. It took a while to build up the requisite cred to do much more than water plants and feed cats, but I've managed to make it a pretty steady gig. Which is great, because my car was really beginning to voice its complaints about all the miles I was racking up doing take-out deliveries in between, which, in a foodie haven like Portland, was not insubstantial. This is the farthest from the city I've been hired. And it's easily the nicest place I've been entrusted to watch over. On a recommendation, no less. Which is a big deal. Like I said, historically I haven't exactly left people with very nice things to say about me. To have stuck out in somebody's mind as anything but a cautionary tale is what I call progress.

It's the first day of October. Friday. I've spent most of my time here on the back porch, curled up with a book in an Adirondack chair, like some kind of heiress. From the edge of the impeccably manicured lawn (not my job this time), a wide field of the invasive beach grass stretches to a gentle swell of dunes that just blocks my view of the ocean. It's visible from the upstairs bedroom, but the weather has been unseasonably warm this week, and I don't see any sense in wasting a minute of it indoors. The sky this evening doesn't even seem real. It looks painted by one of the landscape artists whose works fill the windows of half the shops in every tourist stop along the coast, full of soft clouds glowing purple and gold.

The air is heavy with mist, the roar of waves, and the smell of a campfire somewhere. I can't believe I'm being paid to do this—and far better than usual. Mom's just waiting for me to accidentally set one of these places on fire, a smug "Surprising nobody" already chambered and aimed straight at my heart. I'm not going to give her a reason to pull the trigger. Not this time. Not ever again.

Some evenings I can see shapes roaming around out there in the grass. Elk, looking for a place to bed down for the night. But right now, the dunes are empty. Jake probably scared them all off when we went for our after-dinner walk.

Jake is a dog, by the way. It isn't just the house I'm sitting. He's a four-year-old yellow Lab with enough energy to power the entire Pacific Northwest for a year. Seriously. Tear down the dams, hook some transformers up to a treadmill, put Jake on it, and shout, "Bird!"

Me and Jake get along, though I relish the few moments of peace I get after he's bird-chased himself into a coma.

As if he knows I'm thinking about him, Jake lifts his head and looks at me, his knowing brown eyes studying my hands for signs of Treat. Then his ears perk up, and he shifts his ever-alert gaze to the fence dividing this house from the neighbor's. A shrill sound builds in his throat.

"No whining, or I'll lock you inside and you'll miss out on this beautiful sunset," I threaten, rubbing his belly with my foot. He cuts his eyes back at my hands, but keeps his ears aimed at the fence, sniffing at the air with his wet nose. The smoke, it turns out, isn't from some distant campfire at all—it's coming from next door.

I peel myself from the Adirondack, walk barefoot through the cool grass, and peek over the sun-bleached cedar fence.

It's him.

He's sitting by a stone firepit built into his back deck. The fire spits sparks into the air, and by the glow of it, I get my first good look at his face; he's barely stepped outside since I've been here. If he owns a car, he doesn't drive it. I've never seen him at the mailboxes, and the HOA manicures his yard—though all the potted geraniums out back are shriveled and brown.

He's got a very North Coast vibe. Weathered and rough, looks like he hasn't shaved in a week, combed his hair in a month, or slept in a year. His scruffy beard is speckled with gray, matching the salty streaks in his otherwise dark hair. I think he might be in his early forties, but it's tough to tell at this distance.

I grab my Nikon camera from beneath the Adirondack and zoom in until I can see the fire reflected in his eyes. They're red and glassy, like he's been crying, or sitting in the smoke too long. He lifts a blue plastic Solo cup to his lips, takes a long drink, and refills it from a bottle of white wine. Wait, no—that's champagne. Who drinks champagne by themselves? The kind of person who sits outside on a picturesque coastal evening with their back to the sunset, apparently. He stares deeply into the cup, as if all the mysteries of the universe are swirling around down there, little beads of champagne sparkling gold in the hairs above his upper lip. The alcohol and warmth of the fire have brought a blush to his sun-starved pale skin.

The shutter clicks like a gunshot, and I duck back out of sight. Jake scrambles to his feet, eager to come to my defense, and I have to snap my fingers at him before he starts barking and gives me away. I toss him one of the little peanut butter–flavored squares I keep in the pocket of my hoodie.

I wait a moment, crouched at the fence, listening for approaching footsteps over the sound of Jake's tail whomping the ground. I don't think I've been made. I lift the camera to spy again. Nope, he hasn't moved. I probably could have shot an actual gun, and he wouldn't have looked up from the fire.

That fire sure does look nice, speaking of which. The champagne looks pretty decent too. The first thing I learned upon arrival was that the owners of the house keep it bone dry. Which isn't a bad thing, given how my past adventures with alcohol have ended. The last thing I need on my best gig yet is some nanny cam sending high-resolution video halfway around the world of me passed out and drooling all over the sofa while the dog eats peanut butter treats right from my pocket.

But one drink won't hurt, right? And a little company sounds nice. You can hold only so many conversations with a dog. It's not as if we have to be prisoners on these gigs.

Jake whines again, knowing what I'm about to do in that prescient dog way and doing his best to dissuade me. Before I can stop myself, before I can tighten my grip on the wheel and put my eyes back on the road, I open my mouth, take a deep breath of smoky, damp air, and say:

"Hey, neighbor."

≈

He looks at me with what appears to be great effort. Like he was about to nod off into a heavy, much-needed nap when I interrupted. He doesn't look too bothered. Not like he might were I a car smashing through his fence. See that, Mom?

I take my hand off the Nikon's focus ring and give him a friendly wave. Hopefully he doesn't find it creepy that I'm peering over his fence with a camera in hand. Why am I still holding the camera, anyway?

"Hi?" he says as if he isn't sure I'm even real.

"I thought I was all alone out here." I gesture vaguely at the world around us. Told you I'm a liar. "Seems like everybody else on the street already jumped ship for the season. Winter is coming."

"Call it a slack tide," he says with a somber nod. "We're between holidays, the kids are back in school, the weather's just starting to turn, but the storm watchers won't start arriving for another month. There aren't many year-rounders here." He pokes at the logs with an old hot dog skewer that's coated in rust. The sight of those warm embers sends a ripple of gooseflesh down my legs. Shorts and a hoodie are fine during the day, but the evening chill arrives fast and sharp as a switchblade in a dark alley.

"I've been here for a week," I say, hugging myself to keep from shivering. "This is the first time I've seen you. Just get in?"

"No, I've been here. I don't go out much."

"On vacation? Taking advantage of the quiet?"

"Something like that." The man is a wellspring of information.

"Well, now that you know I'm here, and we both know that we're alone, I suppose I have to wonder if you're going to try to murder me." I say it with a smile and a well-practiced, awkward half wink. He doesn't return them. Jake paces behind me, nails clicking on the composite decking. He clearly disapproves of my choice to engage this man, whose name I don't even know, and definitely disagrees with my pointing out that we're alone and murderable.

"I'm not going to murder you," the man deadpans. It's not particularly reassuring. Maybe Jake is right. After all, he's lived here longer than me. And dogs know things.

But my eyes are drawn back to that Solo cup, and the bottle he filled it from.

"I know you're not *going* to," I say. "I'd kick your ass from here to Sunday. What I said was 'if you *try*.'"

Finally he smiles. I feel like a thief who just found the family vault behind an old tapestry. Now it's time to crack it.

"I'm not going to try either," he says.

"Okay, then. How about you prove it and invite me over for a drink like a proper gentleman?" I'm putting on the act now. Slipping into character as easily as a comfortable pair of pajamas. It's a familiar performance that always gets me where I want to go, and never where I need to be.

"Isn't that exactly what I'd do if I were intending to murder you, though?" he asks, eyes narrowed quizzically. He's having fun with it now. I'm in. I can almost see Mom shaking her head in disappointment.

I shrug and look off toward the ocean, feigning second thoughts. I hear the foamy surf crash, roll up the sand, then recede. It's hypnotizing, that eternal, narcotic rhythm. For a moment, I forget what I'm doing. What I want. Another second or two, and the window of opportunity will close. He'll say look at the time, it was nice to meet you, and have a good night, and I'll go run a bath and fall asleep in front of the TV. We'll probably never talk again.

Would that be so bad? I know what will happen if he invites me to the other side of this fence. I know every line, like a show I've watched too many times.

"I suppose you're not wrong," I say, shooting him a mischievous side-eye. "But what the hell? I could use a little excitement in my life."

He laughs this time. Then darkens, as quickly as that surf retreats into the depths. He stares down into his cup as if reading the sediment. Determining his fate. I feel my tires slipping. Engine surging. He looks back at me, having caught a glimpse of headlights as I slide off the road and careen straight at him. This is his last chance. To save himself. To save us both.

"Why don't you come over?" he asks. "Have a drink with me?"

≈

He fills me a Solo cup of my own as I admire the champagne label. It's a vintage Dom Pérignon. I think that's a good brand. I sniff at it as if I know what I'm doing. It smells like champagne, and that's good enough for me. I take a dainty sip and smack my lips appreciatively. I don't know who I'm trying to impress, as he's been slugging the stuff like it's Rocky Mountain Kool-Aid.

"Goddamn, that's really good." I'm not lying this time. My only experience with champagne is the headache-in-a-bottle variety you pick up at the corner store for a New Year's Eve party nobody has any intention of remembering.

"It's pretty all right, isn't it?" Mike says. (That's right, I got his name first, so wipe that look off your face, *Mom.*) He watches as I take another—longer—drink. It warms me in a way the fire can't, through my veins and to the center of my bones, softening my edges and loosening all the various moving parts. "I'll send a couple bottles home with you," he adds.

"You have *more*?" I can't hide my surprise, which only further illuminates what an interloper I am. I always thought champagne this nice was something you treasured, kept in the basement for that one, truly special occasion. Of course he has a trove of it. He's probably saving the corks to pave his driveway. "What is this, like two, three hundred dollars a bottle?"

"I don't remember."

I fish a pack of cigarettes from the pocket of my hoodie. Smoking in the house is strictly forbidden. I haven't even dared to smoke outside, unless I'm down on the beach, lest some errant ember makes its way inside on the breeze and fulfills Mom's prophecy. But I'm on the other side of the fence now. There aren't rules over here. At least as far as I know. I tuck a cigarette between my lips and light it. "Mind if I smoke?"

"Go ahead," he says with a wave. I take a long drag and exhale into the chilly evening air.

"You want one?"

"No, thanks."

I lean back and enjoy another drink of Dom, swirling it around in my mouth, trying to appreciate it. Then I give up and swallow so it can get to its good work.

"So," I say, noticing Mike's eyes have found my bare legs. "You have a cellar full of expensive champagne. What did you do, rob a wedding reception?"

"No."

"You think anybody's ever done that? Robbed a wedding?" My thoughts are taking on that lazy, liquid quality, and I feel as if standing up might just send me floating off into those clouds with the smoke and sparks.

"That would be lower than worm shit," Mike observes, scratching his chin thoughtfully.

"But you could come away with some serious swag, right? Jewelry, heirloom silverware, a KitchenAid mixer—I'm sure those have street value, especially around here." I unzip my hoodie and pull it open, glancing left and right suspiciously, whispering: "Hey, Sharon. Whaddya need? Copper pots? I gotcha covered, sis. New Dyson? I'll hook you up."

Mike laughs harder than he should.

"And nobody's expecting it to happen, right?" I go on. "So nobody's packing heat. Well, probably not. Do your research. If it's Jimbo and Honeybear tying the knot at the county fairground, stay the fuck away."

We both laugh too hard this time. I fill the weird silence that follows with another drink, sucking champagne mist down my windpipe and erupting into coughs. Sexy, I know. Don't try this at home, kids. I'm a professional.

"For real, though," I sputter. "What's with the stockpile of primo bubbly?"

He blinks, my question bringing him back from some unknowable reverie. "It's for . . ." he begins, then stops to think about his answer. "Well, it's kind of a ritual—"

"I knew it. Here comes murder time after all."

"Not like that. It's just a way to unwind after wrapping on a project. Come up here to escape the hustle and the bullshit and the traffic for a few weeks. Then start the next thing and go back to L.A. renewed, hit the ground running. But that first night, it was all about popping a cork and watching the sun set. . . ." He trails off.

I wait for him to finish, to tell me what else the first night is about, but he doesn't. Off-limits, that topic. Fine. We all have those. I don't point out that he doesn't seem particularly interested in the sunset, or the fact that he's been here for at least a week. Maybe he's also a liar; maybe his champagne ritual isn't exclusive to just the one night. I don't really care, so I refill my cup.

"So what are you, a film director or something?" I ask.

"Producer. I directed a thing years ago. I think it's a rule that we all have to do that at least once. Avant-garde tripe that made the festival circuit and died a slow death in so many direct-to-DVD bargain bins."

"*Many* years ago, that."

"Yeah." He takes a long drink. I'm such an asshole.

"Well, it seems your other stuff paid dividends," I say, looking around at his house and yard. "Unless this place was a hand-me-down?"

"No, I've enjoyed my share of success. Started off making small genre films and programmers, but a few number-one opens gave my name a bit of weight. I'm no Bruckheimer, but . . . you know." He shrugs as if it's no biggie, like I probably know all about it.

I'm not sure I can actually imagine the kind of money that must come with being a name in Hollywood. Would it fit in a briefcase? A big canvas bag? See that? The very idea of such coin seems inherently criminal to me.

"Well, hey! Congrats! Cheers!" I lift my cup. He stares like I'm waving a live grenade. "You must have just 'wrapped' on something, then. Right? Isn't that why you're here? Celebrating? Your ritual?" This guy. Is he even fully conscious?

"Oh. Right. Thanks, cheers." He taps his cup to mine, and we drink.

My fingers are tingling and my feet don't feel like they're touching the deck anymore. I know I should take it easy or the champagne will kick my ass. But as soon as I slow down, this lightness in body and spirit will wane, and I'm not ready for that yet. One night, give me a break, I've been good.

"So what's the next project? When do you go back?" I ask. He actually winces. "Do you hate when people ask you that?"

"A little."

"Will you *pitch* it to me?"

"Nope."

I pretend to be horribly offended. "I bet you have it written down. I'm just going to have to sneak into your house while you're asleep and find it. You know that, right?"

Most guys, at this point, would take the opportunity to pivot the conversation to other things that might happen after I sneak into their house after dark. But Mike just smiles—a sight I'm beginning to like, as it makes him at least appear to have a pulse—and doesn't say anything. It's almost an invitation for me to try. He tops off his cup, then moves to refill mine, but only a few drops roll out. I meet his eyes for what feels like the first time.

"Exactly how *many* more bottles of that do you have?"

≈

We're well into the third bottle, and the sun has dipped low, a red ball of flame balanced at the edge of the world. Mike finally relented and turned around to watch the sunset with me. A narrow sandy trail cuts a path to the beach from his back deck; I can just see the white crests of waves where it carves through the dunes.

"So where do you live?" he asks. "Permanently, I mean. When you're not house-sitting."

"Portland." Not exactly a lie, but if I'm any more honest about it, I'm afraid he'll get weird, tell me to leave. "I'm here for a few weeks, which is the longest I've sat a place," I say, moving away from the subject of my own housing situation. Let's just say that, since I moved out of my parents' place, it hasn't been *ideal*. "They have a dog and didn't want to board him."

I almost forgot about Jake. The backyard isn't fenced and he hates the lead, so I put him inside before coming over. He's a good house dog in small doses, but he'll get bored soon. He'll need to poop. I should go take care of that and crate him if I plan to hang out with Mike for much longer. "I didn't know they had a dog," Mike says.

"I bet you didn't even know anybody lived there at all, did you?" I accuse with a smile.

He shrugs. "I don't think they've been there all that long. It's hard to keep track in this neighborhood. A lot of turnover. Lot of vacation rentals."

I can't quite wrap my head around him. It's as if he's here, but not. Like he somehow exists between worlds. He's a successful movie guy, but my employers never mentioned him living next door. Maybe they just wanted to protect his privacy. But more likely, they have no idea who he is either. I could count the number of producers I know by name on one hand, and I honestly don't even know what they do.

"I see you're a photographer as well as a dog sitter." He nods at my camera.

"Not really. It's just a hobby. I'm doing that thing where you take a picture of something different every day for a year, so you can look back at the end, see where you've been, what's changed. Oh!" I turn to look at the fence, where not too long ago I'd been peering over, gripping that camera like a paparazzo. "I bet you thought I was some kind of crazy fan, didn't you?"

He smiles. "It wasn't my first thought; it's been a very long time since I've enjoyed that kind of attention, and it was always just collateral damage. Nobody cares about producers, outside of scandals anyway."

"But you still can't be sure." Something about this idea makes me giddy. Couldn't have anything to do with a bottle and a half of champagne, nope. "You didn't even know you had neighbors, Mike. Which means you wouldn't know if they were dead and this whole house-sitting business is just my cover story to spy on you."

"Well, you kind of just gave it away, if it's true."

"Unless *that's* all an act too. What if I'm just playing innocent, getting you drunk so I can more easily restrain you? Maybe I'm a deranged starlet who wants you to put her in your next blockbuster? Break your legs so you can't escape until you've made the call to my agent?" Not that it would take all that much effort to keep him here, apparently. Mike would make a horrible horror-story victim. The villain would just get depressed and go home.

But Mike surprises me with a wry, suggestive smirk. It's the most human he's looked all night. The most alive. "Maybe I already thought of all that," he says, "and decided to just play along. My counterploy. Because maybe, like you, I could stand a little excitement in my life."

"Plot twist!" I laugh and inhale another mouthful of champagne and spend the next two minutes hacking my lungs up all over the deck.

"Can I see them?" he asks when I've quieted down. "Your pictures?" I was really hoping he wouldn't ask.

"Will you pitch me your new show?"

"Touché."

He tops off our cups. I really should go check on Jake, but I don't want to leave. Not quite yet. If I leave, I might not get to come back.

Mike gets lost in the sunset, and I join him.

"It's pretty, isn't it?" I ask. One of those stupid questions you ask when you don't know what else to say. Or you do, but you just don't want to. Like, *I'm having a really nice time but I need to go make the dog poop.* A sliver of sun peeks over the horizon. I see it reflected in Mike's eyes. They're watery again, and this time I know it's not from the smoke. That's okay. I get it. Sunsets can have that effect. Especially when viewed through a haze of inebriation.

"My dad always used to say it's important that people never stop appreciating sunsets," I say. It just kind of comes out, unprompted. Thanks, Dom. "As long as we can still be stopped in our tracks and remember what a big deal it is that we're even here, there's hope for us. We're just brief bursts of being on a tiny rock hurtling through the void. Our time is a gift and we shouldn't take it, or each other, for granted." My eyes unexpectedly well up, too, and I turn my head just enough so that Mike can't see. Dammit, Dad.

"I've always found sunsets to be rather melancholy," Mike says.

"You? Shocking. Why?"

"They're reminders that no matter what, inevitably, our day will come to an end too. No matter who we are, how we spent every hour, lived each second, eventually night will fall and that black tide will wash over every one of us just the same. And tomorrow the sands will be scrubbed clean. As if we were never here at all."

"You're a real cheery fucker, Mike. You know that?"

"Sorry."

"Don't apologize. Make it up to me, for killing the moment." He reaches for the champagne, but I stop him, leaving my hand where it landed atop his. "Actually, I had something else in mind."

Screech—crash!

2

MIKE

Well. That happened.

I have no idea what time it is. The clock on the nightstand has been flashing *12:00* since last winter, but midnight feels about right. More or less. Not too late but later than I meant for it to get. Late enough that I've had plenty of time to change my mind about things.

But I haven't.

My eyes trace the familiar patterns on the ceiling, the room washed in cold autumn moonlight, and then I look over at her. She's younger than me by a decade. Pretty and quite aggressive. Insatiable. I've been out of this particular game for too long; my heart was threatening to clock out before she'd even warmed up. What was I thinking? What was *she*? I don't look at myself in the mirror much these days, but I know it's not an impressive sight. Did I even take a shower this morning? I guess with enough champagne, it doesn't matter.

She's lying naked in my bed, the sheets pooled around her waist, this woman I met just a few hours ago. I still can't believe it. I've never done anything like that in my life. Tonight's full of firsts.

And lasts.

Goosebumps lend her tanned skin the appearance of low tide sand, cool and alluring and endless. She's snoring softly, and a few strands of hair have fallen across her face and stuck to her lips. I have to fight the urge to brush them away. I don't want to wake her. Because then I'll have to wait for her to fall back to sleep. And that will only give me even more time to think about things. To change my mind.

Maybe that's what she is. An agent of fate. A benevolent sprite, sand and sea coalesced into human form, here to pull me out of this current before it pulls me under. The notion makes me think of the sign at the end of the beach trail, the one cautioning anybody who happens to come by against venturing into the waves alone. No lifeguards on duty. There are a lot of those signs standing sentry along the North Coast beaches. Agents of fate in their own quiet way, though people rarely pay them any mind. Not until it's too late, anyway.

I slide quietly from the bed. My boxers and bathrobe are puddled on the floor, and I slip into them, the silky material whispering traitorously against my skin, as if trying to alert her. *He's up! He's on the move! Beth!* It doesn't work. She just keeps on snoring. I really didn't expect much else. There's a half-empty bottle of Dom Pérignon on the nightstand. I grab it and head for the door.

She rolls over, her snores stop, and for a second it seems like she might startle awake.

She doesn't.

≈

The window in the office faces the ocean. It's a clear night, and the moon paints the dunes in a ghostly pale hue. There's a ship out there on the horizon, a fishing or cargo vessel—I'm not sure. From here it's just a single twinkling light, a fallen star riding the waves.

I sit down at my desk. Been a long time since I've sat here. Feels a bit like coming home after an extended vacation, everything familiar yet also somehow changed inexorably by the passage of time, and you have to reacquaint yourself, as with old friends you haven't seen in an age. But there's no time for that tonight.

My workspace is clear except for my laptop and a lamp with a brushed nickel base and a green glass shade, both draped in a blanket of dust. I leave the light off and open the laptop. It takes a while to wake up, clicking and whirring groggily. Once it's fully roused, the word processor pops open cheerfully. Right where things left off. I'm surprised it can even remember that far back. I barely can. Back to when I still had so much hope for the future. Back to when I still dreamed.

There's a pale face staring at me from the window, from out there in the darkness, and I nearly jump straight up out of my chair. But this time it's only me, the glow of the screen a harsh key light ruthlessly illuminating the cavernous inset of my eyes, the dark bags beneath them where a year's worth of sleepless nights have gathered. I barely recognize myself, and quickly look away.

The cursor blinks eagerly, like a faithful old dog ready to follow me on another grand adventure. Wasn't Beth watching a dog? I hope it doesn't tear up the place. She'd have trouble getting more work after something like that. I don't know much about her—funny, considering what we just spent the evening doing—but I don't think she deserves that. I should probably go wake her, send her home, before going any further down this path. It's the decent thing to do.

Or maybe it's just the universe trying to get in my way again.

I hold Backspace until the page is blank. The cursor keeps on blinking, but it seems a little less enthusiastic now. Almost offended. *What sort of cruel trick is this? Will there not be an adventure after all?*

"Oh, there will be," I reassure it, taking a swig of warm champagne. "A very short one."

My fingers find their marks as easily as a well-rehearsed cast. Then they begin their dance.

≈

Beth,

First and foremost, I want you to know that this had nothing to do with you. I both appreciated and enjoyed our time together last night. I'm sorry for how that sounds, like I'm turning you down after a job interview. As I'm sure you can understand, this is kind of an awkward letter to write. What I'm trying to say is, it meant a lot to me. Maybe if we'd met two weeks ago, or two months, things would have turned out differently. But I doubt it. This has been a long time coming. And I sincerely apologize for putting you in the middle of it. It probably feels like I sprang a trapdoor beneath your feet. That truly isn't my intention. Maybe I should have stopped things before they escalated, but it felt good to have a connection with another human, even for such a short time. I didn't think I'd ever feel that again.

Thank you for spending an evening with a lonely lost soul. Keep taking your pictures. I wish you the best,

Mike

p.s. I'm sorry if that dog pees all over the house. Please find some way to blame it on me.

p.p.s. I meant what I said about the extra champagne. It's yours, if you still want it.

≈

The sand is cold and coarse between my toes. The salty breeze off the water billows my bathrobe and sends a chill into my bones. It will be October tomorrow. Or is it October already? It doesn't matter. Summer has been hanging on, fighting for life like a cornered animal, but it's a losing battle. Time to let go and accept defeat. I know all about that.

The dog started barking as soon as I walked out, but I don't think Beth can hear it. I glance back and see its outline in one of the second-floor windows, watching me. What did she call him? Jake? Be good, Jake, please, just for a few more hours.

There's something standing at the bottom of the gentle slope where the dune becomes the beach. Two legs and an elongated trunk that I again mistake for something it's not. A warm burst of adrenaline shoots through me. It's hardly the first time I've thought somebody was out here, shuffling up from the beach toward my house, creeping up to my window to watch me as I try to fall asleep. I've gone in search of disrupted sand or streaks of fingerprints on the glass, the sense of that presence so powerful, but nothing is ever there. Loneliness is a vicious drug.

It's just the sign. In the moonlight, I can read its various appeals to leash and clean up after dogs, its forbidding of fireworks or making campfires in the dunes. Above all that, in aggressive block letters demanding to be heeded, are the words DON'T SWIM ALONE—NO LIFEGUARD. This is accompanied by a crude, weathered illustration, like some ancient mariner's map of waters unknown, warning of rip currents lurking in the shallows like living, hungry things. Here be dragons, it may as well be saying with those little black arrows.

The champagne no longer has any taste or effect. My brain understands that there's no point and has simply switched off those particular receptors. I drop the empty bottle into the line of foam at the edge of the wet sand and walk farther, my naked feet slapping the beachface. In the daylight, I'd be able to see the sand change color beneath them, the pressure of my steps forcing the moisture down and away, like the footsteps of some supernatural being. I always thought that was pretty neat.

A breaker rushes up to meet me, soaking me to the knees. The cold ocean water stings for only a second; then my brain turns that off too.

The Milky Way expands above me, glowing. At least, I think that's what I'm seeing. I'm not an astronomer. But it's a breathtaking sight. We really are small. It never ceases to amaze me how big life feels until I come out on a clear night, far from any city lights, and look up. We're just riding the edge of that unfathomable spiral. What's it riding the edge of? And beyond that? What could be out there, so far away from anything we've ever managed to know? Here be dragons, indeed.

Another wave soaks me up to the hem of my boxers. I feel my heart beating now, fluttering around its cage like a startled bird. It, too, understands what's happening. That it's about to be retired of its singular purpose, and it has no idea what to do in the face of such existential finality other than simply go mad.

Something streaks through the sky above. Not a dragon, but a meteor burning through the atmosphere.

"I'm so sorry," I say to the ocean, to the sky, to the darkness. "I tried. I truly did. But I just can't do this anymore. I don't *want* to. Every sunset hurts as much as the first. I can't take another. I hope you understand. And forgive me."

The sky answers with a few more streaks of light. Acknowledgment. Encouragement, even. I've never been a religious person, but at that moment, I can't help but feel as though I've been heard. *It's okay. I'm here. I hear you, and I understand. Come be with me. Come join the stars.*

I lie flat on my back on the compacted sand and gaze up into infinity. The next wave crashes ashore. I feel the surf surging toward me, trembling every grain of sand and shattered shell in its path, like a front line of warriors charging headfirst into battle.

Then something happens. Something as unexpected and strange and wonderful as Beth coming into my life for one evening.

The sky fills with streaks of light. I've never seen anything like it. Meteors, thousands of them, maybe more. As if every star in the heavens is plummeting to earth. As if whatever magic keeping them suspended up there abruptly ran out. They sear through the night sky. I can even see trails of smoke as they pass. I haven't watched a meteor shower since I was a kid, but I don't remember them being like this. It's kind of scary. I hear booms like bombs going off overhead, incredible crashes as some strike the water.

A few miles up the beach, there's a flash brighter than any lightning, followed by what sounds like the earth itself splitting in half. I can't help but crane my neck to look, half expecting to see molten lava erupting like blood from a fatal wound.

But I don't see anything. The world has fallen so absolutely dark I have to blink a few times to convince myself my eyes aren't shut. The moon has all but vanished behind a towering cloud, though I swear the sky was clear just a minute ago.

The winking speck of that ship on the horizon flashes, then flickers out. There's a strange smell on the breeze, a foulness that reminds me of rotten eggs or the stink of a pulp mill. And suddenly I don't feel terribly alone on the beach. It's no reflection this time, it's no sign. Something is out here with me. The same something I've been catching glimpses of in the darkness outside my window, except tonight it's been granted a physical form. I hear it, an unsteady shamble, coming closer, closer.

Beth. It must be Beth, half awake and still drunk. She was roused by the drumfire of meteors blowing through the atmosphere. It probably shook the whole house. She followed me down to the beach. She's coming to see what's wrong. This makes the most sense, if I can just ignore how heavy those footsteps land. The fleshy slap against the sand, as if those feet are bloated to twice their usual size. The wet wheezing, like air being forced from lungs filled with fluid, doesn't sound much like Beth at all, and I've become intimately acquainted with her breathing.

"Beth?"

She doesn't answer, to my irrational relief. Maybe she's hurt. Maybe she's asleep. Maybe she needs me as much as I, right now and so unexpectedly, need her.

The tide reaches me before she does. It slams into my feet, washes over my legs, my chest, my face. I gasp, and it fills my mouth, rushes down my throat, and floods my lungs with burning pain. I hear that dog, no longer barking but howling, and now I'm afraid too. More afraid and uncertain than I've ever been in my life. I reach for Beth, trying to cry out for help. I've changed my mind. I don't want this. I don't want it at all.

And then everything goes black.

3

BETH

How the flipping fuck did I get *outside*?

I have no idea where I am. I must have sleepwalked? I've never done that before. At least, not that I know of. I've been plenty drunk in my time, but wherever I ultimately black out is always where I wake up again. The moon is full overhead. It's a weird color, like one of those creepy blood moons. Was it like that when we went to bed? I can't remember. I barely remember it rising over the mountains as we sat around Mike's firepit. I don't recognize the landscape it's illuminating—like *at all*—and I clearly remember that. Grassy dunes, lonely sands, Mike's backyard, they're nowhere to be seen. I don't even *hear* the ocean anymore.

I blink and rub the sleep out of my eyes, but I can't make them focus. I can make out only vague outlines of what looks like some craggy desert in Utah or Arizona or somewhere. Which is plainly nowhere near Neacoxie Beach, Strawberry Dunes, or any damn place I could have realistically walked even in the sober light of day. The sky is full of shooting stars—big ones. They burn through the night like coals blown from a fire. Most of them don't hit, they just kind of dissolve into nothingness, as if they're falling behind a curtain.

The sky is also full of things that kind of look like clouds, but also sort of like the stuff you see pictures of living down in the deepest parts of the ocean. Incomprehensible, shapeless blobs of life that have never known the sun's light. And the color of them . . . it's like no color I've ever seen. A constantly shifting iridescence that makes my head hurt.

Definitely dreaming here. We don't dream in color, right? That's why the cloud things don't make any sense. I'm trying to apply color logic where it can't exist. How much champagne did I *drink*? And what was it laced with?

"Mike."

I roll over and slap at the ground. It's cold and hard and solid rock. The air *reeks*, too. Not of drunken, sweaty sex but like a sewage treatment plant. It's almost a relief that the smell is at least marginally familiar. I haul myself to my feet.

Is it . . . *snowing*? Or something? Strange, ash-colored flakes drop lazily from the sky. I catch one in the palm of my hand. I wish I had my phone—the screen would provide better lighting than the sickly moon. But even in the muddy light, I see it's not a snowflake. Or ash. It looks like the husk of some insect that shed its skin before emerging as something new and bigger. It has too many legs on too short a body. Like a centipede met a garden beetle. I blow it away, but the feel of it lingers in my palm.

I need to get back—no, no, that would imply I've gone somewhere, which is completely unacceptable. I need to wake up. Yes, that's what I need. Wake up, Beth. Please.

Something screams.

"What!" I spin in the direction of the noise, my voice echoing off those craggy formations and finding its way back to my ears like the anguished cry of a mangled pet dragging itself home to die. Was that *Mike* screaming? That couldn't have been Mike. That wasn't a human sound. I don't know what it was, but it was too close for comfort. It's accompanied by another noise, a piercing warble like a squealing timing belt. I can't see anything in the deathly, burnt-out light of the moon.

"Mike!" I call out again, aware that with every outburst I'm drawing attention to myself. But that doesn't matter, because I'm asleep and dreaming. In fact, it's probably for the better. Hopefully the word will make its way from my mind to my lips and he'll actually wake me up. Maybe I'm hard asleep facedown in the pillow, so drunk even my subconscious can't think to readjust, and I'm asphyxiating into the soft, luxurious cotton.

Except I don't *feel* asleep. That's the most unsettling thing. I feel very awake. Very lucid. Very *here*.

Something else screams. Two somethings. One on either side of me. I hear them moving, like the tines of a pitchfork skipping across concrete. Both of them are making that timing belt trill. Together, they sound like crickets singing. Very big crickets.

"Hello?" I shout, and something runs across my bare foot. I leap into the air, my mind conjuring up images of whatever shed those husks. I kick wildly, my foot striking it and sending it tumbling, screeching in surprise, all those legs flailing.

That's when one of the cloud things turns. They aren't so high in the air as I thought. They're like . . . *right* above me. And they seem to have noticed me.

"Wake up, Beth!" I slap myself. Stomp on my foot. All I feel is pain, and it doesn't wake me up. The cloud thing moves toward me, expanding and contracting like a jellyfish shooting through the deep, trailing swirling streamers of bug husks. It makes a *whoosh-whoosh* sound as it cuts through the thin, rotten air. The shrieking things fall quiet in its wake, clearly having a better sense of self-preservation than me. How was I supposed to know the impossible dream clouds are also predatory?

"This isn't happening. You can't die in dreams." I can't move. The bottom of the cloud thing is splitting open in all directions, like a blooming flower bud, but there are no pretty colors within, only a darkness like nothing I've ever known, blacker than the deepest sleep. The bug husks are sucked into that void as it passes, and in a moment I will be too.

Why am I not waking up? What is happening?

One of those meteors passes right overhead, and the world lights up around me. Shapes scurry in every direction, disappearing into shadows and crevices before I can get a good look at them. In the brief flash, I see even those craggy mountains appear to be moving, covered in terrible life or living themselves, I honestly can't say. Neither would surprise me. I see columns of smoke in the distance, and when darkness returns, the faint flicker of faraway fires. Tiny, more human sounds reach my ears, voices wailing in confused terror, but I can't possibly pinpoint them, and after a moment, they're swallowed up by the chaos.

The jellyfish thing is so close that its repetitive *whoosh* is flipping my hair into my face, and through it I can just see long, limp arms reaching out for me, to grab me, to pull me up into that impossible black hole.

Wake up Beth wake up *wake the fuck up or you are going to die—!*

≈

I catapult from the bed, but my legs are tangled in sheets and my face smashes right into the hardwood floor of Mike's bedroom.

My God, his *bedroom*! Wood floor! I've never been happier to recognize a place. It's dark out, and I can still taste Dom Pérignon and the room is spinning because I'm still drunk. It's great. It's what's supposed to be happening, not being eaten alive by cloud monsters in some dank hellhole. I'm practically giddy as I crawl to the toilet and empty my stomach of some seriously evil nastiness.

"You bitch," I spit, my abdominal muscles screaming as they contract and twist, wringing my guts of every last remaining drop of caustic bile. This is the Beth we all remember, folks. Right here. Naked and retching, half tangled in sheets like some grotesque creature flopping from its cocoon. Happy, Mom? "Dumb, stupid bitch."

When I'm sure no more is going to come up, I stagger to the bed. There's a car alarm going off somewhere outside, but the awful smell is gone. The clock, which had been flashing *12:00,* seems to have died completely. I slap the nightstand blindly until I find my phone and wake it up, the light of the screen searing my retinas. Just as I do, it begins to screech, similarly to what I was hearing in my dream.

There's a text message on the screen, accompanied by an exclamation point. An Amber Alert, or maybe a storm advisory; I can't make out the details. I dismiss it and squint at the time until the numbers come into focus. It's only one in the morning. I turn the screen off and lie down. I should go get water. I should go back to my place. But I don't really want to do anything until my head stops spinning.

I don't know how long I lie there with my eyes closed when my phone starts screeching again. This time I'm able to shut it up without even looking. The car alarm, however, continues to wail in the distance.

"Whose car is that?" I ask Mike, but he doesn't respond. "You alive?" I think I say, and then sleep takes me again.

This time I don't dream at all.

≈

It's midmorning the next time I open my eyes, and the other side of the bed is empty and cold. Mike must be one of those intolerable types who never get hangovers and bound awake at the crack of dawn, ready for anything. I drag myself back into the bathroom and pee for what feels like an hour straight.

"If I don't smell coffee soon, there's going to be blood!" I shout, the sound of my own voice cracking against my skull like a hammer. Wherever Mike is, he doesn't respond. What a jerk. At least the car alarm has finally shut up.

My legs are so weak I have to lean against the counter just to stay upright long enough to rummage through Mike's medicine cabinet. I need painkillers. Hospital grade. And industrial-strength mouthwash. If it doesn't burn away the top layers of my mouth and melt my teeth, it isn't strong enough. He has some weak-ass, generic aspirin. Sure. I swallow four of them. And there's no mouthwash, so I settle for squirting a blob of minty toothpaste onto my finger and smearing it on my teeth. As I'm polishing away the bitter film, I feel something gritty scraping my gums.

Both my hands sparkle with coarse sand. Coarser than the stuff on the beach, little flat flakes that glint like tiny razor blades. It must have come from the beach, though. Where else?

My mind briefly flashes to that alien landscape, to the rocky surface I "woke up" on. But that's impossible, obviously, as that was an alcohol-fueled nightmare. The sand stuck to our feet while we were sitting on Mike's deck. We tracked it into bed, and now it's in my damn mouth. I spit and rinse until there's no more grit.

I swallow a few gulps of lukewarm water. My stomach quivers uncertainly, but it stays down. I'm about to go hunt for Mike when I notice a blue toothbrush in a little wooden stand on the counter. There's also a green one. Nearby is a hairbrush, a few long brown strands tangled in the teeth, which don't look an awful lot like Mike's.

He didn't. . . .

There's a pair of skinny jeans and a bra at the bottom of the clothes hamper. Back in the bedroom, I zero in on the bookmarked novel on each nightstand, the driftwood earring hanger on top of a bureau, the walk-in closet half filled with a woman's clothes.

He did.

"Mike!"

≈

He's not in the kitchen either. The coffee maker is dark and dusty—like everything in the house, I'm beginning to notice. Dust and grime and clutter. Neither Mike nor Mrs. Mike are very concerned with basic housekeeping. I'm a little surprised somebody doesn't come do it for them when they're gone.

She must be away. Visiting family or on a work trip or something, that's why I haven't seen her around. And why he didn't bother to mention her. Didn't want to scare me off. He knew she wouldn't be home, he wouldn't be caught.

I backtrack through the house. The power must have gone out, because none of the lights are working. I glance into dark closets and a bathroom—the sink and tub and toilet bowl ringed with mildew—until I come into what must be his office. The walls are lined with bookshelves crammed with a disarray of titles, from classics to contemporary, fiction and nonfiction. A few are behind glass. Those look like they're a century old. There are a few movie posters on the walls, too, signed by actors and directors. The projects that paid for this house and all that champagne. I've even seen two of them. Seen Mike's name flash across a screen, back when it held no meaning—no "weight"—to me at all. What a small, strange world.

Also among the posters is a faded framed photograph, featuring Mike, much younger and grinning in a way I wouldn't have thought possible last night. Beaming like he was the happiest person alive at that moment, proudly displaying a check for $2,500 from some obscure production company. Obscure to me, at least.

He isn't wearing a ring in the picture. Maybe he wasn't married yet. Maybe he just doesn't wear one; he surely wasn't wearing one last night. That isn't so strange, I guess. Or maybe she's just a domestic partner. Why am I trying to rationalize this?

There's another picture in the room. This one is on the window sill, facing his desk. The picture is of a woman standing at the edge of the ocean at sunset. She's radiant, laughing, the water splashing around her ankles, the wind blowing her sun-singed hair. It's the same color as those strands in the comb.

I step up to the desk and look out the window. I've seen Mike in this same spot, on my walks. Lost in thought. Working on whatever his next thing is, I suppose.

My eyes drop to his laptop. Also coated in dust, but streaked recently by fingers. The lid isn't closed all the way, as though he left in a hurry and didn't quite push down hard enough. I don't know why I do it—with all the other discoveries I'm making this morning, this should be the least of my concerns—but I carefully lift the lid with my index finger, as if it might be booby-trapped and start spewing poison gas. It's probably password protected at the least; Mike hadn't seemed too terribly concerned by my threat to sneak in and read about his next project.

The screen wakes up. It's plugged into the wall, but running on battery, confirming that there's an outage. Maybe that's what Mike is away checking on. There's no password prompt, no log-in. Just a word processor, open to a blank page. The document isn't even titled. Well, that's anticlimactic. Is he having a bit of a creative block? That would explain why he didn't want to talk about it. I have the urge to start hitting Undo, out of spite, just to see if he'd been writing something, but right then there's movement outside the window, and I slap the lid shut.

It's Mike. Dressed in blue jeans and a flannel shirt on top of a plain gray tee, walking up the narrow beach path. He's carrying a bright red bucket. From the way he's struggling, it must weigh a hundred pounds. What did he do, go clamming? And what business does he have looking so normal? So not hungover, guilty, miserable? I just spun off the road and crashed through the side of his perfect little life—why does he look *fine*?

I stride from the room to put a proper damper on his day.

4

BETH

Mike stops when he sees me standing on the deck, my arms crossed and hips angled in that *don't even think of it* way women are born knowing. For a moment, he looks ready to bolt, as if he completely forgot I was still in the house and thinks it's Mrs. Mike standing before him, *I know what you did last night* in her stance and murder in her eyes. He shakes it off and breaks into an uncertain grin, like he's still not sure I'm really here.

"You're not going to believe this," he pants. His energy is infuriating. But before I have a chance to knock that stupid grin into the sand, something comes streaking out of the grass behind him, a flash of gold and big brown eyes and slobbery pink tongue.

"Jake!" I scream. *Oh shit the dog how did I forget about the dog it's over everything is ruined you did it again just like always what is the matter with you*

I drop to my knees and Jake crashes into me with the force of a tsunami, knocking me backward and drenching me with kisses. I'm about to cry. I'm not going to cry. I cannot believe I forgot this poor dog. I literally had one job to do. I'm going to cry.

"Everything is fine," Mike reassures me, still looking around as if he's not completely convinced of that. "The house is all in one piece. He got on the bed, and the couch, but nothing a good vacuuming won't fix. He's also been fed and went on a nice long walk with me."

"You . . . *when*?" I gape at him.

Mike's eyes drop to the ground at his feet. "I couldn't sleep. There was a meteor shower last night. I went outside to watch and I heard him barking. I thought maybe he was upset, being alone, so I brought him over. He slept in the office. He's a good boy."

I can tell that isn't the whole truth, no surprise there, but it does account for why Mike wasn't around to save me from dying in my sleep. From being eaten by cloud jellyfish. Weren't there meteors in my dream too? I feel like I remember that. Reality and dreamland briefly bleeding together, it must have been.

"You should have woken me up. I would have gone and got him," I say. Except I did wake up. And then I went right back to sleep. Because I am literally the worst. Mike looks up at me strangely, and I wait for him to point this fact out too.

"I actually thought you had gone back," he says instead.

"What do you mean?" I string the words together carefully, as if I'm under cross-examination. I thought I had last night's weirdness all sorted out, and now here's Mike, trying to poke holes in my story.

He frowns, as though this is something I shouldn't have to ask. "I looked in on you," he says, almost as if he's trying to convince himself of this. "I was going to ask if you wanted to bring Jake over. You weren't in bed. I went next door and knocked, since he was still barking, but you weren't there either. When I came back, there you were, snoring away." He stares at me expectantly, waiting for me to clear this up in a way that makes perfect sense.

"I was probably in the bathroom," I say. I'm more concerned about the fact that Mike was able to waltz in and get Jake, meaning I left the house unlocked too.

"Hey," Mike says, following my train of thought. "Don't kick yourself. We had a lot to drink and got carried away. But it all worked out. Jake's fine, the house is still in one piece, and my lips are sealed."

"Yeah, speaking of keeping secrets," I say, brushing sand off my shorts and reassuming my stance, anger renewed. Mike goes rigid.

He already knows what I'm about to say. They always do. If his jaw wasn't better attached, it would have dropped right off onto the ground. I fight off the image of Jake grabbing it and running away. "Is there something you want to tell me?"

He looks behind him, toward the beach, as if calculating the quickest method of escape, then back at me, his lips parted and trembling just slightly. He doesn't know how much I know, or what I plan to do with it. But I don't feel like waiting on him to figure it out.

"Are you married?" I ask, point-blank. He goes slack with relief, which is not the reaction I was expecting at all. What did he think I was talking about?

"No. I'm not," he says.

"Then whose stuff is that inside?"

"What I mean is, I *used* to be married. I'm not any*more.*"

"Yeah, heard that one before. Usually right before somebody comes home sooner than expected. A good laugh all around does not often follow."

He slumps down into one of the chairs by the cold firepit. The sight of those charred logs, the black, dead embers, makes me wish we could rewind to last night. To that hour or two around the fire, watching the sunset. How could he find sunsets melancholy, anyway? Sunsets are when the magic happens. Morning, now *that's* a bummer. Case in point.

He takes a deep sigh, thinking over his confession. As if I'm the one who's going to be hurt by it. Although this time I might be. Obviously, I'm not some puritanical girl who's going to go home and shower in holy water—surprising, I know—but I have to spend another week next door. If Mrs. Mike comes back and learns what happened, she might decide to tell my employers. I can already see the review: Homewrecker screwed the neighbor and forgot the dog, zero stars, do not hire, if seen call the police.

"She left," Mike says flatly. "A year ago. Walked out that door right there and never came back. I'm sorry for not telling you. But you don't have to worry about there being any drama. Any more than this, that is."

I can't tell if I believe him or not. I want to ask him why, what did he do, was there somebody else like me, was he pulling his dick out during casting sessions? But I have other questions. Namely: "And you just . . . kept all her stuff exactly the way she left it?"

"Yes."

"That's weird, man. And probably unhealthy. A *year*? And her dirty underwear is still in the clothes hamper?"

He nods sheepishly. "I know."

"Were you hoping she'd come back or something? Pick up right where she left off?"

"No." Mike makes a choked sound that might be either a suppressed laugh or a sob. He nudges one of the rusty hot dog forks with his shoe. "I keep meaning to clean up, move on. It's easy to avoid doing the things you need to do out here. Especially when there's no one around to light a fire under you." He gestures at the empty, lonesome dunes. I guess I get that. There have been times this week where I've felt like I may as well have been on Mars. "Again, I'm sorry I didn't tell you. It just didn't seem . . . relevant."

"At least not until after you'd fucked me," I say. I'm expecting him to retreat even further into himself, to become that husk I saw sitting here last night, drinking alone with his back to the sunset. Instead, he looks up at me, his eyes sharper and clearer than I've seen them.

"So you told me everything there is to know about Beth, then? Didn't leave anything out so as not to spoil the mood?"

Normally, I would take this opportunity to thank him for looking after Jake, and for the champagne, and go back across that fence and make certain he never saw me again. I don't need this. I'm not the one who imploded his life. It isn't too often I crash into a house that's already been burned to the ground, and that makes it easier than ever to walk away.

Except, for some reason, it's not. There's a quiet desperation in Mike's eyes, behind the accusation. Like a part of him is pleading for me not to go, not to leave him alone with whatever ghosts are in that house. Which is far more responsibility than I signed up for.

Jake abruptly breaks away from me and goes to Mike, nuzzling his hands until Mike relents and scratches behind his ears. Jake swishes his tail contentedly, craning his neck to look back at me, firing guilt beams from those impossible brown eyes. Like how dare I even consider prying him away from such superior scritches. What a brat.

"Fine," I say. "The least you can do is make me breakfast when the power comes back. A clam scramble should do it." I walk toward the bucket he left sitting in the sand.

"It's not clams," Mike says, standing up and following me.

"Oysters? Even better." But it isn't oysters either. What it looks like is a bowling ball, washed in with the tide and coated in sand and barnacles. Or one of those glass floats you can sometimes find on the beach or in overpriced coastal home décor shops. But this one isn't the usual soft green or blue color I'm used to. It's black as obsidian, the sheen dull, and the barnacles seem to actually be a part of it, not just aquatic hitchhikers.

I glance up at Mike. That harrowed look is gone from his eyes and he's actually grinning, relieved to have moved on to a topic with fewer sharp edges. Although some of the barnacle things do look pretty prickly.

"What is this?" I ask.

His grin widens. "It's a *meteorite.*"

I stare down into the bucket. A whine rises from Jake's throat, and he takes a step back, ears perking up.

"Holy shit."

"Yeah. Like I was saying, there was a major shower of them last night. I could see impacts up and down the coast, and hear them hit the water. I went out at daylight to see if any of them washed ashore. Jake helped, he homed right in on the thing like he could sense that it didn't belong anywhere near this beach. I honestly expected it to have disintegrated, but, well, look at it!"

None of the meteors in my dream were hitting. Just disappearing halfway between the sky and the ground. Maybe my champagne-drenched brain just didn't pick up on the sounds of them landing.

Or maybe that's what the awful screaming was about. A duet with my phone and strange rocks shrieking through the atmosphere. Who knows what the cloud jellyfish was supposed to be.

By this point, Jake has become a puddle on the ground, tail whomping furiously. When he sees me looking at him, he whines and flops onto his side, as if the weight of his distress is just too much to bear. What's his deal? Is he just mad that not all the attention is being directed at him?

For some reason, I kneel and reach into the bucket. Never touched a space rock before, so why not? Jake is on his feet in a flash, letting out a sharp bark at the same time Mike grabs my wrist.

"Don't," he says, squeezing hard enough to hurt. "Don't touch it."

"Is it still hot?" I ask, pulling my hand away. I don't know, this isn't my field of expertise. But I really don't like the alarm in Mike's voice, as if I were about to grab hold of a live power line.

"Not exactly, but it does burn. Kind of like getting chili pepper seeds on your hands. I had to use leather gloves to pick it up."

"It *stinks* too. What *is* that?" I can't identify the odor. It falls somewhere between rotten eggs and dead fish on the foulness spectrum, but also like nothing I've ever smelled before.

Wait.

That isn't true. I *have* smelled it before. I smelled it last night. In my dream. What is even going on? No way I smelled this thing from the bedroom. Unless . . . If as many of them were falling as Mike says, and there was a wind off the water, the smell *could* have wafted inside when Mike opened the door to check on me.

These explanations are becoming painfully weak. I should just tell Mike about the dream. He could probably clear things up.

"It's pretty ripe, isn't it?" he agrees. "Sulfur and stardust."

Another idea comes to me. One better than reaching into a bucket and fondling an extraterrestrial object with my bare hands.

"Hey, hold on a second." I dart back into the house and grab my camera off the kitchen table, where I'd left it last night en route to the bedroom. Dad will flip out, seeing this. Even if he won't remember it. "Makes a pretty good picture of the day, don't you think?"

"There might be a bigger one a mile or two up the beach. I heard it hit. Felt like an earthquake. I think it even set off the tsunami warning system. You can just hear the siren in Gearhart from here."

"I thought that was a car alarm," I say.

"Those were going off too," Mike says. "It was quite a show. I bet we can find it. *That* would make a hell of a picture."

I really shouldn't. I should take Jake home and clean the dog hair off everything, then clean myself and get back into my routine of reading and daydreaming and being a good little house sitter. I went off the road last night. Not as bad as I could have, that was lucky. I shouldn't push it.

But a change of scenery might get the claws of that awful dream out of my head. It might do us both good. I just need to make sure the door is locked this time.

"And Jake can come with us," Mike adds, sensing my reluctance. I look down at Jake. He angles his head to stare at me with hopeful eyes.

"Okay, deal. I'll even pack us a picnic. Do you have any orange juice?"

≈

Mike drives a Subaru. An Outback, three or four model years out of date. That surprises me. When I think of that woman in the picture, of movie deals and beach houses, I think of a convertible and sunglasses and windblown hair, not a family wagon. Maybe she took the Porsche when she left.

We have to jump-start it. The Subaru has been sitting neglected in the garage for so long there's a black widow living under the hood. Right by the battery, of course.

"We could just take yours," Mike suggests grimly, waving at my Toyota.

"Do you see that thing?" I scoff. "If it goes down onto the beach, that's where it will stay until the end of time. And I can't exactly afford a new car right now."

I do the jumping. Mike doesn't know anything about cars. I leave the Subaru idling to charge the battery and go inside to make lunch and call the bosses, to assure them all is well in case they heard about the meteors striking near their home. I don't know what time it is right now in Vietnam, but it's no real surprise they don't answer, so I leave a pleasantly bubbly voice mail. The power is still out, to the whole development it seems, which makes me a bit apprehensive about leaving, but Mike reassures me that it's just part of life on the coast, with high winds—and apparently the occasional meteor shower—knocking trees into poles. It'll probably be back on when we return and I can spend the afternoon resetting clocks.

It's past noon by the time we're cruising along the sand, the windows down, a salty breeze twirling my hair. I'm so ravenous I have to resist devouring both sandwiches when I open the cooler for the jug of orange juice I'd emptied a bottle of Dom into. I shake it gently and help myself to a long sip. A little hair of the dog. No offense, Jake.

"Mimosa?" I pass the jug to Mike. He takes a swig and nods his approval. "Let me see your phone," I demand, holding out my hand. "I want to Google this meteor shower. I think finding them whole like you did is actually pretty rare. Could be a big deal, who knows?" I remember a meteor or something years ago, flying over Russia. I saw the YouTube videos, the flash and bang scaring everybody shitless, blowing out windows. They found only tiny pieces of that one, I think. Maybe that's all Mike found. What constitutes a "tiny piece" of space rock? What is it supposed to look like? And why would it leave a lingering burn when touched and stink like it was dredged from a sewage treatment plant? So many questions.

"I don't have a cell phone," Mike says. I keep my hand out, waiting for the punch line, but it doesn't arrive. Neither does his phone.

"What?" His words in that order don't make any sense to me. "Like, you didn't *bring* one, or you don't have one *at all*?"

"Oh, I'm sure it's around somewhere. But it turns out if you stop paying the bill, they stop working. Who'd have thought?" He shrugs.

"Why would you stop paying the bill? Don't you have people you need to talk to? An agent? Studio people?" I get that he comes here to be off the grid, but this is ridiculous. Hollywood doesn't just stop because Mike wants a breather.

"Where's *your* phone?" he deflects.

I sigh and fish it out of my pocket. "I just didn't want to drain my battery," I tell him, annoyed. I help myself to another drink, holding the phone up to the windshield. "How is there no service at all?"

"It comes and goes out here," Mike says.

I shove the phone back into my pocket. It's already getting hot, looking for a signal. My Wikipedia deep dive will have to wait.

There are cars ahead. A half dozen, parked on the beach just beyond a sandy access road. People out beachcombing, maybe. Or clamming. Or meteor hunting. I don't actually see anybody, though, except one guy pacing around aiming his cell phone at the sky, and a young girl hovering nearby, watching us approach through a pair of binoculars so big I'm surprised she doesn't just tip over.

Jake whines from the hatch area. Poor pup has been so stressed out all day. The meteor shower really messed with his head. I don't blame him, really; last night was weird all around. Right now he can't decide if he wants to sit, stand, or pace in agitated little circles. Too bad he can't have any mimosa. I'm already feeling the morning's edge soften.

"It's all right, buddy," I coo. It doesn't help. I toss him my last peanut butter treat. He just looks at it forlornly. Wow. Maybe I should get him to the vet.

"Looks like we're not the only ones who had this idea," Mike observes.

The first vehicle we pass is a red Jeep Wrangler—big tires and a removable plastic top—and then a bit farther on, the main cluster of vehicles. An SUV, a couple of sedans, and a nice pickup. I spy another of those strange bowling ball–looking meteors—no, sorry, meteor*ites,* according to Professor Mike, since they survived the fall. It's lying in the sand past the man with the phone. He doesn't show any interest in it. And he seems to have found some bars, since he now has the phone pressed hard to one ear.

He has a crew cut and wears a tank top that shows off toned, tattooed biceps. He looks annoyed by whoever is on the other end of that call, a vein protruding alarmingly on his forehead. If I had to guess, I'd say the girl is maybe eight, with dark, inquisitive eyes, and a cascade of loose, black curls down to her shoulders. She lowers the binoculars and wanders toward the meteorite. Crew Cut moves to shoo her away from it, his face soft but stern. Apparently he, too, knows not to touch them. From experience?

The girl redirects her attention our way, breaking into a broad smile and waving as we pass, as if we're old friends she's been waiting on to arrive. The binoculars bounce heavily off her chest, nearly knocking her over. They look powerful. Expensive as my camera (which Mom made sure to tell me the price of, as if it were my fault, before hiding the credit cards in a place Dad wouldn't find them). I take a gulp of mimosa and lift the jug in a toast. Then I realize it isn't me she's waving at. It's Jake. His tail gives the floor a single whomp, then his attention turns to the dunes, and another whine builds in this throat.

"You know them?" I ask, meaning Crew Cut and the girl.

"No," Mike answers. "We were never really here long enough to get to know anybody." I follow his stare to the other vehicles. Most of the drivers and passengers are, oddly, sitting inside, gazing at us with bleak expressions. A middle-aged woman in a T-shirt and pajama pants, like she crawled out of bed to come down here, leans against the rear bumper of her car, cradling her head in her hands and rocking back and forth as though she's going to be sick. Somebody else partied too hard last night, looks like.

Jake barks. Then, apparently having scared himself, collapses into a quivering ball on the floor and whimpers. I really don't like how upset he is. Like he senses something about this situation that we're both missing. I wish he could talk. Mike doesn't comment, but I see him eyeballing the sick-looking woman. He feels the strangeness in the air too. It's palpable, even if I can't quite identify what it's all about. I wake up my cell phone again. Still no bars for me, and just checking has chunked my battery life down by almost a quarter.

Once we're well beyond the crowd, Mike makes a sweeping turn until we're facing the waves; then he kills the engine. Hopefully one of them has jumper cables, in case the battery craps out again. I don't think we drove long enough to charge it, and the Subaru's an automatic transmission, so we won't be able to push-start it. You become very aware of these things when you drive a car that's held together mostly by duct tape and prayer.

"Why we stopping?" I ask. "You think this is where the big one hit?"

"No, I'm just . . . curious about something." He gets out without offering more, and I get out with him. Jake whines in protest.

"We'll be right back, buddy," I assure him, and close the door.

He yelps in despair, like he firmly believes we'll never come back at all. This is why Jake's people didn't want to board him. He hates being left alone in small places. Even crating him is torture. He was born to run. I'd let him out here, but I don't want him to see us near the meteorite and get even more anxious.

The air is already heating up. This unusually warm fall is going to reach its apex today, I think. A perfect day to spend on the sand. I fill my chest with that clean, rejuvenating ocean breeze, then set off after Mike, sealing our fate.

5

MIKE

What are they all doing here?

There aren't any kites in the sky. No dogs running around or beach chairs set out or sandcastles being built. Did these people all come to look for meteorite pieces? If that's the case, why are they sitting in their cars? And why all the vacant, glazed faces? It feels as if we've driven through a funeral procession.

I set my sights on the meteorite half sunk in the sand. Beth trails close behind. She left the dog in the car, which I'm glad for. He seems so concerned about everything. Maybe that's why there aren't any other dogs out. Jake threw a fit when we found the first rock this morning. I thought he might bite me, just to get me away from it. He'd decided by then that I couldn't be left to my own devices. He wouldn't even let me leave the office after I brought him over last night, not without crying and throwing himself against the door. As if he'd known exactly what I'd been up to down there on the beach, and worried that as soon as I was out of his sight I'd do it again. And I won't say I didn't think about it. Lately it's been all I think about. I certainly never expected a stranger, a dog, and a few falling stars to alter the course of things.

The man on the cell phone looks at us warily as we approach the rock, like an attendant at some tourist attraction who's been yelling at touchy gawkers to keep their hands behind the rope all day. But he doesn't say anything, until the little girl wanders toward us.

"Natalia!" he snaps. "What did I tell you? Stay away from that." He throws me an annoyed look, like it's our fault she doesn't listen. The girl, Natalia, sulks away, then directs her binoculars toward my car. I should get binoculars, now that I might be hanging around on this rock for a bit longer. Or better yet, a telescope. That would fit nicely in the office window. One of those fancy ones you can control with your computer. Punch in *Andromeda* or *Orion* or *Mars,* and there it is on the big screen. Listen to me. One astronomical event, and suddenly I'm Neil deGrasse Tyson.

"She's fine!" the man barks at the person on the other end of the call. "She doesn't need to get back in the car. Would you stop? She's safe out here, I told you. I can see for miles in both directions. I'm more worried about you. Where are you?"

"What is it you're curious about?" Beth asks, interrupting my eavesdropping. We're both standing a few feet from the meteorite now, neither daring to take that final step forward, as though it might blow up. Which is ridiculous, of course. But something about it has my warning bells clanging like last night's tsunami siren. "It smells as bad as the last one."

"It looks exactly like it too," I say. This is what I'd noticed as we were driving by, and now I'm certain: this rock is identical in every way that I can see with my untrained eye. The same size, shape, and coloring as the meteorite I lugged off the beach in a bucket, Jake whining at my heel the whole way.

"Does that mean something?" Beth asks.

"I honestly don't know. You'd think, being pieces of space debris that burned through the atmosphere before smashing onto the beach, they wouldn't look so . . ." I wave vaguely at the thing. The word I need slips through my fingers and darts away into the murk, wanting to be said about as much as I want to say it. "I've seen pictures of meteorites, they're . . . well, they look like what you'd expect. Like hunks of rock. This—"

"Looks like an alien's bowling ball," Beth says, grabbing the word fearlessly and throwing it onto the deck to flop about between us. *Alien,* that is. Not *bowling ball.* But she isn't wrong there.

"Right. Which I thought was just an anomaly with the first one I found. A perfectly round piece that broke off and survived the landing intact. But here's another, *exactly* the same."

She snorts. "'An anomaly.' Maybe you should consult your colleagues back at the university."

"I just thought it was interesting, that's all. I'm not trying to say I get it."

"All right, it *does* seem weird, I'll give you that." She puts her hands on her hips and looks around. "It also seems like we're the only people dumb enough to stand this close to them. So maybe we stop doing that until we know more about them. I mean, that smell, it can't be healthy. It's extraterrestrial. By definition, right? Whatever that funk is, it isn't from Earth."

We both take a large step back at that. The rock has no reaction to this slight on its character. The look on Beth's face, however, tells me she wishes she hadn't said anything. It's a bit creepy, when you think of it that way. Of all the things these rocks have passed by, and through, on their way here from wherever.

The palms of my hands begin to itch where I touched the thing. I wipe them on my pants and tune back in to the man's conversation. What was that he was saying about being safe on the beach? Safe from what, exactly? Certainly not the smell; the breeze is distributing that all over the place.

"No, I don't have an ETA," he's saying in mounting exasperation. "He's still gotta get down here from the marina. We're probably not the only ones who had this idea, so it could be busy crossing the bar. Then he's going to have to tender us all out, since he can't exactly dock on the beach. We're just lucky the weather is nice, the water calm. At least that's one thing that hasn't gone completely sideways today."

"You hearing this?" Beth asks, her voice low, eyes still glued to the rock.

"Yeah. Sounds like they're all going out on a boat. Fishing excursion or something, would be my guess. Last night must have put some kinks in the weekend plans."

"But 'busy crossing the border'? What the hell?"

"Crossing the *bar.* As in, the Columbia River Bar. The boat is probably moored in Astoria. They're waiting for it to reach open water and come down the coast."

"Wouldn't it be easier to just *drive* to the boat?"

"You'd think so. Maybe they just don't want to pay for parking." I see Beth winding up to deliver a scathing rebuttal to that hypothesis, but a small voice behind us cuts her off.

"I like your dog."

We both turn. The girl stands a safe-enough distance from the meteorite that her dad probably won't yell at her again, watching Jake through her binoculars. He's sitting upright now, staring this way and panting, his tongue rolled out and flinging droplets of drool all over the glass. I shouldn't have rolled up the windows. It's so warm out, the temperature in the car probably double what it is out here on the sand. I just didn't want that smell getting in.

"What's his name?" Natalia asks.

"Jake," Beth says.

"Is he coming with us?"

"No."

Natalia lowers her binoculars and looks at Beth. "Are you?"

"We're just passing through," I say. "Is that your family?" I nod toward the lined-up cars. The woman in pajamas is tightly clutching herself, spitting into the sand. Fresh tears streak her cheeks. Somebody gets out of another car, puts a hand on her back to comfort her. Either they're really upset about running behind, or it's not a fishing adventure they're about to set off on.

The girl shakes her head. "They're some of my dad's friends. And neighbors," she says. "He called others. If they're not here in time, Dad said we'll have to leave them behind. Maybe you could come with us instead. And Jake."

"No," the man rasps, and for a second I think he's responding to her suggestion, but he's still on the phone. He glances this way, sees Natalia talking to us, takes a split moment to judge our intentions, then angles away, lowering his voice further. "I haven't told her about all of it," he says. I can barely hear his voice on the breeze, but it's laced with anxiety. "I will, once we're all on the boat and away from this fucking nightmare."

My stomach balls up like an animal defending itself against an approaching predator. Something is seriously wrong here. More than scheduling hiccups and hungover friends.

"Where are you going?" I ask the girl.

"To get my mom."

"Where is she?"

"In Portland. She went there for a conference."

"Why not drive?" Beth asks.

"Because Dad said the roads are bad." She looks in her dad's direction. "He said it would be dangerous, that we might get stuck and not reach Mom."

"Mike." Beth leans close and lowers her voice. "The meteorites. They must have hit cars, damaged roads, bridges even? Houses? No wonder it's taking so long to get the power on." There's champagne on her breath. She made the mimosa just about strong enough to get up and walk off on its own, and I have half a mind to grab the jug and take another deep swig myself.

I feel like such an asshole. Of *course* there was damage. Probably widespread. And panic on top of that. People waking in the middle of the night to the sky falling and blaring sirens and no electricity, now waiting to be ferried upriver to connect with loved ones, maybe seeking medical attention. I glance toward the cars—the woman in sweatpants is being helped back into hers by an older man, her face still red and swollen, her eyes huge with shock and stress. If things are that bad out here, I can't imagine what it must be like in Portland, where this kid's poor mom is waiting. Meanwhile, here I am, out hunting for treasure.

Typical Mike. Staring at the sky while the ground crumbles beneath your feet.

"Why doesn't your dad want you touching the meteorites?" Beth asks. "Did he say?"

"Meteorites?" Natalia asks, genuinely confused.

"Those things." Beth points with the toe of her shoe.

"Oh. I didn't know that's what they were." She furrows her brow in a way that makes me think she still isn't sure. Am *I*? What else would they be? I *watched* them fall last night, maybe even this very one. She probably slept through it, and her dad hasn't filled her in on all the details, not wanting to make a stressful day even worse by causing her to worry about rocks plummeting from the sky.

Without any warning, Jake starts to bark. Not at us—he's looking toward the dunes, his ears perked and alert. The dunes are taller here than at the house, inclining steeply from the beach and rising a good twenty feet to the rounded, grassy ridge. There are places where the slope has been carved out by the tide, leaving an escarpment of compacted sand and grass roots. I can't see whatever Jake senses on the other side. The ridgeline is empty, the sky pale blue and clear.

"Hey!" the girl's dad shouts. "There he is!" He's looking not at the dunes but out to sea. A boat cuts through the chop, a sailing catamaran, probably a thirty-eight-footer, just visible against a thick bank of fog. "I have to go," he says into the phone. "Stay where you are, stay in your car, conserve your battery. We'll be there as soon as we can, okay? Natalia!"

She runs over to him, and he shoves his cell phone into her hand. "Mom wants to talk to you. Go wait with the others." Then he turns, gives me a stoic, knowing nod, and beelines for the dunes, drawing something he had tucked into his belt: a bright orange flare gun. He runs as fast as he can in the dry, slippery sand, grabbing handfuls of beach grass as he climbs to the top of the dunes. There he aims into the sky, pulls the trigger, and fires a flare with a dull pop.

Beth lights a cigarette, watching as the flare blooms dazzling red in the air. The man jumps up and down, waving his arms for good measure in case the catamaran's skipper hasn't seen the signal.

"Well," Beth says, blowing a plume of smoke into the breeze. "Starting to feel a bit like Armageddon arrived out there on the other side of the dunes. Maybe we should try to secure a seat aboard his little ark, what do you think?"

"I'm sure they're just overreacting." Except I'm not. In fact, I'm beginning to suspect that my detachment from the world around me has put me into a state of *under*reacting.

"We should at least get back to the house," Beth says. "My service sucks out here, and I don't want to miss any new information when it comes." She pauses to take another drag on the cigarette, giving me time to contemplate just how lucky we are that my house wasn't hit last night. Well, how lucky Beth is, at least. I'd have been at a safe distance, down in the water. What a wicked joke that would have been.

"I'm also getting a headache," she adds. "I think it's these things."

"Could be the mimosa," I suggest, not mentioning the pain blooming behind my own eyes. I don't want to think about that. About how I had to wash with soap and water for five straight minutes to make my fingers stop burning after stupidly grabbing the meteorite, or how I can still feel my palms itching, no matter how much I scratch at them. What would cause that? Could they be radioactive? I feel fine otherwise, besides the soreness in my lungs that still hasn't subsided since dragging myself coughing and puking from the ocean.

All in all, I'm coming up with a lot more questions about the last twelve hours than answers, and I don't like it.

Beth flips me off and takes a big swig of mimosa to show me what she thinks of my suggestion. I dig the Subaru key from my pocket and put it in her hand.

"Roll the windows down for Jake, would you? I'll be right there. Maybe turn on the radio, see if you can find any kind of emergency broadcast. I'm going to go see what those people know about these things. Make sure we shouldn't go get checked out before going home."

"Checked out?" she asks, eyes widening. "Like, *medically*?"

"Just covering my bases. Don't worry, you didn't touch the thing."

Beth snorts, stuffs the key into the pocket of her hoodie, and struts toward my Subaru.

The notion of her being some cosmic agent of fate comes back to me as I watch her go. Memories of last night flood my mind. The smell of campfire smoke on her skin, the taste of champagne on her lips, the weight of her body on top of mine as we lost ourselves in each other. The meteor shower may have saved my life, but what brought the meteor shower? Maybe it was her. Maybe it was *us*. Two souls hurtling aimlessly through the void, until by chance they collided with such force that it shook the heavens to rubble.

Beth looks over her shoulder at me and smiles. As if she knows what I'm thinking. Like she's thinking the same thing. She even winks, to acknowledge our little secret. That the two of us have gotten away with something so monumental, so impossible, that even the gods took notice.

I smile back.

Then everything goes to hell.

6

BETH

The smile drops off Mike's face so fast I half expect him to follow it to the ground, groaning and grabbing at his chest, done in by the effects of touching E.T.'s damned bowling ball. But whatever is behind his new wide-eyed look is actually behind *me*.

I dread turning around. There's something in the air—and I don't just mean the putrid miasma from the bowling ball. I've felt it since waking up from that awful dream, and it's only gotten worse. First the meteorite he dragged off the beach, now all these freaked-out people trying to escape to sea. Then there's the way Natalia seemed so dubious about the bowling balls being meteorites at all. What did she think they were? I don't like any of it. It feels as though it's all leading up to something, and that something is right behind me.

I turn around to look at whatever it is Mike's gaping at, bracing myself for all possibilities. Or so I think. Turns out the scope of what's possible today is much larger than even space bowling balls gave me reason to believe.

Three shapes are coming this way. Two are brown colored, the third inky black. They shimmer in the sunlight like mirages rising from the sand. It takes me a moment to understand what I'm seeing, and even then my mind stubbornly crosses its arms, stomps its foot, and says, *Nope.*

They're horses. Which ordinarily wouldn't be upsetting. But these are geared up, galloping at full tilt, their riders nowhere to be seen. The ground trembles beneath their hooves. They don't slow at all as they draw closer to us.

Natalia, the cell phone glued to her ear, stares at them with eyes as big around as the cap of my orange juice jug. She steps directly into their path, wonderstruck as a deer gazing into the pretty bright lights.

"Hey!" I shout at her. "Get back!"

She doesn't move, and nobody in those cars, her dad's friends and neighbors supposedly, offers any assistance. They just stare in morbid fascination, gawkers observing carnage that's already come to pass. I see now that they're in the midst of unloading things: coolers and overnight bags and boxes of what looks like canned food. How freaking long does it take to *reach* Portland by boat? One of them, that woman in the sweatpants, is wailing, grabbing at her hair with both hands. Natalia's dad isn't paying any attention at all, still jumping and waving like a madman, trying to signal the boat while his daughter is setting herself up to be turned into a kid pizza.

"Natalia! Get back!" I try again. She listens this time, and takes a rearward step just as the horses blow past. Their eyes are all white with panic, and the lead horse's hind legs glisten with blood, its saddle stained red.

I backstep, too, shielding my face from clods of sand flinging toward me. My legs are already a bit rubbery from the mimosa—coupled with the possibly toxic stench of space debris and now a sight straight out of some biblical fire-and-brimstone propaganda—and my knees fold. I land flat on my ass in the sand. Nobody notices, not even Mike. They're all still staring at those horses, which are already disappearing down the beach, fading into the mist blowing in off the waves.

Jake is barking his head off. I don't blame him. As stupidly excited as he gets at the sight of elk in the dunes, this must be a terrible tease.

But Jake doesn't appear to have even seen the horses. He's focused like a laser on the dunes, on the man jumping up and down, waving his arms, the bright flare still slowly falling to earth above him. Jake's eyes are ready to pop from his skull, and bubbles foam from his lips. He looks flipping rabid.

"Mike!" I shout, stumbling to my feet and loping toward the Subaru. "Mike, let's go, please!" I don't know if I want to get off this beach more for Jake's sake or my own. Something really bad has happened—or is happening—around here. Jake senses it, too, the way dogs can sense earthquakes and heart attacks before they happen. He can probably *hear* whatever new disaster this is, clawing its way toward us from the other side of the dunes. And here we all are, out in the open, our backs to the sea, nowhere to go but the slowly approaching boat.

Jesus Christ, when did this orange juice expire?

Mike hurries toward me, glancing over his shoulder as if afraid those horses might double back for another pass. He's just about to me when the next horror arrives, but this time it's in the form of a police SUV roaring down the beach access road, trailing a cloud of sand. It makes a wide arc, nearly clipping that red Jeep Wrangler, and speeds toward the larger cluster of vehicles. The lights are flashing, but there's no siren. He must have seen the flare from the highway and mistook its meaning.

Mike stops in his tracks to watch as the SUV slides to a stop and a tall, overly muscled cop jumps out with a frenetic energy that immediately puts me on edge. I've known too many guys like that, guys who go around like a bomb with one second on the timer and if you accidentally connect the wrong wires . . . *boom.* He's so amped up on adrenaline I half expect him to pull his gun and order us all to the ground, hands out, faces down, as if we've all taken part in a bank robbery and that boat was our getaway.

"Everybody, listen up!" he barks, holding up his hands to draw attention. As if that were even necessary at this point. "You all need to get into your cars and get off the beach. *Right* now! Go home or to your hotel, lock the doors, and wait for further instructions.

If you don't have a place to go, follow me back to Seaside High School."

Nobody moves.

Not out of defiance but in sheer shock at this new development. It feels like we're all trapped in a bizarre, shared hallucination. I can't help but throw the nearest bowling ball a suspicious glance. *Could* that smell be having psychological effects?

"Come on, people! Move!" The cop claps his hands.

The others look down at the supplies they've unloaded into the sand, mouths hanging open, trying to reconcile whatever they've heard so far with what the cop in front of them is saying now. But what could that be? *Go home*, sure. But *lock the doors*? Is he worried about looters or something?

"We've got a boat coming!" Natalia's dad shouts from atop the dunes, pointing.

The cop follows his outstretched finger and scowls. "Your funeral," he says coldly. "I suggest you get those cars as close to the water as you can and wait. There won't be time to fuck around with all that." He waves a hand at the supplies.

"Why not?" a woman asks.

He looks at me, and I realize I'm the one who spoke out. I feel like I'm in a dream. Like between the mimosa and the bowling balls, I'm on some kind of supernatural cross-fade.

"What?" He's incredulous that anybody is daring to question him.

"First you said go home and lock the doors, now you're saying there isn't time to wait for that boat? Why? What's coming?"

He stares at us like we're two idiots who just wandered into the middle of a movie and have absolutely no idea what's going on, or how they even ended up in a theater. He's not wrong. And that frenetic energy I identified? It's fear. The man is straight-up terrified right now. I'm not positive he even *has* an answer for me, which is somehow worse than anything.

"This is about those things, isn't it?" I press, aiming my jug of liquid courage at the bowling ball. "That smell? Are we being quarantined or something?"

The cop looks at Mike instead of answering me. My heartbeat spikes and my face burns.

"She yours?" the cop asks. Like I'm a dog that got off its leash and took a shit on the sidewalk.

"She's with me," Mike says almost apologetically, and I make a mental note to kick him right in the balls when we get home.

"Get her and yourself into your vehicle. It's for your own safety."

"Come on, Beth. Let's go." Mike moves to guide me back to the car, but I duck away from him. Two minutes ago, I wanted nothing more than to get off this beach. But now I don't want to go anywhere—don't want to even *move*—until I have a firm grasp of what's going on around me. It's like we've found ourselves in the middle of a minefield and one wrong step will surely be our last.

"No," I snap. "Not until he tells us what the hell is happening here. Why are they getting on a boat? Why are you telling us to go home and lock our doors? What is everybody trying to get away from?"

I half expect him to arrest me out of sheer annoyance. It would be a perfect garnish to this demented cocktail. I'm more certain than ever that this all has to do with the poisonous space turds. We've all seen and breathed something we shouldn't have. All that's left is to wait complacently for the cleanup squads.

But before the cop can do anything, Jake's barking reaches such a fervor that everybody takes notice, even Natalia's dad, way up on the ridge. I see something in the cop's face that puts me on full alert: defeat. As if Jake's fit tells him we've run out of time. Whatever he was here to save us from has arrived.

Good job, Bethany, my mom's voice whispers hideously. *As usual, you've ruined everything.*

"Hey!" Natalia's dad shouts. Then he's gone.

I blink, trying to comprehend what I just saw and failing magnificently. One second he was standing there, then he wasn't. Like somebody cut the film and spliced in a reel of empty dunes.

Before I—or any of us—have a chance to make sense of it, a single, sharp, human scream rises from beyond the ridge.

And then that, too, is cut short.

For a moment, time stands still. Even the ocean behind me falls into grave silence. Every person on the beach, including the cop, intently watches the space where the man had been standing, waiting for the universe to stop fooling around and correct whatever glitch has occurred and put him back where he belongs.

The moment lasts about as long as the man's scream.

"Everybody, *go*!" the cop orders. This time, they listen.

Even me.

7

MIKE

Dizziness hits me first. Then denial. *It can't be. That did not just happen.* It feels like the day Sarah walked out the door for the last time, those long minutes bleeding into longer hours, just staring at my hands and refusing to accept the truth that was closing in around me from every angle, crushing me like an empty soda can.

The moment is brief, and then I'm grabbing Beth's hand and pulling her toward the Subaru, the world strangely devoid of sound above the pounding of my heart in my ears. I practically have to drag her along. She's staring dumbfounded at the dunes as if she's just witnessed a mind-bending magic trick. The cop is already back in his SUV and speeding past us. He's bellowing something into his radio as he cranks the wheel and gasses it, spewing an arch of sand into the air as he ascends the slope. He stops at the ridge, at the spot where Natalia's dad was just yanked from view by . . .

By what? *What could* possibly *have done that?* I desperately try to remember a hook reaching from somewhere offstage to snatch him away. But there was nothing.

There was *nothing.*

The cop jumps out with a shotgun in hand and charges into the tall grass, then down the far side of the dunes. The last I see of him is his head, before I have to shove Beth into the car. I have no idea what's going on in her mind, but she's in a daze. There's no time for questions, though; the cop was right about that. We need to get out of here. Get home. Like everybody else was quick to do. As I look, the last set of taillights disappears up the access road. Even the boat has reset its course and is swiftly sailing right on by, having assessed the situation on the beach as a lost cause. Time for us to follow suit.

I reach for the ignition, but the key isn't there. I shove my hands into my pockets, my stomach plummeting.

"The key." I hold my hand out to Beth.

She stares at me as if I'm communicating in grunts. "What?"

"The *key,* Beth, give me the key."

"I don't have it."

How much champagne did she put in that orange juice? "I *just* gave it to you," I say, trying to keep cool. Trying not to shout all the things I want to shout: *Damn it, Beth, why'd you have to start drinking again? How couldn't you foresee that you'd need all your faculties in good working order today!*

"Oh, right." She jams a hand into her hoodie pocket, coming back with only her cigarettes and lighter, which she deposits into the cup holder. Then she tries her shorts. Up front are those silly fake pockets so mind-bendingly prevalent in women's clothing. She pulls something small and metallic from the back pocket, and I nearly lunge for it in my eagerness, but it's only her house key. She tries her hoodie again.

My stomach sinks further. That dizzy denial makes an encore performance. *This isn't happening.*

"What the hell?" she asks nobody in particular.

"Where is it?" I want to grab and shake her until it drops out into my hand, but I resist. That would be a good way to lose an arm.

"If I knew that, I'd give it to you!"

"Get up," I say, calmly as I can. I don't even know what I'm freaking out about, exactly. The boat, the cop, the disappearing man. I know it must all add up, but I can't do the math, and I do not like it. "Lift up." She raises her butt. I pat the seat, dig my fingers into the cushion crack, between the seat and center console, listening desperately for that telltale jingle.

I don't hear it.

"Did you drop it *outside*?" I ask, my voice going shrill.

"*I said I don't know!*" Her eyes are as wide as those horses'. Those *horses*. What was *that* all about? And what happened to their riders? More variables in this awful, increasingly baffling equation.

The image of that man disappearing as though a trapdoor opened beneath him invades my mind. I shake it away. Not now. No time for that now.

Beth gets out and searches around the car for about three seconds before throwing up her hands in frustration. I get out and join her. Clearly this is a two-person job, when one of them has half a jug of mimosa in them.

"You fell," I remind her in a low, conspiratorial tone. As if I don't want anybody to overhear. To know how badly we've screwed up. Not that anybody else is around. The red Jeep Wrangler is the only vehicle remaining, silent and empty and sad, its owner having been plucked from existence by unseen hands. "You must have dropped it by accident. Where was that?"

"I don't know, here? There? Somewhere." She shrugs.

"That really isn't helpful, Beth."

"Gee, sorry! Just let me grab my metal detector!"

I let her have that one. We retrace our steps, quickly losing the trail in a mess of shoe prints and hoof marks and tire tracks. It wasn't this far away—I know that much. She never got this close to the other cars. It's somewhere between the meteorite and the Subaru.

"Goddammit, it's got to be here," Beth mutters. She hasn't seen that we're alone yet. But she will, soon. Hopefully after we've found the key and are speeding back down the beach.

"It's probably just buried," I say—also unhelpful—and kick at the ground. "One of us must have stepped on it, or—"

The blast of a shotgun cuts me off.

≈≈≈

The police SUV is still idling at the top of the dunes, the red and blue lights silently flashing their warning. We stand motionless, for what feels like at least an hour, waiting to see the man's shape rise again from the grass, shotgun resting casually on one shoulder like a hardened action movie hero.

But he doesn't come back. He doesn't fire any more shots either.

The silence is broken by a long, piercing wail. A shriek, that would be a better word for it. It's not the cop, though. It's not a human sound at all, not like anything I've ever heard in my life. It's like metal tearing and a woman screaming in rage and the hungry howl of some feral beast all at once. I can't even process it as real. It's a dream sound. A nightmare sound, impossible to transcribe into reality. But there it is nonetheless.

The shriek blessedly dies away. Beth's mouth hangs slack, her eyes searching the ridge for the source of that noise. I'm not so sure I want to see it.

"Let's get back in the car." I say it quietly, so that whatever produced that sound can't hear *me.*

"What the unholy fuck was that?" Beth whispers. It's a relief to know I'm not alone in being unable to identify it.

"I don't know. Just get in. Please."

"What about the key?"

"We'll flag the cop down when he comes back," I say, my confidence pitifully insincere. It's a defense mechanism more than anything. When the world around you suddenly ceases to make sense, you grasp for any reasonable thought and hold on for dear life.

Beth doesn't call me out. She's grabbing for some way to stay afloat too. Without further ado, we both get into the Subaru and gently tug the doors shut and turn to watch the dunes, as Jake has done since we got out here.

He glances at us with a mournful look. *I tried to tell you.*

"What if he doesn't come back?" Beth croaks. That shriek got into her like a damp chill. She's shaking despite the temperature inside the car.

"He will," I reassure her. "He's trained, and armed. You heard the gunshot. And I haven't heard that . . . *other* sound since."

"I heard the gunshot *before* whatever that other thing was. Doesn't that seem like the wrong order?"

I cannot dispute this, as much as I want to, so I keep my mouth shut. The catamaran is already disappearing into the fog far to the south of us, speeding toward Tillamook Head, its angle suggesting an open ocean trajectory. Getting as far away from land as they can. From whatever the cop was trying to warn us about.

"Don't you have a spare key?" Beth asks. "One of those magnetic lockboxes?" She's so hopeful it breaks my heart to answer.

"Sarah had it." It's the first time I've spoken my wife's name aloud in so long it doesn't even sound right. Doesn't sound real, much like the shriek from the dunes. "She kept it in her purse. It's probably still there." I search for a way to steer the conversation away from lost keys. "Oh, your phone!"

"Genius." She pulls it from her hoodie. Of course, it's the phone she managed not to drop. "Police?"

"Given the circumstances, I think that would be best. Make sure to mention there's an officer in trouble. They'll be here in a blink." And ideally take us with them. I'm glad to be thinking clearly again.

"What is with your car? I can't get any bars!" She starts to get out, but I grab her arm to stop her.

"It's fine. You'll still get Emergency Dispatch. Probably."

Beth dials with trembling fingers and holds the phone to her ear with both hands, as if it's heavy as cast iron. She pulls it away immediately. Red-hot cast iron, apparently. "Are you *kidding*?"

"What's wrong?"

"It's *busy*. Can that even *happen*?" She tries again.

I almost ask her to put it on speaker, so I can hear too. As if that might somehow make a difference. Guy logic.

She ends the call. "Wow."

"That's okay, we'll try again in a few. There are probably a lot of calls coming in."

"About what?" Beth asks. "What do you think that cop was talking about?"

"I don't know. Natural disaster, people freak out. If the highways are in bad shape, it'll be an all-hands-on-deck kind of day." Stay focused, Mike. Don't get caught up in the peripheral details.

Beth holds her phone up to the windshield and practically squeals when a single bar appears. "Oh! It's back!"

"Do you have an emergency contact or anything local you could try? A veterinarian's number?" I ask.

"On a piece of paper at the house," she says, biting her lip, still holding that phone up as if the slightest dip in height will snatch the service away.

"But what about your employers?"

"They're in Vietnam!"

"I mean, can't you call them? Have them put us in touch with somebody?"

"Can't *you*? You *live* here!"

"I don't know any numbers off the top of my head! That's what a contacts list is for!"

"For a guy who doesn't have a phone, that's pretty stupid, Mike!"

We both realize we're screaming and simultaneously hush ourselves, casting wary glances back toward the dunes. Whatever produced that unearthly shriek still hasn't revealed itself. Which is a good sign, as far as I'm concerned. The cop is probably standing over it, shotgun smoking. I try to draw a mental picture of that action hero again, but my imagination locks up on what the source of the shriek might have been. Maybe it wasn't anything—maybe we were just hearing a mix of feedback from his radio, accidentally broadcast over the SUV's PA system. Yeah. That actually makes sense. Kind of.

"Goddamn, Mike," Beth says, voice raspy but calm. "When we get back, you're going to start paying your cell phone bill again. No ifs, ands, or buts." She opens her contacts and hovers her finger above the screen, but can't bring herself to tap. She probably doesn't want to have to admit to them that she'd left the house unoccupied during a time like this.

She quickly scrolls down and finds a different number.

"Who are you calling?"

"My parents." She slumps in defeat, as if this call is going to be even worse. "They live in Portland, so I don't know what help they'll be. Probably none. But if Dad's having a good day, maybe he can tell me how to hot-wire this stupid thing."

"Have you heard from them otherwise? Texts or anything?"

"No." She shudders, taps the number, and puts the phone to her ear. "It's not even ringing." She looks at the screen, swears under her breath, and holds the phone up to the window. The one bar disappears and NO SERVICE takes its place in the upper corner of the screen. She lets out an exasperated sigh and looks toward the police SUV. "If he doesn't come back—and I'm just saying *if*—then they'll send somebody out to check on him, right?"

"Eventually. Depends how stretched thin they are. We might be better off just walking home." Which is the last option I want to consider right now. The cop's orders come back to me. *Get home, lock your doors.* The takeaway being that we should minimize time outside.

"That idea sucks," Beth concurs. "We should just wait."

We're both dancing around the obvious: There's a police officer right on the other side of that dune. We could just climb up there and see what the deal is. Except there's also whatever made Natalia's dad vanish. *She's safe out here,* he'd said into the phone. *I can see for miles in both directions.* Up there, in that tall grass, visibility decreases. He learned that the hard way. And as much as I want to believe that shriek was just radio interference, the cop did shoot at *something.*

"I keep thinking about that smell," Beth says. "It could be toxic. It makes sense that they want to keep people indoors and away from it. Like, maybe it's . . . I don't know, affecting us somehow? You said touching the things made your hands burn. Could that explain those horses? Or that *sound*?"

The horses again. My poor mind keeps doing its best to sweep that bit as far beneath the rug as possible. Their white, terrified eyes; the vacant riding saddles; the blood.

"Do you think we could be hallucinating?" Beth clarifies.

"It would have to be a shared hallucination. Should we compare notes? I'm pretty sure everybody saw those horses. And you and me both heard a noise. Like a shriek of some kind?"

The way she shrinks from the word tells me we heard the same thing.

"There are mountain lions on the coast. It would explain Jake's behavior." At the mention of his name, I realize it's been a while since Jake last vocalized his disapproval. I look for him, but he's melted into the back somewhere behind the seat, panting hard enough to tremble the car. "Have you ever heard one of those? They're scary enough without being high on extraterrestrial happy gas. It's probably been out here since last night, terrified out of its mind by the sky falling. It attacked those riders, made its way up the coast, and went after that guy next. Maybe *it's* being affected by the smell too."

Beth runs a hand through her hair. "I want to get out of here, Mike. Before I start seeing *you* differently."

"Sorry, I don't know how to hot-wire the car either." It's been done in plenty of my own movies, but always as B-roll picked up by the second-unit guys. I was never around for it. I never seem to be around when it really matters. Sarah could tell you all about that.

But I've got a firm hold on my mountain lion explanation now. I can wrap my head around that, and therefore the next logical move seems far less daunting. "Luckily, worst-case scenario, we have another way off the beach." She follows my eyes up to the ridge. To that police SUV.

She grabs my forearm, fingernails digging in. "You're not going up there."

"Beth, that cop probably killed it. He could be up there right now, administering first aid, waiting for an EMT response. He might be hurt *himself*. Bleeding out while we're down here arguing." She's not impressed. That's fine. She can wait here.

I climb over the back seats and into the hatch. Jake remains limp, deadweight, managing to whine woefully only as I slide him aside and pull up the floor mat. There's a tire iron in the spare compartment.

"Oh, that's great." Beth rolls her eyes. "What are you going to do with that if you get attacked? Besides trip and impale yourself?"

"It's just backup. I'm taking Jake with me."

"The hell you are. This dog is my responsibility. I'm not sending him out there with you to use as bait."

"I was more thinking of protection," I protest. Despite my rationalizations, I still don't like the idea of going up there alone. A crazed wildcat is nothing to scoff at. But there's no way I'm persuading her. And from the look of it, I'd have to drag Jake behind me anyway. "Fine. But when I get to the base of the hill, I'm going to lose sight of the ridge. Would you at least be a lookout? If you see anything moving around up there, and it seems like I don't, just lay on the horn. Please?"

Beth scowls, but grabs her camera bag, takes out her Nikon, and attaches the zoom lens.

"Good thinking," I say, and manage a smile.

She doesn't reciprocate. "That makes one of us."

8

BETH

The second Mike opens the door, the thunder of crashing waves floods in. I can practically feel the sea spray against my face as the breeze cools the sweat beading at my hairline. Summer still has its claws sunk deeply into the North Coast, clinging on for dear life. The sand, reflecting the afternoon sun, is hard to look at. I slip off my hoodie as Mike gets out of the car.

He doesn't immediately start for the dunes. First he looks toward the red Jeep that belongs (belonged?) to Natalia's dad. It's empty, parked about an eighth of a mile away and shimmering in the heat haze rising off the sand. Natalia herself escaped with the others, though I didn't see who in particular grabbed her. I wish they'd extended that same courtesy to us.

Mike looks back at the ocean next, searching for that boat maybe, but it's long disappeared. That fog has appeared almost every day that I've been here, rolling in around midday and burning off with the afternoon sun. Another side effect of this strangely warm weather, I'm sure. Today, however, it fills me with deep dread. Like if we're not safely inside by the time it makes landfall, we'll be lost forever in it. Even the most benign things seem sinister and hungry today.

I hold my phone up to the windshield. Two bars appear, so I call my parents again. Nobody answers the landline, so I try Mom's cell. After four rings, a robot voice offers to take a message. I didn't really expect her to answer.

"Hey, it's Beth," I say.

Mike jumps at the sound of my voice behind him.

"I just wanted to check in with you guys. It sounds like things might be pretty bad in the city, after last night? I'm sitting a house on the coast. Neacoxie Beach. I'm okay, but things are still a little chaotic. Power's out, roads closed, people freaking out." I don't go into poisonous bowling balls and shrieking dune creatures and vanishing men. Unless the same things are happening there, it would only convince her I've backslid into substances much harder than mimosa, and she'll be even less likely to pass on the next part of my message. "Anyway, if Dad's around—you know what I mean—would you have him call? I have a car question. He shouldn't worry if I don't answer, cell reception is weird here. Tell him I've got some good pictures for him." That last bit was just for her. I hope it stings. I can't believe I'm even thinking about such petty shit at a time like this. Like mother, like daughter.

But it's better than the things I *should* be thinking about. Like what I heard Natalia's dad saying to the woman on the other end of that phone call. *Stay where you are, stay in your car, conserve your battery.* The cop said something similar. *Go home, lock the doors, wait for further instructions.* As much as I try to rationalize how those suggestions could possibly apply to a meteoric event, I can't do it. Makes as much sense as telling people to arm themselves because a tornado's coming.

Mike finally heads out toward the dunes at a determined pace, clutching his stupid tire iron like it's a broadsword. If he runs into a mountain lion up there, he'll be killed for sure. If that's even what it is. Would a mountain lion really attack three riders on horses, then flee down the beach to ambush two grown men?

If it's scared enough, maybe. If that fetor from the bowling balls drove it mad. If the smell is behind our own increasing paranoia—and that of everybody else who's been downwind of them today—how long until it drives *us* into a murderous rampage too? Is this how the zombie apocalypse begins?

A picture of Mike pops into my head, stumbling down the dunes and running toward me, swinging that tire iron and screaming like an animal, eyes red and strings of saliva whipping about. It's as ridiculous as it is horrifying. I have half a mind to yell at him, call him back, but he's right: reaching the cop's SUV is the best plan. And speaking of which, I have a job to do.

I slide into the driver's seat and stick my legs out into the breeze. God, that feels good. It's so hot in the car. The air current fans more of the stink in, so I pull my shirt up over my nose. Because that's really going to help. Poisonous particles travel a million light-years through space, resist burning up as they fall to earth, but are stopped in their tracks by my cheap cotton filter. Movie logic—it's going to get us all killed. At least me and Mike.

I turn on the camera, sighing with relief at the full battery indicator. Jake clambers to his feet like a drunk peeling himself off the pub floor. He stares at Mike, ears alertly perked, a whine building in his throat.

"It's all right, Jake. I know he's your new favorite human after last night, but you're stuck with me until he gets back." Jake shoots me some dubious side-eye, then ramps up the whining. "You know what? Fine. Knock yourself out. Please."

I pop off the lens cap and aim at Mike. He's lost a bit of the pep in his step, now that he's near the base of the dunes. I scan the ridge through the viewfinder. Nothing up there but the swaying grass. Even that gives me the creeps. What's hiding in there?

"Can you hear anything?" I ask Jake. He plops his butt on the floor, tail sweeping to and fro across the plastic mat. The whining stops, but his eyes bug out like they're trying to escape from his skull and roll all the way home to the safety of his bed.

Mike stops at the bottom of the hill, assessing it like a mountaineer at the base of Everest. It's steep enough here that I'm amazed the SUV made it to the top without tipping over. Mike's best bet is to follow the trenches those beefy tires tore into the sand.

While he stalls, I take aim at the Jeep and zoom to max. Empty, the windows up. I wonder if Natalia's father left it unlocked. And did he leave his key behind too? Beyond the Jeep, the beach is deserted. No sign of the horses. Farther south, a column of oily black smoke rises into the sky, and my first thought is the house. But, no, the fire is much farther down the beach. Seaside, maybe. Where the cop suggested we follow him. Great.

I turn to find Mike staring at me expectantly.

"Sorry," I mutter, and give the ridge another sweep with the camera. Still nothing up there. Nothing I can see, anyway. I reluctantly communicate this to him with a thumbs-up. Mike won't have to wade into the grass to reach the SUV, but something could still be waiting just beyond my sight line. This is all such a bad idea. I should just lay on the horn. Scare Mike shitless, bring him running back. Lie about seeing something, go try the Jeep instead.

Before I have a chance, Mike begins his ascent, the loosened sand making each step a comical effort. Any moment he's going to slip, put his hands out to break the fall, and drive the pointy end of that tire iron right through his eye.

But he doesn't fall and, more important, doesn't impale himself. Two steps in the right direction.

Jake watches intently. His tail is still. Is that a good sign or bad? Surely he wouldn't let his new best bud be torn to pieces without at least a word of warning, right? Unless he knows it's too late.

Shut up, Beth!

Mike reaches the ridge and stands there, out in the open like an asshole general surveying the battlefield. I suppose there's a chance the cop is just on the other side of the dune—I can't see if Mike is speaking or not. And while that may be the case, I'd much rather he just get into the SUV and shut the door like an intelligent man with a reasonably strong will to live. Or at least turn around and give me a sign that says all is well, our imaginations have clearly been getting the best of us, c'mon up and we'll have a good laugh about it all.

"What are you doing, Mike? Give me something. Or get in the car, get on the radio. Better yet, get down from there."

Jake growls an agreement. I don't like that. Growl is worse than whine. He's upgraded the threat level. Next is bark. After that, it really will be too late. I know in my gut that Natalia's dad is dead. So is the cop. And in a moment, the heroically stupid Mike will join them, leaving me here, with nowhere to go and God knows how much time to ponder it. I don't want to be alone in that fog.

Jake lets out a single shrill yip and flattens his ears.

"Don't you do it, Mike," I whisper. "Don't even think about it. Not without at least calling for help first."

He turns and looks at me. For a moment, I think he heard me, or heard Jake, and I wave for him to come back. Instead, he holds up an index finger and mouths: *One minute.*

"No!" I shout just as he turns away. "Not 'one minute'! What's wrong with you? Why? *Why!*"

Mike marches down the other side of the dune and disappears.

That's when Jake starts to bark.

9

MIKE

She's going to kill me when I get back.

Beyond the ridge, the dunes drop steeply before leveling off into a wide swath of beach grass and weeds. Past that, a scrubby coastal forest forms a natural buffer between the dunes and the various residential developments along the highway. Saddle Mountain rises prominently in the distance, but to the north, the hillsides of Astoria are hidden in a smoky brown haze. There's a small military training base just to the northeast of here. Sometimes, on our sunset drives, Sarah and I would be stopped by soldiers on the beach because live-fire exercises were happening out there beyond the tree line. But if there's a cavalry, they've already moved out.

Directly between me and the tree line is an impact crater as big across as my car, from headlights to tailpipe. I don't see any sign of Natalia's father, the cop, or a mountain lion attack, though. That brings me both a measure of comfort and deep unease. Seeing is believing. But the real horrors live in those places we can't see.

As I descend the slope, I'm plunged into silence so heavy I can feel it perched on my shoulders, wrapping itself around me in a crushing embrace. The ridge of the dunes mutes the ocean entirely, until all I hear is the whisper of a breeze and the hushed rustle of beach grass and the soles of my shoes squeaking in the sand.

And then I see some of those blades of grass are stained red. Blood, still glistening and tacky. That brings me to a stop.

"Hello?"

My voice is so loud in this new quiet that it startles me. I get no response, human or otherwise. I don't even hear any birds out here. No hum of traffic moving along the coast highway, no wail of sirens as emergency response vehicles rush about, tending to the disaster.

I've never seen so much blood outside of a movie set, splattered around following an act of violence. Roadkill, sure. But not real *human* blood. I don't know how I know it's human, but I do. Might have something to do with the cop's shotgun, which is lying in the sand at my feet.

It's been sheared in half, as if made of paper, the barrel separated from the rest just above the trigger guard.

That could explain the shrieking sound. Metal being sliced. But what could cut a shotgun in half like this? Not a mountain lion—that's for sure. And I don't imagine the cop stood idly by in the meantime. Whatever happened, it happened *fast*.

I step forward, my shoes feeling full of concrete, and kneel to pick up the two shotgun halves. There's a sticky dark substance coating the barrel end. It looks like tar but has no odor. Having learned from my earlier mistake, I don't dare touch it. Maybe it's just oil from inside the barrel. I toss the shotgun aside and stand up.

"Hello? Officer . . . ?" I don't know his name. I'm sure it was there on his shirt, but I didn't look. I don't know the name of Natalia's dad either. "If either of you can hear me, please say something. I'm here to help." I'm sure they're just overwhelmed with relief.

It feels as if I'm being watched. Like no matter which way I turn, something is creeping up behind me. I glance back at the ridge. The cop left his door open, but I haven't heard any radio chatter. You'd think, with the state of things on the coast right now, there would be plenty of activity on the police band. And there's nothing coming from his lapel radio either, wherever it might be. The strangeness keeps stacking up. Soon I'll need a stepladder just to see over the top of it.

A trail of little brown blood splats in the sand leads right to the impact crater. The crater itself is about half as deep as it is wide, the grass around it flattened beneath soil ejected from the pit. As I near the rim of the crater, I finally see the meteorite itself, or at least a piece of it, half buried at the bottom. It's smaller than the others, oddly enough, considering it actually produced an indentation in the earth. The exposed surface is black like lump charcoal, rough and angular and oblong, with streaks and flecks that glint in the sun. In short, it looks like a rock. It looks about as I'd expect a meteorite to look.

It looks nothing like the thing I hauled off the beach in the bucket. Nothing like the thing lying in the sand near my Subaru at this very moment. Near Beth and Jake. It doesn't stink either. That might actually be the worst part. At least a hint of that knock-you-flat malodor would be enough to tell me this and the others came from the same place.

But if the other things *aren't* meteorites, what are they? And more important, where did they come *from*?

My palms tingle, as if to remind me that I'd stupidly stuck my bare flesh on the thing Beth called a space bowling ball, a term that now feels far too cheerfully benign. I jam the tips of my fingers deep into my palm and dig around, chasing the itch. The thing hadn't even felt like rock, now that I think about it. It was heavy, sure, as something composed of iron and nickel and whatever else is out there should be. But when I'd grabbed it, it felt *meaty* somehow. Like the shell of a coconut. I probably should have mentioned that part to Beth. She would have demanded we go straight inside until we figured out what was going on. We'd be safe indoors, together, not stranded out here in the middle of it.

There's something else at the bottom of the crater, atop the violently disrupted soil. I make my way slowly toward it, rivers of sand rolling down to begin their slow task of burying the rock. With the nearly constant coastal breeze, it won't be long before the hole is filled completely, its otherworldly contents swallowed up and forgotten for untold eons.

But the other thing down there isn't otherworldly at all. It is very much a product of this planet.

It's a human hand.

10

MIKE

That's it. That's all there is. Five fingers and a bit of wrist, cleaved from the rest of the arm as cleanly as the shotgun barrel and sitting in a thick, brown pool. It's so coated in blood and sand I don't even know which of the missing men it belongs to. My eyes trace a trail of muddy droplets up the curve of the crater, across the displaced sand, and into the grass. The rest of him is lying just a few feet away from me.

It's the cop. That's one mystery solved.

His head is missing from the nose down, his eyes still open wide in a mask of fear and surprise. Below the neck is just a mess of shredded uniform and bloody bits spilling into the dirt.

I fall flat on my ass in my hurry to put as much distance as possible between me and this horror, scrambling to my feet and managing a weak lurch before hitting the ground again. I repeat the strange boogie, retreating a few precious inches at a time, until the ground falls away beneath me and I tumble into the crater and smack my head against the meteorite. That gets me moving. I'm on my feet and out of the hole in a single flailing leap, as if I'd felt that severed hand reach up and tap me on the shoulder. *Excuse me, I think I'm lost.*

Black flowers bloom at the edges of my vision, and my head fills with helium. *No! Not here! Not now! Keep it together!*

I cannot seem to tear my eyes away from the man's corpse. He wasn't eaten. Just ripped apart and discarded, and in far cruder fashion than what happened to the shotgun and his hand. No mountain lion did this. I'm not hallucinating any of it either. I can no longer hide the unfathomable engine powering this nightmare behind a curtain. Something is out there, in the dunes. Something that arrived last night while we were all staring awestruck at the sky. It deposited strange, smelly orbs up and down the coast, it briefly blocked out the moon on an otherwise clear night, it has people so frightened they're ready to set sail rather than risk waiting for it to find them.

Is this the thing that had been coming for me last night? When I'd dragged myself from the surf, the moon was bright overhead again. I'd looked for my visitor's footprints as I staggered back toward my house, fighting off images of the bloated, wet feet that could have produced such a sound; of pallid, sandy lips curled into a terrible grin. But, as always, I found only signs of myself. By the time I had brought Jake over and was at my computer deleting that letter, I convinced myself my imagination had managed to fool me again, that the palpable strangeness in those lightless seconds between drowning and sitting bolt upright, gasping for air, had just made it more real than ever before.

Now I'm not so certain. I don't exactly see any sign of whatever killed the cop, either, but I can hardly deny it happened. But if something really had been on the beach with me, why didn't it attack? And where did it go?

The cop's lapel radio is nowhere to be seen, or heard, but his pistol is still holstered to his hip. The thing that killed him can cut metal like soft cheese and reduce a man to gristly leftovers in a blink. If that thing's still out here, my tire iron will prove fatally insufficient.

Undoing my hard work, I inch forward and reach toward the holster with one hand, forcing myself not to look at anything but my own intact fingers. With a rubbery tug, his handgun is mine. Not that I have any clue how to use it. I've been on plenty of productions with prop guns, but that's the business of the weapons wranglers and talent. How hard can it be? Point and shoot, just like an autofocus lens. There's probably already a clip loaded and a round chambered.

I sprint for the ridge, vaguely aware that if I trip, I'll likely blow my own brains out. Honestly, that would be a better fate than what befell the cop. Faster, for sure.

The grass grabs at my ankles, slowing me down. The sand is slippery as ice. Everything has developed a malevolent will. I can hear all the noises around me now, as if somebody cranked up the volume, the silence itself becoming a deafening static in my ears. Chirps and chitters and rustles and thumps, the world suddenly full of menace and teeth. Why did I have to come out here? Why didn't I just get in the SUV the moment I saw blood? I could still pretend there was an aggressive mountain lion on the loose, had I done that.

As I huff my way up the ridge, I'm greeted by the rumble of waves—and the insistent bleating of a car horn. *Beth.* She's seen something. Or she's just trying to light a fire under my ass. It works.

Without stopping to look around, I dive into the SUV and pull the door shut and try to catch my breath. It's quiet again. A better kind of quiet. Safe. Whatever is out there, it can't get me in here. Beth lets off the horn, and in the side mirror, I see her lift her camera and aim it toward me. I give her a wave and she returns a middle finger. That's fine. I deserve that.

The engine is still humming; all the gadgets appear to be properly working, including the radio, despite an unnerving absence of chatter among police units. Now would be a good time for me to get on the air and make a distress call, but I can do that once I'm off this cursed dune. Away from all that grass, and whatever's hiding in it, watching me.

I shift into reverse, but before I can lift my foot from the brake pedal, the front end of the SUV dips forward, sinking into the sand, the shocks creaking beneath added weight. Except nothing's there. Nothing but granules of sand scattered across the hood, and a smear of blood right where the thin metal covering the engine has gone slightly concave. Was that dent there all along? Did he hit a deer or something?

The SUV is positioned at just enough of an angle that I can't see the grass over the hood, but I *can* see the tops of the trees beyond the meteorite crater. There's something *off* about the view. A slight bend of the light, a warping of the treetops and the mountains. A flaw in the glass, must be.

The distortion moves ever so slightly, the bend in the skyline shifting position. The movement is accompanied by the unmistakable pop of metal under stress, and the indentation deepens. There's a sound, all but masked by the hum of the engine. A constant, high-pitched chitter, like a cricket trying to sing harmony with an old iron gate swinging in the breeze. It's an alien noise (*please, find a different word, Mike*), somehow both mechanical and organic.

Just like that shriek.

Beth, impatient as ever, lays on the horn again. The unexpected bleat causes me to jump—and blink. In that sliver of a second that my eyes are closed, something happens. I'm glad I can't see it. That I can only hear the screech of sharp points peeling back the top layer of hood, the heavy thump of impact that turns the windshield into a webwork of splintered glass.

I slam the gas pedal to the floor. The tires spew a geyser of sand out over the grass. My hands, operating independently of my other systems, crank the wheel in a desperate bid to get me facing the opposite direction of whatever just smashed into the windshield and toward my goal as fast as possible. While I appreciate their initiative, it backfires spectacularly.

The tires find traction, rocketing me backward just as the front end swings parallel with the steep dunes, which proves too much for the top-heavy vehicle. My stomach does a slow somersault as the passenger-side tires lift up off the sand. Before I can even think of correcting, the SUV—the whole point of this ridiculous odyssey, our only hope of escaping this haunted goddamn beach—tips.

And rolls.

≈

It happens in slow motion, briefly transporting me to those loud carnival rides I masochistically enjoyed as a stupid child. The deafening roar of steel and gears and motors, people screaming in joyous terror as their guts were turned inside out and brains smashed against the insides of their skulls.

This time, the ride goes off the rails, and the only one screaming is me.

It took me a lot longer to hike up the dune than it does to come back down. The sandy hill doesn't unfurl gently down to the beach as it does from my backyard, to that signpost and all its warnings. Here the dunes are tall and abrupt, as if a particularly strong tide had rudely pushed them up into a pile. It might not have been so bad had I followed the trajectory of the tire tracks. Instead, the vehicle rolls straight down and right over a ledge, where the hillside has been sheared away by the elements. The free fall is brief, and concludes with a coda of cracking glass and metal groaning in protest. Pain lights up on every quadrant of my body, each impact accompanied by a blaring alarm in my head. I can't keep track of what's being broken and bruised as I rattle around inside the SUV like an ice cube in a cocktail shaker. At least I'd remembered to put on the seat belt, breaking my streak of supremely idiotic decisions, though I think that was muscle memory more than anything. Amazingly, the gun doesn't go off and put a bullet or three right through me.

The SUV comes to a stop just beyond the base of the hill, lying on its side, the tires still spinning as if there's yet a chance of pulling off this getaway. I'm crumpled between the steering wheel and door like a greasy hamburger wrapper, staring up at the passenger-side curtain airbag, which billows gently in the breeze passing over the smashed-out window. I can feel pieces of glass in my shirt, my hair. The roof panel is between me and the Subaru. I can't see Jake, but I hear him howling in despair. He's still in the car.

But Beth isn't. "Mike! Ohmygod! Mike?" Coming this way.

"I'm okay!" I shout. Each word is a knife plunging through my ribs. The worst pain is on my left side, just above my hip. Prodding the area, I find the cop's small laptop came free of its mount during all the excitement and ended up between me and the door, where one of its corners dug into my flank with enough force to tear open the skin. Blood seeps through my shirt, thick and dark, almost black. I suck air through my teeth and hold it in, my lungs igniting, and delicately place my hand on the laceration. Boy, that's a lot of blood. I should look. I don't want to look. As long as I don't look, how bad can it really be? "Beth, stop! Stay away!"

I hear her feet come to an abrupt halt. "What's the matter?"

How do I even begin to answer that? I'm not even sure what just happened myself. Except that there was something on the hood. Something I couldn't see, but that could apparently see me. I unlatch the seat belt and rotate until I'm kneeling on the driver's-side window through the airbag, feeling things deep inside me grind and pop in ways I don't think they're meant to, not even at my age.

"Just listen to me! Get back in the car!"

There's a thick security-glass partition between the front and back seats, and a metal mesh screen between the passenger and the cargo area. Not getting out that way. I could probably punch through the windshield, but I'd likely lose a lot more blood and the use of my hand in the process. There's no other way but up.

That's when I hear it. Outside, scraping along the exposed undercarriage, poking curiously at the pipes and frame, still chirping and shrill. Above me, I can just see the side mirror through a corner of the window opening that's no longer covered by the deflating airbag. The mirror is cracked, and now angled in such a way that I have a partial view of the ground, but I still can't *see* whatever is making that noise.

And Beth won't be able to either. Even were it to materialize, the SUV is between it and her. What is she doing, anyway? I haven't heard the Subaru door shut, but I also don't hear her approaching.

"Beth! Do not come over here!"

She doesn't respond. She must think that keeping quiet and still is the best course of action at the moment, and I cannot find the words to convey to her how wrong she is.

The singing, unseen thing keeps prodding. Searching for a way into the SUV. Soon it's going to move around to the other side. It's going to see Beth standing there. Then she won't have time to make it back. Jake seems to sense this too. He's going on about it just as he did last night, during the meteor shower. As if he knew this was all coming. And once again, here we are, ignoring his warnings. We truly don't deserve dogs.

I reach to sweep away a pebble of glass digging into my knee, and my hand brushes against cold metal. The pistol. I grab it just as the SUV trembles from the thing leaping up onto the sky-facing side with the grace of a cat, having heard the mournful wail of the breeze passing over the opening. In a moment, it's going to find that opening. It's going to pull aside the airbag curtain and come in.

I press the safety button, resisting the urge to squeeze the trigger just to be sure I've got it in the right position. I don't dare take my eyes off the opening above me to check. I train the gun on the airbag. How will I even know when it's coming in? Will there be a shimmer? A heat haze distortion in the clouds? Grains of sand raining down into my eyes and blinding me? Why not.

Before I can imagine even more fittingly absurd ways for this to end, something rips the curtain away and a face appears, staring down at me. Two eyes and a mouth, open not in a shriek of hungry rage but in a word I actually understand.

"Hey—!" Beth says.

The gun fires all on its own.

11

BETH

A bolt of lightning strikes me right in the face, with a clap of thunder so loud I'm pretty sure my head just burst like a melon dropped from a ninth-floor window. Everything—Mike's surprised face, the rolled SUV, the beach—is swallowed by a blinding white flash. Which seems wrong. I always figured death would be a black screen. A void. Maybe it happened so fast I skipped the tunnel and the end credits and flew, howling, straight into the light.

Then the white fades to misty blue. When the spots clear, I'm lying flat on my back in the sand, staring up at long fingers of that dreadful fog as they begin to close around us. My lungs fill with heavy, warm air, my head with an eardrum-shredding shriek. It's not me. I couldn't scream right now if I wanted to. How could I, when my head just exploded?

He shot me. In the face. Why would he do that? How am I even thinking this right now when I'm dead? Am I not *actually dead?*

I blink. That's good. My eyelids still work. I'll just expand out from there, working one part at a time to determine what's missing.

I roll my head to one side, and another flare of pain blurs my vision. When it clears, I see Mike scramble up through the window and out of the wreckage. What a dipshit. Seriously, what was he thinking? I swear, when I'm inevitably banned from pet-sitting anywhere in the immediate solar system and forced to turn to a life of crime, remind me never to hire him as a getaway driver.

Mike is blubbering and shouting something. It isn't him doing the shrieking, though. No human can produce a sound like that. And it's no mountain lion either. It's the sound we heard earlier.

It's the sound I heard last night.

In my dream.

I know, I *know*. But if the smell of the bowling balls could make its way into my subconscious, why not this? Which means whatever is making that noise, it appeared here at the same time as the bowling balls. It's been creeping around Neacoxie Beach since midnight, and we're the only two fools who didn't know about it. Until now. When it is entirely too late.

I lift my throbbing head to look toward my feet. Something isn't right. (Whatever *that* means anymore.) My vision is warped, the beach and dunes and distant contour of Tillamook Head appearing to bulge toward me, probably owing to my brains leaking out through the hole Mike made in my head. Even stranger, the wind has kicked up some sand, but rather than blowing it right into my face, the individual grains are suspended in midair, just past my feet. As if they blew up against and stuck to a pane of glass dampened by the mist.

"Beth!" Mike shouts. I barely hear him. Every ounce of my focus is on the beach beyond my feet. As that weird bulge begins to split open, I realize the sand was stuck not to a pane of glass but to a canvas, on which the beach is only painted. Something on the other side is pushing, tearing its way through, revealing the void behind the world.

The darkness is coming for me after all.

And it has teeth.

That dark maw widens, revealing rows of devilishly sharp points glistening in a black, oily sheen. It isn't the shrieking void at the edge of existence that I'm staring into but a set of sinewy jaws stretching open to swallow me whole.

Not sure that's an improvement.

I blink, expecting never to open my eyes again. And when I do, the thing shoots forward, and those dripping jaws clamp shut on my right thigh.

Now I'm the one screaming. An awful, guttural howl, my fingers digging trenches in the sand as this impossible horror drags me toward the dunes. As soon as those jaws closed, the thing disappeared again, except for those floating granules and a thin line where the jaws aren't quite sealed, thanks to my leg.

The pain is hot, like I've been set on fire, those teeth sawing back and forth through my muscle and grinding up next to bone as it pulls. There's a sharp buzzing sensation rocketing up my spine and spinning around inside my skull like a blender gone mad, pureeing my brain. Blood pours from the spot where my leg vanishes into that mouth. It's so red and bold it looks fake, splashing into the warm sand like paint.

A rapid succession of gunshots is followed by sudden and overwhelming relief as the monster skitters backward across the sand, leaving me—and my leg—behind. The world splits open again, giving me another look at all those teeth, now stained with my blood. Then it disappears, retreating up the dunes. I'm able to track it only by a trail of sandy depressions and the nauseating waver of its outline.

Should I keep screaming at this point or laugh? I've been pretty messed up on some seriously questionable products in my life, but this is beyond anything my poor body has ever been forced to endure. The pain is real. So is the blood. But nothing else that just happened is. Everything else is a nasty joke. Obviously, the bullet should have killed me immediately, but when I managed to hang on, the universe sent me a little something-something to push me over that final ledge.

Yet here I remain. Still breathing. Still bleeding. Still screaming.

An arm around my waist. Helping me to my feet. It's Mike. He's real too. He's still here.

"What was *that*?" I wail, clutching at my leg. So much blood. Seeping through my fingers, vivid and viscous. The spots are back in front of my eyes, like somebody's tossing rocks through the surface of my vision just to watch the ripples.

"I don't know!" Mike cries. He's bleeding too. What a circus. "We have to move."

That sound rises from the dunes again. That shriek of twisting metal and gnashing teeth. It makes me want to stop, drop, curl into a ball, and get dead just so I won't have to listen to it anymore.

Then it's joined by others. One, two, maybe more. The chorus digs deep, like utensils scratching across a plate, burrowing into my head like something alive and hungry. There was more than one in my dream too. How could I forget that? And how the hell did Mike not hear them? He was the one actually *outside*.

"Come on, Beth!" Mike urges, shouting over them.

I try to pick up my pace while keeping pressure on my thigh as we limp pathetically toward the Subaru. Mike supports me as much as I support him, both of us leaking blood and gasping with every footfall, as if we're barefoot and navigating a gauntlet of glowing coals and scattered nails. Jake yips and paws at the window, cheering us on.

The shrieks all stop at once. I risk a look back.

I still can't see them, but I see the waves caused by their movement and the displaced sand as they tear out of the dunes toward us.

"Mike—"

"Don't look!" he roars. "Just go! Faster!"

Faster, yes, sage advice in any scenario where the goal is to outrun death and dismemberment. We hobble and heave and grunt, the dry sand squeaking beneath our feet like tiny mocking laughs as it slows us down. How are we not gaining any ground? Why does the Subaru look just as far away as it was when we began? Jake spins in mad little circles. I hear the things behind us, gliding effortlessly across the sand, closing the gap in seconds.

"We're not going to make it. We're not—"

"Shut up, Beth!"

Mike pulls his arm away and I nearly fold to the ground. That would have been the end, for sure, but the adrenaline surging through my veins keeps me upright in an absurd, drunken stagger. He passes the pistol to his right hand, extends his arm behind him, and fires blind until the gun clicks empty. Great. Our only defense, and he wasted one bullet on me, while the rest he shot into . . . what? The dunes? The sky? Not *them*, that's for sure. I hear no cries of pain, no thumps of lead sinking into flesh or whatever they're made of. Do they even exist at all when those jaws aren't open for business?

The soft sand becomes firm farther from the dunes, and we pick up speed. So do the shriekers, whatever it is they have for feet ripping up the beach like rototillers. It sounds like they're in pouncing distance when Mike flings open the Subaru's hatch and pushes me in on top of Jake. He slides in behind me, crushing us both into the back of the rear seats, and pulls the hatch door shut.

The first shrieker slams into it hard enough to dent the door. The thing screams in rage, and its buddies join in. I clamp my hands over my ears before the discord splits my damaged skull right down the middle. Jake can't decide if he wants to bark or howl or melt into a quivering blob.

Mike pulls the cargo cover over us and secures it in place.

We lie there, the three of us packed together in the dark like oily little fish in a tin. Only it's not oil slicking me and Mike but sweat and blood. Mike wraps himself around me, and I let him, despite the heat. The contact feels safe, and I need that right now more than I ever have before.

"Don't move," he whispers, as if I need convincing.

I never want to move again. I squeeze Jake as he tries to squirm away. He's my buoy and Mike is my life jacket and if I lose either, I'll be pulled into the roiling, bottomless depths of this madness.

One of the shriekers jumps onto the roof, tapping curiously at the metal while another pounds on the doors. Did I close the driver's door when I got out? The ocean is a muted grumble, and there's no airflow, so I must have. I guess we'll find out soon enough.

"We'll be okay," Mike breathes into my ear. "If we just keep quiet and don't move, we'll be okay."

He can't know that, and I don't care. It's something. And for the moment, it's the best we have.

12

BETH

I don't know how long we've been under the cargo cover. Time has no meaning in the sweltering dark. Long enough for somebody to come looking for that cop. Long enough for somebody, anybody, to find us. But nobody does. Or maybe they drove down the access road, took one look up the beach at two seemingly abandoned vehicles and a wrecked police car, turned right around, and noped outta there. I don't blame them.

My head stayed in one piece—that's a plus. Once the adrenaline of outrunning giant invisible mouths full of very sharp teeth waned, it was pain's turn to show its true face. And pain's an ugly bastard. My eyes are pulsating and my teeth ache and there's a terrible ringing in my head.

The bullet just grazed my scalp; when I pull the sticky clumps of hair aside, I can feel the shallow groove it carved. My skin there is on fire and my skull feels like it's about to crumble apart like graham cracker pie crust. I've managed not to poke the spot for almost thirty full seconds now, but I'm going to need some kind of medical attention soon. So will Mike. His bleeding stopped, but he jerks every time he takes too deep a breath, like somebody's sticking a fork in his side, which is bruised from his hip to the bottom of his ribs.

And poor Jake is panting so hard I'm afraid he's going to suck his tongue into his lungs and asphyxiate himself. I finally got him to stop growling at the things outside, but then he started farting. And when I say farting, I mean if we were any closer to an international border, it might be taken for an open act of aggression.

"I have to get out of here," I announce, rolling back the cargo cover. I'm not sure whether it's the light that blinds me or the fresh surge of pain. This is worse than any hangover.

"Beth, no—" Mike tries, but I'm already sitting up. The fog has come to rest on the beach like a cloud that got tired of hanging out in the sky (*cloud why does that word make me anxious what happened with clouds recently*). Visibility is less than a hundred yards. Even if somebody came down the access road now, I'm not sure they'd be able to see us. I don't see the shriekers, not that that means much. They could have retreated to the dunes, moved farther down the coast, or they might be sitting five feet out the window. I don't see any wavy distortions, no grains of sand suspended in midair or freshly laid tracks. That's good.

"I don't understand what's happening," I whisper. I barely even want to breathe, and not because of Jake's farts. We have no idea how good the shriekers' hearing is, or if they even *can* hear. Mike did his best to debrief me on what happened beyond the ridge, but the whole story stopped making sense once he got into that SUV and something he couldn't see jumped onto the hood. "How can something be . . . *invisible*?"

It looks for a moment as if he's going to attempt an answer, but then he wisely keeps his mouth shut. I don't want science. I want to know how something that, as far as I'm aware, doesn't exist—and admittedly, I zoned out during high school biology for a few months—just chased us across the beach.

I examine my leg. It looks almost as bad as it feels. Like somebody tried to lop it off using a pair of rip saws. There's a lot of blood on the floor. That can't all be mine. How much blood can we lose before we hit the point of no return, anyway? And how fast do we replace it?

"All of that out there . . . it definitely happened?" I ask. "That wasn't a hallucination?"

"As far as I can tell." Mike doesn't look like he's ready to believe it, though. "But I have no idea what they are or where they came from," he adds.

"The meteor shower. I mean, did one of them hit some kind of . . . I don't know, *laboratory* or something? Punch a hole through the 'Top Secret: Don't Even Think of Opening This' door and let these things out?"

"Maybe," he says super helpfully. I don't know what I expected. What sort of answer could he possibly give? "Let's just hope there's some sort of system in place to clean up the mess."

"*How?* We can't *see* them!" My head is pounding hard enough to blur my vision. "People were trying to escape out to sea! The cop was telling everybody to get home and lock their doors!"

"He also said to 'wait for further instructions.' Which suggests to me there's some sort of plan in motion. We just need to wait." He looks up and down the beach. "And honestly, I think we're in a good position to do that. Those things already seem to have forgotten about us. I wonder if they can't see through the windows. Or maybe they just lost track of us in the fog?"

"What *I* don't understand is why you didn't get on the radio and tell somebody we were out here." I know it doesn't do any good to make him feel shitty. But it helps to redirect my anger. After all, we wouldn't be sitting here if I hadn't dropped the stupid car key to begin with. *Quit it. Don't let Mom get into your head. You're supposed to be done letting her do that.*

My parents. Dad hasn't tried calling back. How is he handling this? Two years ago, I wouldn't have worried. He was always so levelheaded, even under her tyranny. He would have developed a plan, followed instructions, made it all seem like Mom's idea. But now? On his best days, the slightest deviation from routine can send him into a rage. On the worst, he doesn't even know where he is. Will Mom even bother with him, if some kind of rescue effort comes knocking? Will she just leave him behind to putter around the house, to continually ask the walls if Beth is coming over for dinner? It won't surprise me at all if she uses all this chaos as a way to escape him.

When Dad's memory started to slip, it was me—the daughter who always ruined everything—who ended up being his constant, lingering in Mom's environment like poisoned air after a nuclear disaster. It's been a special kind of hell for her. Sometimes I wonder if Mom wishes her mind had been the one to go, the atrophy of old age wiping me from existence.

"I'm sorry, Beth," Mike says. "It all happened so fast." He lowers the back seats and rear console and scoots forward, squeezes into the front passenger seat and opens the glove box with a clunk that shakes the car and can probably be heard for miles. We both freeze, waiting for the shrieks, for the pounding on the windows that will undoubtedly break them this time. A whine forms in Jake's throat, and I snap my fingers. He flattens his ears, sniffs at the stain of my blood on the carpet, then gives me the same indignant look usually reserved for when I tell him the elk don't want to play.

When nothing emerges from the fog to attack, Mike digs through the glove box and finds a little travel-sized first aid kit. Extracting it from the compartment seems to cause him physical pain, like he's pulling a nasty splinter out of his palm. Or his heart. I bet his wife put that first aid kit there. What's her name? Sarah? I still don't know what happened between them, but I silently thank her for her foresight. There's no first aid kit in my Toyota. Maybe a used Band-Aid beneath one of the seats, some emergency panty liners in the console, a half-melted tube of ChapStick in the glove box.

"Come up here," Mike whispers.

I slide closer to him. Every movement I make rocks the car, announcing to whatever is within earshot that we're still here, nice and marinated, slabs of meat in a barbecue.

Mike gently pulls my bloody hair aside. When a small strip of my scalp peels off with it, I bite my lip to hold back a scream. Mike drops the clump like something he just fished from a clogged drain. Sweat stings my eyes. He dabs at the graze with a damp antiseptic wipe, and it's all I can do not to throw him out of the car. "I am so sorry," he says again. "That could have been really bad."

"Oh, *could* it have?" I can't give him too much grief for this one.

I would have done the same thing in his position. Only I wouldn't have missed. At least he had the presence of mind to grab the gun, not that it does us any good, now that it's empty. Maybe one of us can use it as a club until our arms are bitten off.

"You said you only found part of the cop," I say, steering the conversation away from my poor head, not that this new topic is a whole lot better. "What about the other guy?" I wish we'd gotten his name. Natalia's dad.

Mike shakes his head. "There was a lot of blood in the grass. Could have come from either of them. But no body."

"I think that's his Jeep parked up the beach," I say, glancing in that direction, which causes Mike to miss his target and jam his finger straight into the gouge and halfway through my head. That's what it feels like, anyway. I push his hand away. "Stop. Enough."

"Sorry." He looks toward the Jeep.

It's right on the verge of being swallowed by the fog. I can just see its shape out there. The last connection we have with a world that only yesterday still made some measure of sense. It was a violent, beautiful, heartbreaking, wondrous place, that world. It was a mess, but it was ours. Now the fog is pulled over it like a shroud to save me and Mike from having to look at the ugliness of its corpse.

"I'm sure you're right. But I bet his keys are on him. Wherever he is."

"That's what I was going to ask—if you happened to find them."

"Nope."

"Too bad. Being on level ground, you might have had a harder time rolling that one." I try to smile. I'm not sure what face I actually pull off, but Mike scoots a few inches back from me.

"I didn't see him," Mike repeats.

"Maybe he has a spare set hidden somewhere? Like you should have done?"

"Maybe. But that's a long walk from here. And then we have to hope those things don't catch wind of us while we're looking. And if we don't find a spare set, we have to make it back."

"Thanks for the report, Admiral Optimist. You know, there was a positive outcome to that scenario too," I say. But I don't believe it either.

Then he says the words I've been dreading. That I knew he would say—but not so long as we were on some other topic. "I have to clean your leg."

"You don't. It's really okay," I lie. "It doesn't even hurt anymore."

"Take your pants off."

"Wow, mister. I don't know what kind of girl you think I am—"

"Beth," he says solemnly, meeting my eyes. It's the first time we've really looked at each other since the world became something different and unknowable. Since the air itself learned how to open up and bare its teeth. I force myself to hold the stare until he says: "Now."

≈

I can't look at it. I don't need to. And I don't need to take my shorts off either, *Mike*. Instead, I gingerly roll the tattered hem back, adhered flaps of skin trying to peel away with it, and Mike's expression is all that's required to know it's worse than a mosquito bite. The color has drained from his face, and that's got nothing to do with his own loss of blood.

"It's . . . it's dirty," he chokes. What does that mean? Sand? Dog hair? "I need to clean it out. Thoroughly."

I can't help it. With one eye closed and the other squinted like there's something grim on TV and I haven't fully committed to watching yet, I look. My leg is marred by two rows of deep, messy punctures just above my knee—one on the top of my lower thigh, one on the underside, where the jaws clamped down. The individual holes are clotted with sand and dry blood, yes, but there's also a gross, black, oily substance all around the wound.

"I think this is saliva," Mike says, making it all that much worse. "Or some kind of bile. It doesn't seem to be corrosive or anything. Does it burn?"

"Actually, yes—now, can we please stop admiring it and get it the hell off me?" I'm trying not to hyperventilate, but I just can't with this. *Bile?* No. Nopity nuh-uh. I'm done. Going back to sleep, and when I wake up, it'll be this morning again and none of this will have happened. Why not? Last night I had a nightmare that killed the world. Why not a daydream that restores sanity and order?

I gag down a pulpy swig of mimosa. It reminds me of a time I crashed in some college guy's crappy apartment. Woke up and grabbed the closest can of half-drunk soda to wash the taste of so many bad decisions out of my mouth. Only it wasn't soda in the can—it was a mouthful of warm chewing tobacco spit. I left the contents of my stomach on his floor and stumbled out and somehow made my way home. Well, to my parents' home. That was the last time my key worked.

Mike tears open a sanitizing wipe and goes to work, first cleaning away the black slime, then scooping grit from my leg. I force down another chunky, orangey gulp, then lie back across a flattened seat, leg resting on the center console, and clench my teeth to keep from screaming and drawing their attention.

Jake rests his head next to me, watching with unblinking concern. His wet nose issues little puffs of air, rustling the hairs entwined with the upholstery. He lifts his head now and again to look out into the fog. My heart loses its rhythm every time he does it. Can Jake *see* the invisible bastards? Or can he just pinpoint them with his super canine hearing?

Jake flops over onto his side and pants into my face. His eyes are wide and bright and pleading with me to fix things, to bring him some relief from this ridiculous heat. For real, it's freaking October! Does the temperature have something to do with the new hell we're living in?

"Soon, buddy. We'll figure something out, just hang on a few more minutes." He blinks, seemingly comforted by my reassurance. As if I actually have any sort of plan. As if anybody does. *Go home and lock your doors, wait for further instructions.* What a joke.

"This isn't good enough," Mike says. The disinfectant wipe looks like bloody sandpaper now. He spies the cooler with our lunch tucked behind the driver's seat. He leans over me, pops it open, and finds the fifth of vodka I pulled from his freezer, a jug of tomato juice (who doesn't like a good Bloody Mary with lunch—c'mon!), and the sandwiches I assembled from what little I could scavenge from his fridge. "Is this all you packed for lunch?" he asks, staring into the cooler incredulously, as if I'd filled it with cleaning supplies.

"Yes!" I snap. I know where this is going. I know I've Bethed up once again. "I wasn't planning to be out here all *day,* okay? I thought we were going to have *fun,* not perform fucking triage."

"You didn't bring any water." It's just an observation, but it comes off like an accusation. As if I did it on purpose, out of some incredibly prescient malice. I've been accused of that my entire life, and his words make my insides twist up.

"There's a whole ocean right there! You're welcome to go get some." I can taste the venom in my words, bitter and burning on the tip of my tongue. His tone, the look on his face. It's all too familiar. *Oh, Beth,* I can hear Mom chiding. *I didn't think you could possibly make things any worse, but you continue to blow through my expectations like a semitruck through a guardrail.*

"For us to *drink,* Beth." Mike deflates. As if this is our last chance for survival. As if we had a chance to begin with.

"Tomatoes are mostly water," I mumble.

I can't even meet Jake's eyes. His stare is the worst. There's nothing accusatory in it. He still trusts me. He still believes I'm the smart human who was hired to take care of him and keep him happy and safe. That pink tongue of his is rolled out across the back of the seat like a worm dying in the sun, his breath hot against my skin, each exhalation a plea for me to give him a cool drink. How did I not even think to bring water for him? I should just open the door and get out. I don't deserve to be in here, in the hot safety of the car. Maybe the shriekers will fill up on me and move along.

"I was hoping to use it to clean up your leg too," Mike says. "But this will have to do." He grabs the vodka.

"Will it, though? Maybe just Band-Aid that bitch and let them do the rest at the hospital, whenever we get there, preferably after they've knocked me right out." The nearest hospital is in Seaside; I know that from the instructions left for me at the house. Seaside, where the cop directed anybody who didn't have a home to go back to. I wonder what that situation looks like right now. These invisible creeps could get into the high school without anybody knowing until they opened their mouths. I think I'd rather be here.

Mike blots my leg with a paper napkin, then cracks the lid of the vodka bottle. For some reason, he sniffs at the cold liquid inside. As if confirming it's of a sufficiently fine grade for medical use. I almost ask him for a sip. It seems only fair, given what he's about to do, that I get a little anesthesia.

"I have no medical training," he informs me, as though he's afraid I might sue him later. "I have no idea if this is adequate, but I don't want to take any chances."

"Wait—"

He doesn't. He tips the bottle and pours cold vodka directly into the punctures. I jerk bolt upright like a vampire bursting from a coffin. My fist, acting of its own free will, swings into the side of Mike's head. He topples back, nearly dropping the vodka and spilling it all over the floor. As if we needed even more tragedy today.

"Son of a *bitch*!" he hisses, blinking to clear the stars from his vision. "I don't want it to get infected. You don't know what that thing could be carrying."

Why'd he have to say something like that? What an awful thought—I want to reach into my mind and grab it and rip it out and stomp it to death.

"Don't care," I say. "You're done."

I snatch the first aid kit, rip open a gauze patch, lay it across the worst of the punctures, and haphazardly tape it down. I can't shake the thought of that thing's awful teeth in my skin, that slimy black goo seeping into my bloodstream, the fact that last night the sky opened up and unleashed honest-to-God *monsters* upon our world. But at least I don't have to keep staring at the evidence now.

I look at Mike. "It's my turn to play doctor."

He pulls up his shirt, as if to show me how unnecessary that is. He's got a lot of scrapes and bruises, but the worst is a single, wide tear down his side, like somebody tried to shank him with a wooden spoon. It bled badly, but the bleeding has stopped. He doesn't even have to worry about monster bile. What an asshole.

"Does it hurt?" I ask.

"Not anymore."

"Don't worry. I'll fix that."

13

MIKE

The tide's coming in. It's been rising for a while, but I've only really noticed in the last hour. It seems every time I glance out the windshield, it's crept a bit closer, inching toward us like a cat stalking a bird. Before we know it, it will be on us, and there will be no getting away.

Staring meaningfully into the tangle of wires behind the panel beneath the steering column isn't helping either. Unsurprisingly, the owner's manual doesn't have a chapter on emergency hot-wiring. If only Beth's phone could get a strong-enough signal for internet. You can find how-tos for just about anything on YouTube. I've read plenty of characters who steal cars, but always by force. Crimes of opportunity. Or they were appropriately equipped, courtesy of plot necessity. I should have rewritten them. Demanded higher stakes. Challenged them. That extra research would have paid dividends today.

Beth calls 911 again, and again gets a busy signal. At this rate, her phone will probably die just as she gets through to somebody. Now, that's a good plot beat. Can't let the characters off too easy—how will they ever grow? Sarah sure didn't show me any mercy. But that's where the parallels between our life and our fiction end. Protagonists are supposed to rise from heartache and ashes, not drown in them. Or maybe I'm not a protagonist. Maybe I'm just a side character, here to deliver some crucial piece of exposition before being killed in spectacular fashion. But if mine is just a supporting role, who's the hero of this story? Maybe that's another difference between reality and fantasy: In real life, sometimes there are no heroes. In life, sometimes everybody loses and darkness swallows the world.

Beth exchanges the phone for her camera and aims up the beach into the fog. She's looking for the things she's taken to calling shriekers. Tracks in the sand, swirling wisps of mist as they glide through the fog like wraiths. I'm honestly glad we can't see them. If I saw what she described—that yawning maw of teeth—I might just snap. I also can't shake the gnawing feeling that I've already snapped. That by skirting my fate last night, I slipped into this terribly broken limbo realm. That this is what awaits you if you miss your train: madness and monsters.

Beth sucks air through her teeth. "Mike. Look at this." She passes me the camera and points out the window. "You can just barely see one of those bowling balls in the fog."

It takes me a moment of fiddling with the focus ring, but I find what she's talking about. Bowling ball. At this point, that's a better word than *meteorite*, because it looks less like a space rock than ever. In fact, if the things had looked like this to begin with, I'd never have suggested coming down to the beach. I'd never have put one into a bucket and taken it back to my house. I'd have driven straight to the hospital to have myself committed.

A fleshy, creeping, purplish-brown vine protrudes from the object, stretching slowly toward the dunes. There's something undeniably predatory about it, like it's searching for something to grab hold of and squeeze the life from.

"What do you make of *that*?" Beth asks.

"I don't. I can't." I no longer possess the emotional energy to be even adequately mystified. I feel the way I used to after week-long development marathons, losing track of days, stumbling home drained and gibbering, Sarah guiding me to the couch and shoving a glass of wine into my hand before losing herself in a tumbler of icy vodka.

The memory sticks me like a needle. That woman was too good for me. Never on any of those nights did I ask about *her.* What was she seeking comfort from in that frosty glass? I took her for granted. I'd earned her love and assumed that was the mountaintop. She never stopped working for us, for our marriage, so why did I think I could? Why did I assume that if things were okay at the beginning, they would just stay that way until the end?

"I mean, it's . . . like . . . *sprouting,* right?" Beth asks. "Am I just making that up?"

"You're not making it up. That's what it looks like to me too." I can't think about it further than that. That's the problem when your whole life—when the entirety of your species' existence—is restricted to a single speck adrift in an insignificant corner of infinity. When something slams down from beyond the known borders of reality, how are you supposed to approach it? Stories explained the unknowable before the advent of science. What happens when science is left shrugging its shoulders?

I guess it comes back around to us, right? The storytellers. But I'm certainly not up to the task. I've gotten away with being successful in this business largely by virtue of being male, lucky, and just skilled enough to fool everybody into believing I know what I'm doing. I fish my ideas from the crowded shallows, all of us splashing about and bumping into one another and getting our nets tangled. Our catches are familiar, derivative, but satisfying enough when drowned in spice and sauce.

Sarah, though. *Man.* Sarah was brilliant. She sailed beyond the horizon and cast her line into the deep and reeled in things inexplicable and mesmerizing and terrifying. I used to envy her talent. I don't anymore. I have no interest in pondering what else might be out there. Because I know what happens now when you hook something that's more than you can handle. It eats you alive.

"It's almost like the bowling balls . . . are *seeds.* Or *spores,*" Beth says, waving a hand in the general direction of the thing. "Yuck."

"Let's stick with bowling ball," I say, kicking the words *seed* and *spore* into a closet and locking the door. "The tide's coming in," I add, to change the subject to something only slightly less awful.

"How high will it get?"

"Where we're parked? Pretty high." Silence fills the car. Much the way the seawater will in a few more hours. Right around sunset, probably. I wonder if Beth will still find it so provocative, the sunset, as we're choking down our last, briny breaths. Or will she finally see it my way?

"You didn't see anything else out there, did you?" she asks. "On the other side of the dunes?"

"No." But we've reached a point where anything is possible. I almost tell her about what I thought I saw on the beach last night, but that's a can of worms I'm just not ready to open. We have enough problems without bringing my own sanity into the mix. Unless . . . could she have seen that thing too? Or heard it, outside the house, before it staggered after me? Strangely, I almost want her to have witnessed it. I would be somewhat relieved to know the shambling presence came into the world from the same place as the shriekers and bowling balls. "Why?"

She bites absently at her lip, staring through me.

"Beth. *Why?*"

"I was just wondering. If there was anything else we need to be worried about."

I can't tell if that's the whole truth or not. But if she didn't offer it up willingly, she definitely won't if I press the issue. "I still think, for the time being, if we stay in the car, we'll be all right."

Beth quietly digests that, looking like I just diagnosed her with a terminal illness. She pulls up her parents' number and calls them again. It rings to voice mail. She sucks in her bottom lip and bites on it once more.

"Beth—"

"Stop, Mike. Just . . . shh. Don't talk for a minute."

I don't. I look back at Jake, who's sprawled across the folded-down seats. His panting has slowed to long, heavy sighs, his eyes dull and languid. He needs water, of which we have none. He needs cool, fresh air, but I don't dare open the door. He's our best shrieker alert, able to home in on their movement like a finely tuned tactical instrument, but he's on backup power now, his batteries running out of juice.

Beth looks at him, then at me. "I'm going to call for help."

"You've been doing that."

"Not with the phone." She focuses out the rear window. At the wrecked SUV. "They might not be manning the phones, but the radios? I refuse to believe everything fell apart that fast. There are others out there like him. And they *have* to be communicating with each other. We could reach another unit directly."

"Beth, no!"

"Did you try? Before you hit the gas and rolled the car, did you pick up the radio and say Mayday? Or whatever?"

I really don't want her to be right, but she has a point. "No, I didn't." You tell yourself you might do okay in an apocalyptic event. You'll keep your head on, be smart, be a hero. But really, most of us will just be bait. "But I also didn't hear anybody talking, like you seem to think they would be."

"You were in there for, like, ten seconds. There might have just been some downtime."

"You can't really want to go back out there."

"Want to? No, I don't. But versus sitting here, waiting to drown? Or for you to blow us up?" She waves at the exposed wires beneath the steering wheel. "It's worth a shot. It's our *only* shot, at this point."

"Absolutely not." I cross my arms to show her I mean business.

She isn't impressed. "It's been a long time since we've heard one of those things. I haven't seen any fresh tracks in the sand, and besides the hellvine over there, nothing else has changed on the beach. They probably gave up and moved inland, where they can actually see things. There are easier meals to be had than us."

"And if they haven't? It's not like either of us is particularly swift at the moment. I doubt we could outrun them this time."

"There's no 'we,'" she snaps. "*I'm* doing it. This hurts like a bitch, but I sure as shit can run through the pain if I have to, especially without you hanging off my shoulder."

"I said no."

"And I don't recall asking for your permission. I'm just telling you so that you can prepare yourself."

The assertion takes the wind from my sails, but not because she stood up to me. I've again proved a sorely inadequate partner, and now she has to take matters into her own hands. And I don't want to lose Beth too. If I can just get ahold of myself and articulate that, maybe she'll stay. But I can't.

She holds out a hand, but she isn't looking to be comforted. "The gun," she demands.

"It's empty."

"He probably has an extra clip in the car."

I could refuse to give it to her, but why? She'd just beat me over the head with her cell phone and take it.

She checks the chamber for a round, ejects the old clip, and tucks the pistol into the waistband of her shorts. "If I raise my hand above my head," she says, holding up a clenched fist as an example, "it means they're out there. Lay on the horn. Hopefully the sound will draw them away from me. Otherwise, just stay quiet."

"Okay," I say, bile rising in the back of my throat. She's going. She's leaving me. And I'm sitting here with a stupid look on my face, unable to stop it from happening. History is repeating itself.

"Also . . . *where* exactly are we?" she asks.

"About three miles north of Neacoxie Beach, near an access road," I croak. "I don't know what it's called."

She nods, then reaches for the door.

Something occurs to me. Something that seems to have, unbelievably, slipped right by us both, like those rip currents, so easy to forget about until they've pulled you off your feet and dragged you out to sea. But it could explain why Beth hasn't seen any signs of movement out there. "Wait."

She looks back at me, impatient, and I point down. It takes her a moment to get my meaning.

Beneath the car.

14

BETH

I hadn't even thought about them being right under our feet. Waiting patiently in the shadows for one of us to step out. That would explain the lack of movement outside. But how do we know for sure? I mean, without finding out the hard way. I could open the door and look, but I'd risk losing a fairly vital organ—like my head, what's left of it—in the process. At least then Mike would know that venturing out is not a fantastic idea. Not that he needs a whole lot of convincing.

"Jake would have barked," I insist, looking at him for affirmation. Jake barely has the energy to cut his eyes in my direction. It's getting into the afternoon, and temperatures should start dipping once evening approaches, not that I intend to be here that long. But that won't help his dehydration. Or mine. My throat burns for water. Even a drop. The waves taunt me. I can practically feel them against my skin.

"They do make a noise," Mike whispers, like if they are down there, they'll understand what he's saying, know that he's onto them. "A chirping." I know exactly what he's talking about. Last night I likened the sound to a squealing timing belt, but I keep that bit to myself for now.

"When I was in the police car, I heard it," he goes on. "It was constant. I don't know if it's the sound of them breathing or what, but . . ." He trails off, then squeezes between the seats to join me in the back, lies flat, and sticks his head and neck down into the footwell, his ear to the floor. Like he's listening for the drum of approaching hooves. It works about as well as I expect it to. "Maybe they only make the sound sometimes," he says, sitting upright.

"Really helpful, Mike. Thanks." It does give me an idea, though. I grab my camera. I'm going to get my money's worth out of this thing today. Well, Dad's money's worth. I'll have to let him know. If I ever see him again.

Swallowing the sudden lump in my throat, I flip out the LCD and rotate it until it faces up, then slide to the door.

"What are you doing?" Mike asks.

"Just be ready to pull the other way, if something grabs me," I tell him, trying not to imagine how that would probably end. Mike toppling backward, clutching a pair of legs and nothing else. Jesus, Beth, stop that. Those are very bad thoughts.

I tug the handle, then push the door open a crack. The draft rushes in, cooling the sweat on my face and rustling through Jake's fur. He groans and lifts his nose to sniff. I watch him, waiting for a reaction, an indication that something is nearby. He lays his head back down, but his nose keeps twitching, sorting through whatever scents are on the breeze. I turn to the door and push it open a bit more, waiting for the attack, the spray of sand and spit as the shriekers rush out of hiding.

Nothing happens. I've never been so happy for absolutely nothing to happen.

I stretch out on the seat, until my feet brush against the opposite door. One of Mike's hands closes around my left ankle, the other finding the small of my back and gripping the waistband of my shorts. His hands feel like they're made of stone, weighting me down, crushing me into the seat. I've never been too bothered by tight spaces—good thing, considering where I've been living for the past year—but the Subaru feels like a coffin. Jake's hot panting against my arm and Mike back there like he's lying on top of me. There's no room to get a deep breath. No room to move.

"Give me space," I hiss.

He shifts his body so as to stop mashing me into the seat. "Sorry." But he stays at the ready.

Keeping as much of my arm inside as I can manage, I lower the camera until the lens is aimed beneath the car. There are no shrieks of surprise, my hand remains attached to my arm. I crane my neck for a view of the LCD.

The sand under the car is undisturbed. There aren't any floating grains betraying an invisible presence, no shimmer of distortion. A drop of sweat rolls down my nose, and I relish the breeze against my skin.

"Beth?"

"Yeah?"

"Anything?"

"No." I reluctantly pull myself back and pass the camera off to him. He looks at it like it might explode in his hands. "We're clear for now. Keep an eye out, though. And keep the door open." I give Jake a pat. He tilts his face into the air current, his eyes half-closed. "Also?" I give Mike my cell phone. I hate how final this all feels, but it's necessary. "If my parents do call, and I don't make it back, just . . . you know, make it sound good. Please?"

"'Sound good'?"

"Yeah. Not, 'Oh, Beth, she was half drunk and got out of the car when I told her not to and got killed immediately.'" *I don't want to give her the satisfaction*, I don't say.

"That shouldn't be too hard. I mean, to make you sound good. Not that I have to *make* you sound good, you *are*, is what I'm saying—"

"Maybe just don't answer the phone."

"I can do that."

Before I can stall any further, or listen to Mike dig himself clear through the earth, I step out onto the beach.

≈≈≈

I nearly collapse. It's as if the heat in the car caused my muscles to wilt. Or maybe it was the blood loss. My head grows so fuzzy I stumble and have to reach out for support, slapping my hand against the side of the Subaru with a metallic thud that sounds like cannon fire in the quiet of the fog.

"Are you okay?" Mike whispers.

I nod, fighting the urge to vomit. The alcohol, the lack of adequate hydration and sustenance, the heat, all whipped up nice and pretty on top of the worst mind fuck of a day ever—it's no wonder my body is already trying to call it quits. I'm somewhat, and for the first time ever, grateful for the mistreatment I've inflicted on myself over the past two decades. I've built up some tolerance.

Although it sounds like the engine died, the police SUV's roof lights are still strobing pitifully. That means there's power. Enough to run the radio. All I have to do is take one step after another until I'm there. Easy-peasy. But there's something else I have to do first.

"My hoodie," I say, extending my hand back into the car. Mike stares at me like I'm insane, but he passes it to me anyway.

I don't go to the SUV. Not yet. I turn around and walk toward the water's edge. Toward that line of white foam that's inching closer to us every minute. I can feel my energy returning with every step through the fresh air. Well, as fresh as can be with the hellvine over there still giving off its noxious aroma. The thought of those smell particles going up my nose, accumulating in my lungs, taints the ocean breeze's rejuvenating effect—and this is from a smoker.

The water rushes over my toes, and my body aches with relief. I want to just stand here forever. Or to keep walking until the ground disappears beneath my feet. I want to go under, to be completely submerged, cleansed of everything this awful day has thrown at me. But there's no time for that.

I dunk the hoodie into the cold surf until it's good and drenched, then make my way back toward the Subaru. Droplets of water hit the sand with a soft patter, but I don't think they'll hear that.

Something passes in front of the sun. A heavily diffused shadow briefly falls over the beach, and then it's gone. I squint at the sky, into the brightest area of fog. What was that? A cloud? I don't hear anything, and it must have been pretty close or very big to eclipse the sun like that. Hot-air balloon? Or a military helicopter? They can make those quiet, I think.

I pick up my pace. As I near the door, Mike's face resolves into clarity, and I see the worry recede. What did he think I was going to do, swim away and abandon him here? I reach in through the open door and fling the drenched hoodie across Jake.

He jerks, startled, then relaxes, the water pooling around him. His tail slaps the seat with a single, heavy thump of gratitude.

"Good thinking," Mike says.

"There might be a helicopter," I say, pointing. "I can't hear it. I just saw something up there, in the sky."

"There's a Coast Guard base in Astoria," Mike says. "Might have been one of theirs. They could be patrolling, looking for people stranded, like us."

The thought of being airlifted off the beach is so real I want to reach out and grab it. But I'm not quite close enough yet. I need to get into the SUV. I need to get on that radio, let them know where to look.

"Remember the horn." And then I'm off, before he can say anything more.

I resist the urge to run. If I run, I know I'll trip. Knock the wind out of myself. They'll hear that, for sure. No matter how far away they might be, they'll hear, and they'll be on me in seconds. If the helicopter is looking for survivors, they won't just do one quick pass, they'll circle the area. I have time. A little. I ignore the nagging voice telling me if anybody is looking for survivors, they'll be looking in Seaside, in Astoria, in Long Beach, not this deserted stretch of nowhere.

One step, two steps, three steps. Walking is good. Walking is not dying. The pain in my leg is getting more vivid by the step, the injured muscles stubbornly unwilling to do their job, but I grind my teeth and limp through it.

The SUV is as far ahead of me as the Subaru is behind when a shriek rises from the dunes. The sound seems to cause the ground to quiver and give way beneath me, and suddenly I feel as if I'm up to my ankles in the sand. I can't move one direction or the other. I can only stand there, sinking helplessly, my useless legs conspiring against me.

You're not sinking you're not stuck move Beth!

The fog thickens impossibly, until I can't see an inch past my nose. More shrieks join in. Talking to one another triumphantly. Sounding the alarm that the dumb human got out of the car, it's dinnertime. How did they hear me? Is it not sound that attracts them? Can they *smell* me? Taste my fear and desperation on the air? Can they feel disturbances in the fog, like spiders lying in wait in their webs?

There's another scream. This one is nothing like the others. It's a sound that absolutely belongs here on earth, but that doesn't make it any less harrowing.

It's an elk. Being torn to pieces up there in the dune grass. It bellows as they devour it alive. I can hear it thrashing about fruitlessly. I flinch at every rip of muscle and flesh, each snap of bone further anchoring my traitorous feet into the sand. Is it one of the same elk Jake and I watched walk past the beach house? Is the poor animal's picture on my camera, obliviously munching away beneath one of the last sunsets it—or we—would ever experience?

Am *I* on somebody's camera? A cell phone somewhere? Is somebody looking at my blissfully blasted face, remembering the brief moments we shared, and imagining what horrible fate I'm enduring today? Is some vision of my demise giving them a taste of bittersweet satisfaction?

Too bad. It's not happening. Not here, anyway. Not now.

I grit my teeth and run. My legs wobble in protest, my knees threaten to lock up as my shoe soles squeak in the dry sand, my breaths come out in short, sharp huffs. I know they can hear me now. They're coming for me, those dripping teeth, those snapping jaws. The pain shooting up my leg is bright. That shadow passes in front of the sun again, and I look up. I still can't see the helicopter through the fog, but I think I might hear it. There's a distant, soft *whoosh-whoosh* of something.

The shriekers hear it, too, and immediately fall quiet. The elk has given its final anguished bleat as well. Which, on one hand, great. On the other, the new silence amplifies all the noise I'm making.

I reach the SUV and haul myself up onto the sky-facing door, being as quiet as I can (so, not at all) and dropping down through the open window (which is a much smoother process when somebody isn't shooting you in the face). I bang my bandaged thigh on the steering wheel on the way down, nearly biting my tongue in half to keep from screaming.

There's movement outside.

I clap a hand over my mouth and contort into a ball between the steering wheel and seat, trying to make myself as small as possible.

There's that chirp. That steady cricket singing, that timing belt squeal. The creature brushes against the SUV, prodding curiously at the undercarriage with what sounds like a very sharp blade. If their teeth are for biting and tearing, then whatever they have at the ends of their other appendages are clearly for quicker, cleaner work. Like cutting a shotgun in two. I hear only one of them. A scout sent away from the dinner table to check out the new racket coming from the beach. I keep as quiet as I can, even trying to will my heart into taking it easy for a minute. Now would be the time for a gigantic, hideous spider to skitter across my foot or for a sneeze to come on.

But the universe takes pity on me. This time. I'm sure fate has something far worse in store.

That shadow again. And the *whoosh-whoosh*. It's a huge sound, like a jet engine winding up on the tarmac. Up in the dunes, a new sort of shriek rises. Not angry or hungry, like the others. This one seems almost . . . alarmed? A warning, maybe? The chittering outside ceases immediately, and I hear the shrieker retreating swiftly through the sand. The warning cry falls quiet again.

I count slowly to a hundred, to be sure the shrieker has ample time to move far away, then take my hand from my mouth, tuck my head between my knees, and puke up half a jug of mimosa and tomato juice. Incredible how quietly you can retch when it's a matter of life or death.

No more drinking, Beth. For real, this time. If you somehow manage to get off this beach, it stops. It all stops.

I've sworn some variation of that to myself before—once in a similarly inverted car. This time I mean it. I thought I'd meant it the other times, but the pledge feels different now. Everything feels more real today. More absolute.

I wipe the last orange strings from my lips and set to scavenging the console and glove box. I can't seem to catch my breath. No matter how deeply I inhale, I can manage only a tiny gulp. *No more smoking either. And maybe it's time to take up jogging.* Resolutions are easy to make when the odds of seeing tomorrow are slim at best.

There's a black all-weather patrol bag deep in the passenger-side footwell. Mike must not have seen it, not that I blame him. On each end, a water bottle is tucked into a netted compartment. I crack one open and take a greedy sip, my throat wailing for me to just chug the thing, but I resist. That's Old Beth behavior right there. Mike and I will share one bottle; Jake will get the other.

I paw through the rest of the bag's contents. There's a first aid kit, a real one, along with a flashlight, a tactical knife, a cotton face mask, and some black duct tape. I also find four extra clips for the pistol and load one. I nearly cry out victoriously when I spy a fruit and nut bar, but my excitement fizzles quickly when I realize it's just an empty wrapper, leaving me even hungrier than before. I do a hasty search for any other snacks he might have squirreled away, without luck. Not even a pack of gum.

Mike was right: the radio has been quiet, no chatter between units or from Dispatch. It is a bit unsettling that nobody is talking out there. Then again, if the shriekers are sensitive to noise, maybe a communications blackout was issued.

I carefully unseat the radio handset and put it up to my mouth.

This is it. Our last hope of rescue. Please, somebody has to be out there. Somebody must be listening. Mike and I cannot be the only two to have survived this. The universe cannot possibly be that cruel.

"Hello?"

15

BETH

An answer comes so much faster than I could have hoped for.

"Who is this?" Her voice is tiny, cracking a bit on the last syllable of her desperate question. As if she's just as surprised as I am to hear a voice on the other end of the radio. As if, like me, she barely believes it can be real. "Are you there?"

I turn the volume down until I can just hear her. There's no scramble of feet outside, no chirping.

"My name is Beth," I say as quietly as I can. "I'm—*we're*—stranded on the beach—" I clap a hand over my mouth again, this time to cough through my nose, spraying dusty snot all over my fingers. My chest is so tight. I swear the car is shrinking, the steering wheel pressing me into the seat.

"Where are you making this call from?" the woman asks. I don't know who she is, a dispatcher or another cop, but I don't like how scared she sounds. The people on the other end of the radio are the ones who are supposed to have it together. They're the ones we need to save us—they can't be afraid.

"Three miles north of Neacoxie Beach," I recite. Oh, wait. I get what she's asking. There's an ID tag stuck in a clear plastic window on the side of the patrol bag, so I read from it. "Officer Theo

Sullivan's car. It's wrecked." I wait a moment for a response, then remember to lift my finger off the transmit button.

"You said 'we.' Is he okay?" There's unmasked hope in her voice, and it breaks my heart. What's the best way to answer a question like that?

"He's dead," I say, opting to rip off the bandage. I'm not going to tell her what Mike told me, in case they knew each other, were friends. I'm not going to tell her that Theo's shotgun was sliced in half, his hand lopped off, his body turned into pulled pork. Not even if she asks. If she asks, I'll lie and say he died instantly. But she doesn't ask. She doesn't say anything. "Hello?"

"I'm here." Even softer than before. "You . . . you know this for sure?"

I should just say no. Say I watched him run into the dunes and never come back. I've already done enough damage today. How long has she been waiting by the radio for a voice to come through, a voice she recognizes, bringing good news, bringing hope? It isn't fair that I have to be the one to take that away from her.

"I do. I'm sorry. But he helped a bunch of people get away first. He was very heroic." She goes quiet at this. "Listen, we have no way off this beach. Our car won't start, and this one, Officer Sullivan's, it's trashed. They have us pinned. And the tide's coming in."

"'They'?"

Did she just ask that? Like, with a question mark? Who else could I possibly mean by *they*? Marauders?

"You know. The *things*." Gesturing like she can see me. "They make a shrieking noise, and they're invisible." It still feels ludicrous to even say this.

"Oh. *Them*."

I just cannot even. *Oh. Them?* What? Like I told her we were surrounded by a herd of angry cows. *Sure, sure, Farmer Booya's herd—they're an ornery bunch, ain't they?*

"I'm sorry, are there . . . are there *other* things out there?" I'm not sure I really want the answer, but the way she said that, it sounds as though the shriekers might not be the biggest of our problems. Which is, of course, impossible. Please, God.

"Yes."

"Different from the shriekers?"

"The *what*?"

"The invisible things." I know that dazed, faraway quality in her voice too well. I'm sure she's still reeling from the truth bomb I just dropped about Theo, but I need her to come back to me, before I lose her completely. The present is all that matters right now, and I do mean that as selfishly as it sounds. "Tell me about the others."

"Different. *Worse.*" Her voice trembles and goes shrill. The memory of them brings her back. "They haven't found me. I've been here since last night. Hiding. There just wasn't time to do anything else. They came out of nowhere. And now I'm the only one left—" She breaks into heavy sobs.

This is exactly what I dreaded. I can almost picture it: A darkened office, chairs and papers scattered, blinds shut, her beneath a desk, taking calls when she can, hoping one of them will be Theo, or another officer, or a loved one, coming to save her. Instead, she gets me. There's nobody to save either of us.

Except, no, there's still one more chance. A very small one, somewhere above the fog, passing to and fro in front of the sun as if to communicate to me that it's there, standing by for my signal.

"Listen," I hiss. "There's a helicopter out there. Looking for survivors, I think. Do you have any way of reaching them?"

"A helicopter?" As if she's never heard the word. "I don't think so."

"You don't think what? That you can reach them?"

"No, I don't think there are any helicopters. Not around here. It's too dangerous—"

"I *heard* one," I insist, even though I'm not at all certain about that. I heard *some*thing. And if it isn't a helicopter flying above the fog, what can it be?

Scratch that. Don't wanna know.

Or maybe I already do. That's the real issue here.

There was something else in that not-a-dream. Something in the sky. An incomprehensible mass of colors and jellyfish tentacles that I mistook for a cloud. It heard me, that thing. It came for me, right before I woke up. Could one of those have been drifting over Mike's house as I slept? Is that how it bled into my sleep? And if there are shriekers, bowling balls, and cloudfish in the world, what else could there be? The woman on the other end of the radio saw something we haven't, something that wiped out a dispatch center, an entire *police force,* from the sound of it. How many other abominations are running rampant out there?

I'm sweating buckets. It feels like somebody is sitting on my chest. Like I'm inside a can crusher. I need to make a plan and get out of here.

"It could be military," I say. "The helicopter. Stealth." Still trying to rationalize a massive object passing quietly in front of the sun. Hoping fiercely for it to be anything but a cloudfish. "Deployed from some base farther inland, where these things haven't reached yet."

My suggestion is met with a moment of startled silence, as if she's struggling to fathom just how wrong a person could be. Then she lets me have it, like an open-palmed slap across my face.

"Beth, they are *everywhere.*"

A face pops into my mind. It's that little girl's face, the one we met on the beach. Natalia. That confused, highly skeptical look she got when we told her the bowling balls were meteorites. Because of course she knew that wasn't the case. Unlike me and Mike, she hadn't been completely cut off from the world. Her dad might not have filled her in on every detail, but she sure knew this shit wasn't normal. I don't know what the woman on the other end of the radio looks like, but I can hear in her voice that she's making the same face. *Oh, you poor, stupid thing. Where have you been?*

"What do you mean?" I ask. I need her to say it. To make it real. Otherwise, I'll just keep denying it, all the way to my sandy grave.

"It happened last night," she says. "I'd just received a noise complaint. Dogs barking. Sullivan responded. Only, when he arrived, he said it was every dog in the neighborhood. I could hear them, too, in the background. Not angry but *howling,* like you sometimes hear on the Fourth of July."

"But it wasn't fireworks," I say. There's something on the windshield, something that brings everything together with a snap and a cold, plummeting sensation in my stomach. I can't pull my eyes away from it. "It was meteors."

"No," she says. "I mean, yes, that happened next. But first there was just . . . silence. From the dogs, from Sullivan, like our connection had been lost. I felt something like vertigo for about five minutes. And then it was chaos."

I can barely hear her. I can't focus on anything but the windshield. I have to get out of here. I have to get back to Mike and Jake. I have to tell them what I know. What I didn't know I knew until just now. I can still see the meteors in that strange dreamworld, searing through an alien sky before burning into nothing. But, no—that's not right. They weren't burning up, they were *crossing over.* Falling there, but landing here. And they weren't the only things. The air was filled with tiny husks, the shed skins of unknowable creatures drifting down like snow, illuminated in that dreadful, sick moonlight.

There's a light accumulation of those awful little husks caught beneath the windshield wipers. Wherever I went during that dream, Theo Sullivan went there too. And others—I heard them. I heard them *screaming.* Because it wasn't a dream at all. And just as the meteors and the husks and the shriekers and everything else slipped across the threshold going one direction, I and Theo and who knows how many others went the opposite way. Me lying in bed, Theo responding to an annoyed neighbor's late-night noise complaint.

"How long was he gone?" I ask. "How long was the connection broken?"

"I don't know," she answers. There's a tremble growing in her voice. "We were completely overwhelmed by then. I was transferring calls to Astoria, to Tillamook County, but it was the same there. It was the same everywhere."

"But when he did come back. When you spoke to him next. Did he say he . . . had gone someplace *else*?"

This is followed by another brief silence, and then she says, "You went too." Almost awestruck, like I just told her I toured with her favorite band.

"I don't know." Unexpected tears prickle at the corners of my eyes. "I don't know what's happening at all anymore. I don't even know what's real."

"You're lucky," she says. "You made it back."

"Did some people *not*?" I didn't even consider this. I'm still trying to wrap my mind around me being *lucky.* To have woken up to face not just another day but this of all days. But apparently there was an even worse outcome?

"Most didn't, the last I heard," she says. "It wasn't so noticeable here, at first. Middle of the night, the roads empty . . ."

I listen as a newsreel of carnage flickers in front of my mind: drivers vanishing from their cars on busy freeways; jets disappearing from the sky, taking half the passengers with them, only to return minutes later in irrecoverable nosedives. Whole neighborhoods swallowed by alien landscapes. It seems to have been a complete roll of the dice what stayed, what went, and what was returned to its proper place when this bizarre collision of time and space had passed. I'm beginning to understand what the woman meant when she said I was lucky. Theo Sullivan traveled over in his SUV, presumably armed and sober. I wasn't even wearing *clothes.*

And all of this, of course, was only the beginning. Because at the same moment so many people were lost, other things took their place, and they weren't any happier about the situation.

"I'm sorry," she concludes. "I'm so sorry I can't help you."

I barely hear her. I'm too busy trying to make some sense of what she's just told me, to find any semblance of pattern or reason that might give me a hint as to what's happened, and why, and what might be next.

"You don't have to apologize," I say when I can figure out how to form words again. "It's not your fault. Unless it is, in which case,

I'm coming over there." How I'm making jokes at this juncture is anybody's guess. A defense mechanism, maybe. A shield against the beating fists of madness.

It works, though. She chuckles. Or clears her throat. I can't really tell. "Who's with you?" she asks. I forgot I mentioned there being two of us.

"Just a friend." How strange to think of Mike as *just* anything anymore. We haven't known each other a day, but I feel like I know him better than anybody right now. "And a dog." Jake isn't *just* a dog either. Both of them, they might be all I have left, yet somehow that's more than I had before the world ended. "How about you? Is there anybody you're waiting to hear from?"

"My parents and my sister. I spoke to them early this morning. They live in Astoria. They know somebody with a bomb shelter. They were supposed to let me know when they were safe."

I should get going. My head is feeling light. The gas, or whatever the bowling balls are spewing into the air, is gathering inside the SUV like a toxic cloud. I wasn't paying attention to the smell before. I've grown somewhat used to it, since the entire beach reeks. But the high concentration in here is gonna kill me if I don't leave.

Only I don't want to leave her. I get to go back to Mike and Jake, while she has to await her fate alone. And that is simply not right. I don't know her, but I didn't know Mike before yesterday. Even just a few minutes can change a person's life. It might have been dumb random luck that hell spat me back out, but I don't want to believe that. I want to think it was so I could do something besides take up better people's oxygen for once in my life, even if it's simply to spare a few minutes for a fellow human being.

"I'm sure they're okay," I tell her. "Cell networks could be going down, or just congested. Or maybe they got caught up helping other people." Which didn't end so well for Theo, so maybe that wasn't a great example.

"If you two get off the beach, do you have someplace to go?" she asks. The earnestness of her concern makes my heart swell.

"Not really. The Seaside high school was supposed to be safe."

"It's not." She doesn't elaborate. She doesn't need to.

"Thanks for the tip. Maybe this whole mess will be over by the time we get out of here, anyway."

"You think so?"

"Sure. I mean, that's how it always is in movies. Aliens show up, give us a bunch of attitude, level a few cities, then die from, like, rain or chicken pox or something."

She does laugh this time. It's a good sound. Maybe that's how we'll defeat them. Humor. Or at the very least, we'll go down puns blazing.

"And if we know anything about movies, it's that they're always one hundred percent accurate."

I get a moment of thoughtful silence instead of a second laugh. Dang. I'm going to have to go soon, and I'd rather do so on a high note.

"Will you try to reach Astoria?" I ask her.

"I might. Whatever happens next, I'd like to be with my family when it does."

"Hey, that's still a Hollywood ending."

There's the second laugh. It makes me smile. But then she cuts it off with a sharp inhalation. "Something's here. Something's inside."

My heart slams against my ribs hard enough to knock me forward. I grab the steering wheel for balance, and the front wheels grind as they try to turn, wobbling the vehicle. "What is it?" I whisper. I don't want whatever it is to hear me. She must be wearing a headset, but still.

"I don't know."

"Are you hidden?"

"Yes." She can barely form words between shaky gasps. "Under my desk, behind my chair."

"Is it making a cricket sound?"

"Hm-mm." She must have a hand over her mouth to stifle any escaping sobs.

"Okay. It must not be a shrieker. They make that noise, all the time. Just don't move, and don't talk. I'm right here. Just . . . focus on that."

Brilliant, *focus on that,* what are you even talking about, Beth? I don't know what to say to somebody in a situation like this. I don't know how to be encouraging. Even my dad only dared give out subtle compliments, for fear of sparking Mom's wrath. What am I going to tell this woman? *Think about the sunset, it'll save us all*?

"You're going to sit there and not move, and it will pass right on by," I hiss as confidently as I can. She keeps toggling her microphone, and I can hear it in the background. It makes an awful sound as it moves. A quivering, thunderous slap of wet rubbery flesh, like the bottom of a nasty bog took shape and dragged itself free of the earth. It sure doesn't sound like it's going to pass right on by.

It's making a high-pitched squeal too. No, that's coming from her: building in her throat and escaping, maybe through her fingers, with every tortured breath.

"Quiet," I order.

"Beth!" she squeals.

"Please—" Please *what*? Did you not even get her *name*? You horrible, horrible bitch! What is the *matter* with you? "Please, keep quiet. Hold your breath if you have to."

Boom-squilch. Boom-squeeelch. How did it even find her? Did it hear her talking to me? Oh my God, did I drive my stupid car right through her window too? Why didn't she hang up on me? How couldn't she see me coming?

BOOM-SQUIIILSH.

"Don't listen to it," I beg, practically sobbing. "Listen to me. I'm here." I don't know if she can even hear me, but I can hear everything happening on her end. "I'm not going anywhere. Not until it's gone. And then we're getting off this beach and we're going to come get you. Do you hear? We *will* come get you, and we'll drive to Astoria, and—"

She screams. Like something from a Hitchcock film, over the top and distorted. But real. So real it freezes my blood and cools the marrow in my bones. The thing remains chillingly silent, besides the slimy, heavy slap of whatever unearthly appendages it uses to fling her office chair aside and pull her from her hiding place.

Her cries become inhuman. Or at least my mind twists them that way. To keep me from losing my marbles as I listen. I promised to stay, after all. I didn't even bother getting her name, so keeping her company as she's violently extricated from the world is the least I can do.

It goes on and on. I don't even know what I'm hearing—sounds like sticks snapping across knees; like strips of thick, sodden cloth ripping down the middle; like buckets of paint spilling across the floor. Her screams die off long before the unimaginable beast stops desecrating her body. I sit motionless and listen to every last bit of it. My penance for bringing this upon her. Her headset fell off at some point and landed a few feet away, sparing me from an audial tour of its insides. She must have been squeezing that talk button so hard it stuck, gripping the wireless receiver like an extended hand that might yet pull her free.

Then it's all over. The room on the other end of the airwaves is quiet. So quiet I'm beginning to think her headset died. Then it moves again.

BOOM-SQUEELCH. One short step.

SQUIIIIIIIILSH. No step. I think it just leaned over to examine the headset. To determine if it's something worth chowing down on. I want to say something to it. To threaten it. To give it my location and tell it to meet me at sunset to find out how it likes the taste of hot lead.

But I can't. I reach down and switch off the radio. Neither of us has any more use for it.

≈

I sling the patrol bag over my shoulder. It weighs five thousand pounds. Balancing it, I grab the window frame, but I don't have the strength to lift myself. That conversation sapped me utterly.

Perching on the steering wheel is enough of a boost that I can get my forearms out, gaining a bit more leverage. I still feel like I've had more functionality after a four-hour pub crawl, but I manage to get back out into the open air.

There's a second bowling ball half buried in the sand by the back tire, which explains the powerful odor. Either Mike didn't notice it when he passed this way on foot, or it was beneath the SUV up on the ridge and he dragged it down with him. Either way, it's been hard at work tainting the air here. The Tacoma Aroma has got nothing on the bowling balls. I also smell the sharp fragrance of leaking gasoline. The bouquet makes my eyes water and turns my stomach.

More creeping tendrils sprout from this ball too. They grow fast. One creeper is wrapped around the SUV's exhaust pipe, while another stretches lazily across the sand, searching for something to grab hold of. Or maybe waiting for something to wander by. How big can they get? How far will they reach?

Delightful questions, these. Pity I don't have time to sit around pondering them.

The fog is beginning to burn off in the afternoon sun. I see a bit of blue sky up there, but nothing else. I don't hear anything either. *It's too dangerous to fly right now.* It's dangerous to be sitting out in the open too. Time to quit dawdling.

Something snaps around my wrist.

It's cold and damp and covered in what feels like thousands of bee stingers. The pain is electric; every muscle in my arm turns to jelly. What happens next is instinctive. A primal reaction when something startles the piss out of you, especially when that something is a predatory alien creeper vine.

I scream.

Not a short yelp either. I bloody howl, because those bee stingers *burn.* The vine constricts, driving them deeper into my arm. Feels like they're boring straight into my wrist bones. I yank the other way, and the awful thing squeezes tighter. I hadn't even seen it, coiled up and waiting in the front wheel well like some kind of snake. I really need to start paying closer attention to my surroundings, especially now that those surroundings all seem to possess pulses and appetites.

The shriekers respond to my outburst. So does Mike. Every living thing in the immediate area code heard my racket.

"Beth! Are you okay?" Mike shouts. Jake barks his concern too.

I don't answer them. I don't want to give away my position any more than I already have. The grass along the ridge bends flat as the shriekers mow through it, chirping eagerly. I tug the pistol from my waistband and fire three shots in their direction. They skitter back, briefly revealing themselves to me as they hiss their disapproval. And then they're gone again.

But they don't retreat back into the grass. They're learning. The loud pops aren't to be feared. Not until these bullets start connecting.

Hey—now, *that's* an idea.

The bowling ball is a much easier target, what with my actually being able to see it. Luckily, the hellvine took my nondominant hand hostage. The first bullet connects dead-on, ringing like a hammer striking a moss-covered rock, and goes zinging off into the ether.

The second shot misses completely and burrows into the sand.

The shriekers close in. The air wavers all around the SUV. They're going to pull me down from my perch and slice me in half and slurp out my insides. That maddening chirping will be the last thing I hear as I choke on my own blood.

I fire a third shot. Why not? For science!

It hits the bowling ball and again ricochets off, this time striking the SUV's undercarriage. The sulfury sewage smell of the bowling balls is soon accompanied by the pungent odor of burning fuel and melting plastic.

"*Come on*!" There's smoke too. That's neat. The bullet sparked and ignited the leaking gasoline. I couldn't have pulled that off if I tried.

Mike lays on the car horn, having decided to make himself useful. Except now I see the error in my plan: If he draws the shriekers over there, I'll be effectively cut off. That is, if I'm not literally cut off first. They'll be between us, and there's no way they'll lose interest this time and go back into the dunes.

I swing the pistol away from the impervious bowling ball and find one of those shimmering patches. I can't guess how many bullets I have left. A few. No way they'll let me reload. These have to count. I know I can't kill them all. Maybe I can't even kill one. But I can cause harm, this I do know. It's what I'm best at, after all.

I pull the trigger.

This bullet connects with a meaty, satisfying thump. A jet of sticky black goo hits the sand, with more dripping down the shrieker's body, betraying its location far better than the shimmer. It doesn't cry out in pain, which is a little disappointing, but it skitters blindly sideways, right into striking distance of another hellvine.

And strike it does. The vine shoots out, indifferent to the shrieker's invisibility, and coils around its leg—or whatever appendage happens to be within range. This time the shrieker *does* scream. And the rest of the shimmers fall back toward the dunes.

They're afraid of it! Holy hellvines, they haven't attacked me, because they don't want to get caught too!

Which, on one hand, yay! On the other, it can't be a good sign for me if even the monstrous deadly aliens avoid contact with the vines.

If I could see the shrieker, I have to imagine it moves so swiftly that it's just a blur. With little more than a cloud of sand and the swoosh of sliced air, it divides the hellvine into two. The cut end doesn't release its grip, though. Those stingers keep it firmly attached to the shrieker. It rejoins its buddies, yowling in frustration and—I hope, I really really hope—agony. The same kind of excruciating burn that's enveloping my arm.

The sky splits open on the ridge, emitting a wail like nothing I've heard yet today. A haunting warble that brings the others to a halt. It keeps its jaws open, the shrieker that made that sound. I see its shape through the thinning fog.

It's the one that bit me. I don't know how I know this, but I do.

Like we've been bound since it first revealed itself and showed my poor, bewildered mind that I hadn't even begun to imagine the horrors this universe had in store.

The others open their mouths too. There's at least a dozen of them. They're all smaller than the one on the ridge, though no less terrible. Deep within each pair of open jaws is a worm-looking thing. Tongues with circular mouths lined with needle teeth of their own. They look like lampreys, because the shriekers weren't already nightmarish enough. The powerful jaws are apparently just for holding prey in place. The tongue-worm does the dirty work. Even if we survive this, no shower will ever get me clean enough.

The tongue-worms all aim toward the sky. The toothy mini-maws are ringed with glistening black beads that I can only assume are eyes. Unblinking and all-seeing, like a spider's eyes. They don't hold the position long before retracting, jaws snapping shut, and then they all disappear, creating a tiny landslide of sand as they scuttle back up the dune to join the big one. It finally shuts up.

Was I just given a stay of execution? Did the big boss on the ridge tell them I wasn't worth the risk?

Something passes in front of the sun again. It's not a helicopter. I know this because I can see it now. And I've seen it before. I watched it detach itself from that alien sky and drift down to swallow me whole. The shriekers saw it last night too. And they knew to hide and shut up.

It's a cloudfish. But this time, I'm not going to be stolen away at the last moment by some cosmic roll of the dice. That's already happened, and this is the new normal.

"No. No no *no*!" It's coming right at me. My poor hand is purple, the blood either being blocked by the pressure or extracted by the ten bajillion hypodermic needles stabbing into my skin. The flames are still lapping up what remains of the oxygen, their heat tickling my face.

Mike lets off the horn, and in a minute he's going to do something stupid like walk over here to save the day. He won't even see the cloudfish. Those long, dangling tentacles will grab him and pull him up and fling him into the black void of the cloudfish's mouth. Then it will be my turn.

The knife! There's a knife in the bag! Snap out of it, girl!

The pistol goes back into my waistband—amazingly without a bullet shooting straight down through my leg—and I grab the knife from the patrol bag. I open the blade with my teeth, position the sharp edge against the fleshy mass, and push. There's a hiss like leaking propane, the escaping fumes burning my eyes and wilting my lungs. I can taste the sour air and rot, surrounding me in an aura of fetid corruption as viscous, purple slime oozes from the cut.

The cloudfish, if it can detect the smell, is undeterred. I wonder if it's actually meant to *attract* predators? Do the bowling balls smell *tasty* to them? Drawing them near so the hellvine can grab hold? If not the shriekers or the cloudfish, then there must be something in that other world that likes this scent. How long do we have until the wind carries it to the appropriate nose? Until we have a new friend join us on the beach of doom?

The flames spread to the rear tires, putting off an oily black smoke. Between that and the hellvine's leakage, the air is officially death. The few errant tufts of beach grass nearest the blaze curl back from the heat.

I slice deeper. Sweat stings my eyes as I saw through meat and sticky purple pus; right above me, I can hear the cloudfish, the deep, resonant *whoosh-whoosh-whoosh* of air being pulled into that gigantic black mouth.

Come on come on comeoncomeon!

The knife blade reaches the metal door, and the severed part of the tendril goes limp. The main body of it lashes about furiously, looking for my arm again, or maybe my throat. Meanwhile, the cloudfish's tentacles begin to unfurl, to stretch toward me. With only the stingers to contend with, I'm able to rip the hellvine off my wrist and fling it into the sand. I take one look toward the Subaru and know there's no way I'll reach it.

I bang my thigh on the steering wheel again as I drop. It doesn't hurt quite so bad as last time. I have too many damaged parts and not enough pain to go around. It's hot, though—I feel that. And if the cloudfish doesn't pass on by, I'm gonna barbecue in here.

It doesn't. Of course it doesn't.

Those tentacles, like football-field lengths of spaghetti dipped in every possible color and more, are already poking around at the SUV. They're strong; the slightest touch rocks my metal cage tauntingly. One of the tentacles finds the open window and snakes in. It's covered in something that kind of looks like suction cups, but at the center of each is a sharp-pointed hook the color of sun-bleached bone.

Should I shoot it?

Stab at it?

Either way, it's going to grab me and yank me straight up, like plucking an obnoxious little weed from the ground, root and all. I shove myself as far into the footwell beneath the steering wheel as I can, just as the tentacle lands with a heavy thump against the driver's-side window and deflated airbag. It pokes around, pats the seat, the steering wheel. It has to feel that heat, has to know it's dangerous, that it needs to retract if it doesn't want to get burned. *Right?*

It finds the opening beneath the steering wheel, the tiny space this sobbing, choking human is just managing to cram herself into. I imagine that woman on the other end of the radio, stuffed beneath her desk. I can still hear her screeching as she was torn apart. I hope I don't sound like that. I hope it just sucks me straight up like a black olive at the end of a noodle and that's it. Over. A brief, nice view of the beach and *fin.* Roll credits.

I slash at it. Again and again. "No!" every time it tries to press into the footwell. "No!" *Slash.* Mike is laying on the horn, but the cloudfish doesn't give a shit. Cloudfish wants *this* snack right here. "No!"

Without warning it jerks and shoots back up through the window. I risk a peek. The hellvine is latched onto the cloudfish! *Tentacle wars!* This might be my chance to escape.

But the cloudfish has zero patience for this nonsense. The tentacle retracts, snapping into the air like a whip and bringing the bowling ball and all its hellvines with it. The stringy thing vanishes into the cloudfish's mouth. It reaches through the window again, but rather than grasp for me, it smashes easily through the windshield, hooks around the frame, and *lifts*.

Like, *up*.

The vehicle shudders and groans, pitching sharply downward as gravity tugs at the burning back end. One of the rear tires erupts with a loud, fiery pop that makes me yelp. Through the rear window, the beach gets smaller beneath me, while above, the cloudfish seems to inflate, its body growing to nearly twice its original size as it hauls the car into the air. And we're moving, toward the water. It's trying to get away from the flames, not smart enough to realize it's taking the fire with it. I need to get out of here before it catches on.

I cut away the airbag to find the driver's-side window stubbornly intact. I try the door handle. It works exactly as it should, which is a new one for today. Except the door opens only slightly, then swings shut again, seemingly confused by this unexpected new orientation. I wrap one arm through the steering wheel to keep from falling out until I'm good and damn ready, cram the pistol into the patrol bag, and sling the patrol bag over my other shoulder.

Instinct is a powerful thing. Instinct says, *Falling bad.* Otherwise, I would just jump. Before the cloudfish takes me higher than is probably safe to drop. We pass right over the Subaru. I look straight down through the sunroof, and Mike stares back.

I wave. He waves. We are officially insane.

I need to jump. I'll break every bone in my body, but if I don't let go soon, the fall will definitely kill me.

I unhook my arm from the wheel, shoulder the door open, and roll out. The door bangs back against my skull as I drop, and in that moment, it occurs to me that waiting until we were over the water would have meant a softer landing.

My stomach comes right up into my throat before slamming back into its proper place hard enough to crush my bladder and force everything out of it. Which, given the mimosa and all that, is an embarrassing amount. If anything breaks, I don't feel it. Too much adrenaline. I crumple like something delicate knocked from a tabletop, roll, and spring back up, the patrol bag still slung over my shoulder, the knife still clutched in my right hand. Have I been holding on to it this whole time? How did I not stab myself?

Mike flings open the door. “Beth! Get in!”

There’s no hesitation this time. I run.

16

MIKE

I don't even know where to begin. Did she reach anybody on the radio? What is that giant thing in the *sky*? Is she *hurt*? Is she *burned*? How did she *set the car on fire*?

The last one doesn't even matter at this point. The huge, disgusting blob drifting out over the water releases the SUV, which plummets, trailing black smoke and flames, into the water. There's a small eruption of ignited gasoline that blasts molten rubber and scorched pieces of metal in all directions, and then the ocean swallows it all up.

"I guess," Beth wheezes, "it doesn't like spicy food."

I have no words. Just . . . nothing. I really can't do anything but stare at the waves where the SUV went down. At that iridescent blob hanging weightlessly in the sky, a long tentacle unfurling until it just brushes the surface of the water, then curling up to join the others beneath what I can only assume is a mouth. It doesn't come back toward the beach, but it doesn't drift any farther away either. For the time being, it seems content with becoming a fixture in this increasingly alien landscape.

"What happened?" I manage to ask, summing up all my questions in one nice little package.

"I talked to somebody," Beth says, brushing at a muddy clump of sand on her elbow and finding blood, seeping from a fresh wound.

I can't see any broken bones poking out anywhere. She got lucky. "A dispatcher—in Seaside, I think."

"And?" I know I need to give her some space. A moment to unscramble her thoughts and let her pulse settle down to below a few thousand beats per minute. But I can already tell that I'm not going to like what she tells me, and that has me on edge. Inside me is a very short fuse, and at this moment, everything is a flame inching closer, closer.

"And there's nobody coming," she says. "We are completely on our own."

There it is: Flash. *Boom.*

"Well, thank God we can stop wondering," I snap. How did I actually let myself believe she might return with good news? How could I let myself hope that good news is even a possibility in this shitawful world?

I should have known better. I should have known the moment Sarah walked out the door that there is no future for me in which a happy ending exists. In which even *hope* for it exists. I've wasted too much time with hope. I've hurt so much longer than I needed to.

I should be happy Beth made it back to me in one piece, but right now, all I see is the person responsible for getting me into this situation. For the pain I'm still feeling, the pain that would have ended yesterday at sunset, according to plan, had she not peeked over that fence. "I appreciate you risking your life to learn that we are for sure going to die out here," I finish, seething.

"It's not a total waste," she says, not picking up on my tone.

That pisses me off even more. "Oh, right. We learned that at least that giant thing doesn't like 'spicy food.'" Jake raises his head and stares at me. "We'll just siphon the rest of the gas from the tank. Make a flamethrower."

She looks at me uncertainly. "You could do that?"

It's the last straw. I spin on her like a cat that's been poked one too many times, teeth bared and back arched and hissing. "No, Beth! I don't know how to make a fucking *flamethrower*!"

"Well, why *not*?" she spits. "Aren't you a *producer*? Produce something useful, Mike!"

Jesus wept, what does that even mean? I just watched a floating carnivorous blob of rainbow snot lift a burning police SUV and fling it into the ocean. There are no jokes anymore. There is no sarcasm. Everything is real. If you can think it, dream it, it's here.

My whole body lights up. I feel like all my flesh has been peeled away and splashed with vinegar. "A producer who what? Moonlights as Jason goddamn Bourne? No! I don't use guns and I don't hot-wire cars and I don't make flamethrowers! I mean, I could make a Molotov cocktail, but we have to see what we're throwing it at, and I can't build radar goggles out of car parts either!"

"Well, that's too bad!" she snarls, spraying me with spit. We've been building to this. Since she first reached into her pocket and came back empty-handed. I've felt it in my stomach, like the dread and anticipation of climbing that first hill of a roller coaster. Now we've crested, and there's nothing left to do but scream as we plunge into the roaring chaos.

I grab the jug of orange juice and champagne, squeezing the plastic so hard it collapses beneath my bony, pulsing fingers. There are only a few good swallows of the stuff left. The sight of those pulpy dregs sets me on fire all over again. "What's 'too bad' is you somehow managed to make it to the car with *this* but not the *Christ-forsaken key*!" I fling the jug at the windshield. The cap is loose, and juice sprays across the glass.

Jake erupts into a fit of snarls, his hackles raised, lips curled back to show me his teeth. Good. Bring it on, dog. I look at Beth, expecting her to lash out, to spew a nonsensical stream of expletives or even slap me. I *want* her to. I want to return fire, to roar and shove until Jake lunges at me, rips my hands apart so that I can lie here and bleed to death. I want to shriek so loud I put the *shriekers* to shame. I want her to give me a reason to walk out of this car and be done with it all for good.

She doesn't.

Beth shrinks like I raised a hand to hit her. She slides into the far corner of the hatch from me and tucks her knees under her chin like a child. The sight of her like that smothers the fire. This isn't the first time somebody has puffed up and shouted and demeaned her. It's probably not even the tenth. Or hundredth. That armor she wears is as effective as the shriekers' invisibility, but it has a weakness.

Before I can apologize, take it all back, tell her I didn't mean it, something slams against the hatch door. A shrieker scout, drawn by our racket from the dunes.

Beth whirls and punches the glass. "Fuck you!" she howls. "Fuck all of you!" She punches the glass again and again, until I grab her wrist before she goes right through it.

I try pulling her into an embrace, but she shoves me away.

"Why did you give me the key, Mike?" she demands, as if I should have known better. Her eyes are red, tears streaming down her cheeks. I'm so shocked by the reversal I can't even answer, not that I have an answer. "*Why?* Why would you do that? Can't you see what I am? Wasn't it obvious I'd somehow manage to muck it all up, like I do *everything*? Why did you give me the key? Why did you let me into your *house*? Into your *life*? *I wish I'd never met you*!"

She breaks down into heavy, ugly sobs. I scoot forward and wrap my arms around her again, and this time she doesn't resist. She just trembles against me.

"She died, Mike. I was right there and something got her and there was nothing I could do about it. Nothing but listen and be glad it wasn't me." I have no idea who she's talking about, but the words are a knife in my gut. "I don't understand why I keep getting second and third and millionth chances," she cries. "I don't understand why I'm still alive. It doesn't make any sense."

"I don't know either," I say. "But I'm glad you are." I mean it. Despite everything, I *mean* it.

She squeezes tighter and wails into my shirt. The shrieker outside doesn't attack the car again. A quick glance over the ocean and I see why: the floating thing has drifted a bit closer to shore, to us, the commotion we're making. It's the size of a hot-air balloon and ethereal. It seems to be deflating, and as it does, it slowly descends, until its tentacles just nearly brush the crests of the waves. The shrieker must be aware of it too. Knows what threat the strange, ghostly blob presents if it comes this way. I see the trail the shrieker makes in the sand as it skitters back to the dunes.

A flash of motion on the ridge draws my eye.

There's another shrieker up there, its mouth wide open. It's larger than the others, I can see that much from here. For some reason, it makes me think of a queen bee amid her workers. Beth's camera is on the floor next to us. I gently pick it up with one hand, not daring to take my other arm from around Beth, and aim the camera at that open mouth.

Something lies at the center of that throne of teeth. An eel-like body, ending in yet another mouth and even more teeth. The thing appears to be staring right back at me, but that could just be my imagination.

I lower the camera, and it's gone.

≈

With the fog cleared, the late afternoon sun beats relentlessly down on the Subaru, heat shimmering off the hood. It feels like July, not October. Autumn has been off to an unusually warm start, but this is ridiculous.

The tide rolls in, long fingers of foam reaching for us, the cadence of ebb and flow bringing it closer by the minute. It will be after sunset when the tide reaches its high-water mark, I think. I'm going to drown in the dark after all.

I tear a strip of duct tape, from the patrol bag Beth brought back, and seal a crack in the hatch window. The shriekers don't appear to have any notion of just how close they are to breaking through and reaching us. I don't think they can see through the windows. I'm not really positive they can *see* at all, in the sense that we do.

It takes all Jake's energy to raise his head and give me a forlorn look. He's forgiven me for losing my temper. Damn good dog, this one.

"I know, buddy. I'm sorry. It'll start to cool down soon." I pour a bit of water into my cupped palm and he halfheartedly laps it up before slumping heavily onto his side.

Beth put the sunshades in the windshield earlier, but they haven't been terribly effective. She's down to her shorts and bra, her skin glistening. Sweat rolls down her nose and drips onto the fresh bandage on her wrist, where the tendril grabbed her. It wasn't a bad injury, not compared to her leg. Some broken skin and a rash. I don't like how she keeps scratching at it, though. My own palms have stopped itching, but I only briefly grabbed the bowling ball itself. I never came into contact with the thing inside. There was a basic first aid kit in the patrol bag, some disinfectant, but who knows how useful it is for this?

"Why don't the windows have a manual override?" Beth asks, wiping her forehead with the back of her hand, then scratching at her wrist again. "That's a serious safety oversight."

"Most people stuck in a car in hot weather could just open the door and get out," I offer, grabbing the remaining bottle of water and passing it to her. She shakes her head, like a stubborn kid being offered broccoli puree. "Drink. You're still dehydrated."

"It's warm."

"Beth."

"You'll regret this later, when you're dying of thirst," she says, but relents and takes a sip. A glance out the rear driver's-side door doesn't reveal any wavy outlines, so I risk opening it a crack. Jake sits up; Beth freezes mid-drink. All of us are waiting for that telltale shriek. When it doesn't come, I nod for Beth to follow my lead. She cracks her door too.

Beth moans in relief as a draft washes over us. Jake's tail thumps dully against the upholstery. He sniffs at the air. The malfunctioning sewage plant smell is getting worse as the tendrils creep across the beach. Are they taking root as they go, establishing new footholds? Worst of all, there are what appear to be little flower buds sprouting along each shoot. I don't even want to think about what might bloom. Hellvine indeed.

I prop myself against the back of the driver's seat, opening a clear line of sight toward the dunes, one hand on the door, ready to pull it shut. All calm out there. The grass along the ridge rustles in the breeze, but that's it. The blimp monster has ridden the air current out over the dunes and risen higher into the sky again, not having found anything interesting to grab hold of. I can't fathom how it keeps itself aloft, or propels itself, but so long as it keeps heading in that direction, I'm happy letting the rest remain a mystery.

"What are you?" I ask Beth. She stares at me, eyes narrowing in apprehension, like she suspects I've finally snapped. I quickly elaborate. "'Don't you know what I am?' That's what you said, earlier. So, tell me, what are you?"

Now she focuses out her window, squinting sullenly into the reflection of the sun off the ocean waves. "I'm a mess."

"You're not."

"You don't know me, Mike. You haven't even been aware of my existence for twenty-four whole hours. Don't kid yourself that just because we banged it out, you have any idea what my story is."

"So tell me. My schedule cleared up unexpectedly, and I've got nowhere else to be." That gets a small laugh out of her, a nice sound to hear.

"I'm a human car wreck. That's what my mom says."

"She sounds like a peach."

"She is. Full of razor blades and worms. But . . . she's not wrong. Losing the key like that? On a wide-open beach? Total Beth move. No, Mike, don't argue. It's a pattern. I know it. Plop me down in any situation, and if there's a mistake to be made, I will make it. A worst-possible course of action, I'll take it. That's me. That's my life story. A bulldozer in a china shop. You entrusted me with the smallest possible amount of responsibility, and I blew it. It's just what I do."

"You can't blame yourself for triggering—" My tongue sticks to the roof of my mouth. I don't know why, maybe because even with everything that's happened, the idea still seems so ludicrous, so impossible, that my mind keeps trying to censor it. I unstick my tongue and shut off the filter. "For triggering an alien invasion," I spit out. The words land between us like they were hacked from diseased lungs.

"We're saying it now?" Beth asks. "Officially?"

"If you've got a better name, by all means. You're pretty good at that."

"Hey, maybe you can find me a job in the movies when this is all over."

"Maybe I can," I say. As if I even had a job in the movies before it started.

She keeps staring at those waves, her face glowing in the sun, thoughtful. Then her eyes drop to the pistol. I've been glancing at it too, ever since she pulled it from the patrol bag. We both know its purpose is twofold: It can defend us to a point. But it's also a way out. On our terms, on our clock. At least until the high tide stops giving us a choice. Like the words *alien invasion,* it's something we've managed to avoid talking about. But I can feel us getting closer with every roll of the waves.

Beth scratches at her wrist, then gives her leg a brief squeeze. She's in a lot of pain, but she's not about to let me know it. Her eyes land longingly on the empty orange juice jug, drying on the windshield. "Mike," she says tentatively, as though she's not sure she really wants to. "Last night, something happened."

"No shit."

"Not the meteor shower, though that was part of it. But . . . truthfully, I don't think 'invasion' is the word for it either. I think this . . . is all some kind of accident. A mistake." That gets me sitting up straighter. "And everything that's happening," she says, gesturing at the world around us, "is because of it. Like the world broke, and got slapped together again. Except, not. Somehow the shape is the same, but not all the pieces are back in the right place." She takes a deep, frustrated breath and lets it out in a *whoosh,* dragging her fingernails through her hair. "Let me try that again. I had a dream.

At least, I thought it was a dream. Do you remember when you came inside to check on me, and you said I wasn't in bed?"

"Yeah." I don't like where this is going.

"Mike, I wasn't in the house at *all.*"

"What do you mean?"

"I was *somewhere else.* Not for long. A few seconds or a few minutes, I can't say. The shriekers were there. Invisible, but I could hear them. And so was that cloudfish, and it had friends. There were meteorites falling too. And this *stuff* in the air. I thought it was ash, but it was these tiny husks of . . . I don't know what. Insects? Just floating down from the sky like snow."

The image makes me shudder. I can't help but think of pictures I've seen, taken from deep-sea submersibles. There's always a constant shower of detritus down there, at the bottom of the world. What's that layer of the deep called? The *midnight zone*?

"The air there, it stank, too, because there must have been bowling balls nearby."

"Wait—"

"You're getting it, aren't you? Wherever these things come from, I was there. I don't know why you didn't cross over, or why I did, or how any of it happened at all, but it did. The meteor shower, the bowling balls, all of it came from this other place, during that window of time."

"Beth." I don't like her choice of words. *Crossed over.* They make a frightening sort of sense.

"We weren't the only ones," she goes on. "The dispatcher I spoke to, she said lots of people did. People and animals and even *things.* Not just cars but buildings, maybe whole towns, maybe *countries,* for all I know. Whatever that other place is, *wherever* it is, it's like we passed through each other. And we each left bits behind. Do you hear what I'm saying, Mike? Just like the shriekers are stranded here, there are people who didn't make it back."

"The dispatcher told you all of this?" I ask. I don't mean to sound skeptical, and I'm not—at this point, I don't know that it would even be possible.

But the hurt is plain on Beth's face. "You don't believe me," she says.

"That's not it." I consider telling her about my own experience, about the thing that approached me on the beach a moment before the tide washed over me. As much as I'd like to confirm beyond a doubt that it was just some shambling monstrosity from another world, rather than from the recesses of my own mind, I'd have to explain to her what I was doing in the water, and that's a rabbit hole I'm still not ready to go back down. That was last night, and I'd very much like to leave it there. "What else did you see?" I ask instead.

"Not a lot," Beth answers. "It was night there too. There wasn't an ocean, at least not where I was. It felt like I was in a desert. In Moab. The moon was a weird color, and not very bright."

"The moon was there?"

"Yeah?"

"*The* moon? Ours? Luna?"

"I think? But now that we're talking like this, I don't know if it was really there, or if I was just seeing it through . . . through whatever usually keeps these two places separated." She reaches out and brushes at the air, as if feeling for a curtain that could be drawn back, if you could only just grab hold of it.

Not that you'd want to, knowing now what's on the other side. Another world, filled with nightmares, blasting down the interdimensional interstate parallel with our own. Before some cosmic wind pushed it into our lane for a split second. Long enough for a collision. Not a total wreck, but enough to leave behind remnants of paint and some dents. Enough that it will take more than a little polish to buff out. I can't even begin to imagine what sort of cataclysm caused this. And at this point, it doesn't really matter. We need to start thinking forward, not back.

"Could you breathe over there?" I ask.

"Yeah. It wasn't easy. That could have been the shock, though."

"Stand up? Gravity felt the same?"

"Uh. Yes? I didn't move very far. But I did jump once. Didn't fly off into the sky."

So they came from a somewhat Earthlike place. Maybe they even came from Earth itself, in another version of reality, where everything went really sideways. Which would be too bad. Means we can't count on the air melting them if we just wait it out.

"Why?" she asks, wide-eyed, like we're on the verge of a breakthrough. I love her for it. I'm beginning to love her for a lot of things.

It hits me like a swell, this sensation I never thought I'd feel again, lifting me off the seat, and I have to steady myself to keep from being knocked over by it. It's exhilarating, and as much as I just want to ride it as far as it will take me, I also know that people caught in life-or-death situations can develop complex and lasting connections across short periods of time, and it would be dangerous to dive headlong into unfamiliar waters without first carefully reading all the signs. Not just for me but for her too. Beth is more than capable of keeping me afloat, but I'm not sure I can do the same for her, and that's a mistake I don't ever want to make again.

"I'm just talking out of my ass, Beth. I have no idea. This is all science fiction to me." I see disappointment in her face, but that's better than giving her any false hope. I have to wonder, though. What *if* we are the only two people who've had the opportunity to just sit around and puzzle it all out?

What if we're the only two people now, period?

"It's kind of funny, when you think about it," I say. "Humans are one of the most destructive forces this planet has ever known. We're capable of rendering the entire place uninhabitable a dozen times over, all in the name of who gets to be king of which mountain. Imagine what we might have accomplished if we'd had any idea something was coming to take it all away from us. What would we have done differently with the time we had left?" I can't help but think of Sarah. Tears prick my eyes, and I bring the camera back up and stare at the dunes again, mostly so that Beth doesn't see I'm crying.

It's good timing. One of the shriekers is making its way down the dunes, about halfway between us and the abandoned Jeep. But something is different. It seems unsteady, drunk. Also, I can *see* it.

Not clearly; it's like somebody sprayed it with a deep, purple paint. It's about twice Jake's size, with six legs that I can make out. It collapses at the base of the dunes with its jaws stretched wide so that little worm-looking thing can peer out. At the top of the dune, another set of jaws open. These look big enough to bite that other shrieker in half.

The queen.

Did she just exile that other from the group? What's happening to it? Could we be in luck? Could the air be poisoning them after all? And why does that purple color look so familiar?

Before I can pose any of these questions to Beth, something else catches my eye, down in the lower corner of the viewfinder frame. I zoom in as much as the lens will allow, my heart bouncing around in my chest. It's hard to get a clear focus with my hands shaking like this, but what else could it be? Right there among all those footprints, glinting in the sunlight.

"I see the key."

17

BETH

"What? *Where?*" There's no way. We *scoured* the sand for that cursed thing, it can't possibly be sitting in plain view for Mike to see. I snatch the camera from him and smash my eyeball to the viewfinder.

"Right there." He points. "Between the waterline and that driftwood log. The sunlight's catching it, now that it's at this angle."

He's right. The bastard flicks cheerful little stars of light at me. *Oh, hi—were you looking for me?* I could scream. The fog has completely burned away now, and I can even see the beach access road. It's like we've been stubbornly picking at a lock for the past several hours, and the mechanism has finally clicked into place and the door opened in front of us.

"I think we can reach it," Mike says with a resolute nod.

"Can we make it back, though?" The cloudfish has drifted inland far enough that I don't see it at all now, but I'm not about to count on that. It's been hanging around in this area all day. It knows something is here. And then there's the ever-present threat of the shriekers. "We've lost our fog. There's no way they won't see us."

My words trigger something in him. He stares at me, one side of his mouth curling up into a half smile. "Beth, what if they *can't* see us?"

"What? No. They surrounded me over there, and they all opened their mouths. They have these *tongues,* and I swear I saw eyes on them." And even more teeth, but that's not really pertinent.

"I know what you're talking about," Mike says, nodding excitedly, "but what if they can see us only when they have their mouths open? Like, the invisible part is some kind of protective shell? When it's closed and they're invisible, they're also *blind*?"

There's one hole in his theory: the shriekers knew the hellvine was lying in the sand by the SUV. They kept their distance well before they opened their mouths. Could they smell it? Hard to believe they couldn't. But wouldn't it stand to reason that if they could smell with their mouths shut, they could probably also see?

Luckily, Professor Mike's class is back in session. "That noise they make," he says. "That chirping. I wonder if it's some kind of echolocation? Like the way bats 'see'? I bet when they make that sound, part of their shell opens up, to both emit the sound and to catch the sonar bounce back. It probably happens lightning fast, which is why they still seem invisible to us."

"*Why* do you even know this?"

"They must lose track of us when we get in the car," he goes on, not hearing me. "The chirping is building them a picture of their surroundings, and when the moving human shapes go into the unmoving car shape, we may as well be gone completely. Even if the echo lets them see through the doors, there's wiring, the seats, so much they aren't familiar with." He pauses. "You said there was no ocean when you crossed over."

"Not that I could tell." I can't help but feel a spark of excitement.

"That could be screwing with their systems too. This giant, loud, constantly moving body of water. They might be as terrified of their new surroundings as they are confused by it. Hunkering down in the dunes, lashing out at any new thing that comes along, all while trying to avoid their own natural predators."

"Yeah, the spider's more scared of you than you are of it," I say. "Heard that before. Sorry, spidey, when you come into my house, you get the shoe." If only I had a shoe big enough to stomp out the shriekers.

Mike looks out at the water. "If we run for the keys," he says, calculating, "and one of them is up there, surveying the beach, it will detect us. You're absolutely right. Even if we go slowly. But if we go in the water? There's a chance we might just . . . blend in. Like we do inside the car."

"What do you mean, 'a chance'?"

"Meaning, I could be completely wrong and we're about to die horribly. But if I'm not . . ." He lets that hang, so that I can weigh the odds myself.

"What about that?" I ask, pointing at the strange-colored, not-very-invisible-anymore shrieker at the bottom of the dunes.

"I don't know, it looks sick," Mike says. "Maybe it's dying."

I look back at the glint of sunlight on the sand, just as a wave breaks and rushes in, reaching nearly to it. A few more minutes, and the ocean will snatch the keys away, and that will be the end of our story. Maybe the end of humanity's story. Mike and I might already be the epilogue, dragging out that inevitable final line, word by torturous word. If we're going to go out, we may as well go out swinging.

"Let's do it," I say, opening the cooler and grabbing the remaining sandwich I'd packed for us in a completely different lifetime. Just the thought of stale bread and salty cold cuts makes my throat itch for a drink, but I push the thought out of my head. Permanently, I hope.

I dump the sandwich out of its baggie. Jake's head snaps in my direction, sniffing at the air, eyes cutting longingly at the soggy, wilted shape. Soon, buddy. We pull this off, I'll let you clean out the fridge.

I tuck the pistol into the baggie. It just barely zips up, but I think it will work. The gun is probably water resistant, but I don't know about salt water. If it gets wet, I can't expect it to function perfectly when I absolutely need it to, but leaving it behind means it will definitely be useless if this goes south.

The baggie goes into the waistband of my shorts, and I secure it in place with duct tape, wrapping it around me a few times to make sure it won't get pulled free and lost at sea.

Mike flinches at the loud *scriiitch* of the tape roll. "I guess that means I'm on horn duty again?" he asks, dejected.

"Let's leave the whole splitting-up thing for the stupid, disposable characters in your movies. If we're going to die, we die together."

"I don't think I'd want it any other way," he says with an honest smile.

≈≈≈

Mike peels off his sweaty, filthy shirt while I crack open the driver's door and use my camera to spy beneath the car. In a way, we're a bit like the shriekers, aren't we? Tucked safely inside our little Subaru suit of armor, our perception limited by what we can see and hear through the windows. Every time we open the door for a better look, we expose ourselves to their teeth. How can we get them to keep their shells open? Expose themselves to our bullets?

There's still nothing beneath the car, but the shrieker at the base of the dunes turns toward the sound of the door. I can just hear it chirruping, and I try to keep absolutely still.

"Beth?" Mike says. I don't respond. I want that thing to look away before I get back in the car.

A growl rises in Jake's throat, and Mike clamps a hand around his snout. The growl turns to a whine, and the shrieker shifts slightly.

The lens cap slips from my fingers and lands in the sand.

That's all it takes. The shrieker is on its feet and moving. It's not as swift as it was earlier, but it still crosses the beach with frightening haste. I try to sit back—and bump against the steering wheel, which in my panic feels like something solid and heavy pinning me in place.

"Mike!" I screech. He grabs my bra strap and pulls. I'm just able to hook the door handle and slam it shut. The shrieker bangs against it and cries irritably.

Then it stands up.

Its shell is covered in a layer of fuzz the color of a fresh bruise, and that piece of hellvine is still attached to its leg. New creepers have sprouted from it and wound their way around the shrieker's body like bulging veins.

"It's *infected*," I say. "The hellvine is *growing* on it."

The shrieker opens its mouth, and the tongue-worm rises lethargically to stare right at me, all those wet eyes sparkling. There's nowhere to hide. Mike doesn't move. A rumble builds in Jake's throat, his dark eyes about to pop from his skull, his body shaking in anticipation, ready to lunge at the thing the moment Mike lets go of him.

The tongue-worm stretches forward and gently taps the window, leaving behind an oily smear on the glass. Its eyes twinkle, as if, at long last, it understands the nature of the barrier between us, and knows it won't take much to break through. I feel the pistol against my waist. No, not yet. That glass has kept us safe so far—I won't blow it out until we have no other choice.

I lift the camera and aim. The tongue-worm immediately retracts, and the outer jaws close most of the way.

"Yeah, you better watch it," I growl, and through the opening of its slightly parted jaws, those eyes flicker. Then they disappear completely as the shell seals shut over them and the shrieker ducks from view.

"That's the weak spot," Mike says. "And now we know why the queen booted it from the club."

"I'm sorry, 'the queen'?" I turn to look at him.

He nods toward the dunes. "A shrieker, bigger than the others." I know exactly which one he's talking about. "She—it—seems to be in charge. When that purple stuff first started showing up on this one, she threw it out. Don't want that spreading to the rest of them."

"Well, great. Now it's here, which kinda screws up our plan."

"Yeah," Mike says, scratching at his face.

It reminds me how bad my wrist itches beneath the bandage. Burns, more like. Mike went at the spot where the hellvine snagged me with antiseptic wipes until I thought he was going to rub the skin right off, but I'm glad now that he did. I'm especially glad I was able to pull off the piece of vine before it became permanently attached.

"We could wait until the water is high enough. That might run it off."

"And then the key will also be underwater. No, we need to do this now." There's not much in the car that will be of use against the shrieker, except the gun, which will only attract the wrong sort of attention. But Mike was right about the things' sensitivity to movement. Curiosity might not kill the shrieker, but it could at least get it looking the other way.

I peel the sandwich off the bottom of the cooler. Mike gapes at me, probably expecting me to take a bite. I've consumed far more questionable things straight from unfamiliar refrigerators in the haze of a hangover.

"As soon as the next wave comes in," I tell him, "I'm going to throw this out. With a little luck, it'll take the bait, and we can run."

"Because luck has really been on our side today," he mumbles. But maybe it has. We're still alive. We've found the key. A sandwich being the very thing that saves us in a dire moment? Sure.

In a side mirror, I watch the shrieker shuffle into shade at the Subaru's rear bumper. It looks like a huge, tailless scorpion, its head long and flat and all mouth, like a crocodile's. I kind of wish it was still invisible, not gonna lie. It heaves and shudders as it lies there. How long until those hellvines immobilize it completely? Will the shrieker eventually just turn into a giant bowling ball, sprouting enough new tendrils to cover the entire car?

I scoot to the driver's seat. Mike gets into position, gripping the rear passenger door handle. The waves roll in, and back out. And in, and out. When the water surges right up to kiss the Subaru's front tires, I push open the door and fling the sandwich over the roof and toward the dunes. Glued together with warm mayo and meat slime, the sandwich lands with a soft plop, and the shrieker lunges toward it, making it about five feet before its legs give out and it face-plants into the sand. The shrieker drags itself forward on two feet, its jaws opening to give the worm inside a view of the object that came from the car. Maybe it will eat the sandwich. That would kill it for sure.

"Now, let's go." I step out, right into ankle-deep water. We both shut our doors as quietly as we can and quickly wade into the ocean. The water rises past my knees, then my hips. Searing pain radiates from the bandaged bite on my thigh. I want to scream and slap my hands against the water.

"You okay?" Mike asks, coming up behind me.

"Not really."

"The cold water will numb it in a minute." This is far less reassuring than he thinks.

The shrieker isn't moving at all now. It's slumped into a pile right on top of the sandwich. Jake's tail wags inside the car as he stands at attention, watching it through the rear window. I can't hear him, though, which is good. And the others haven't emerged from the dunes to investigate, as far as I can tell. So far, this plan is working out far better than it has any right to.

"Do not let go of me," Mike says, finding my hand and squeezing. There's an unfamiliar sharpness in his voice, and his grip could crush concrete.

"I won't. I promise."

We trudge awkwardly through the churning surf. The current makes the sand shift beneath my feet, creating the dizzying sensation of the ground falling away, of being tugged out to sea. When I lose my balance, Mike's hand clamps tight. My leg is on fire, and my wrist itches so bad I just want to tear it apart with my fingernails.

"Stop," Mike says, not giving me much choice in the matter. I follow his stare to the dunes.

There she is. The queen. Poised on the ridge, jaws open, tongue-worm surveying the beach.

"Mama's awake," I say just as a swell washes over us, and I suck down a lungful of water, coughing and spewing as discreetly as possible. "Do you think she sees us?"

"I don't know. Down." He kneels, and I follow suit, until only our heads are exposed. The unsettled sand makes me feel like I'm standing on bugs. Something slippery slides past the back of my leg. I'm sure it's just seaweed. There was no ocean *over there,* I have to keep reminding myself. Anything that got caught beneath the waves on our side would have drowned.

"I can't tell what she's looking at," Mike says.

"Probably just our buddy," I suggest, even though the worm's eyes are very clearly aimed right at us. I knew this was going too well. And there are definitely *things* beneath the surface. Fleshy things that are not just seaweed.

A big wave knocks us both under, and I catch a glimpse of little silvery shapes in the water.

"Take it easy," Mike is already saying when I come up, gasping for air. "We're okay. Keep your feet on the ground—"

"Shut up," I hiss. "Let's go. There's something in the water."

"It's just fish."

"What?" Looking around, I see he's right. There's all sorts of them tumbling through the waves, and even more scattered along the beach, dead and drying in the sun. Did they cross over, too, finding themselves in the desert with nowhere to go? Or is something happening out there in the water?

"She's gone," Mike says.

Sure enough, the ridgeline is empty. But did the queen lose interest and withdraw to the other side of the dunes? Or did she come down onto the beach? I've never felt so trapped, which is ridiculous, with a wide-open beach in front of me, and the Pacific Ocean to my back.

Mike's hand gets me going again. We continue the cold, dizzying slog until we're in line with the driftwood log. I can't see the key, though. Not even a glimmer from this angle. Mike squints. He doesn't see it either. Fantastic.

A dead fish smacks into the back of my leg, and I jerk it away instinctively, driving my knee into the small of Mike's back and sending him tumbling forward, swallowing a mouthful of salt water.

"Sorry," I mume, somehow still skeeved out by all the lifeless little bodies despite everything else I've seen today.

"It's got to be right there," he spits, pointing.

"We aren't going forward until we know for sure. We can't waste any time wandering around, not with queenie on alert."

We both scrutinize each and every granule of sand.

"I see it," Mike says, staring toward the driftwood. His face is unreadable.

"Where?"

"Right there." He points. His eyes are locked, not wanting to lose whatever he's focused on. I still don't see it, but I guess I have to trust him.

"Don't get too close to the hellvine," I warn.

The bowling ball that brought us to a stop at this cursed place hasn't moved, but one of the tendrils sprouting from it has crept dangerously close to the driftwood, waiting like a viper, half-buried by windblown sand. I can't get over how fast they grow, like the blackberry weeds Dad was always battling. One moment, they're cute little shoots peeking over the fence, and the next, your entire yard is lost beneath a thorny tangle.

Mike takes a step shoreward. I unseal the baggie and grip the pistol. I should have cleaned it. It's probably full of grit and will misfire at a critical moment. Sorry, humanity. You needed a Sarah Connor, or an Ellen Ripley, or even a Katniss Everdeen. You got me.

We inch forward, shambling from the tide like a couple of sea monsters. Our bare feet slap the sand, betraying our approach. The sickly shrieker has returned to the relative safety of the Subaru's back bumper. It doesn't appear to notice us, or if it does, have the energy left to do anything about it. Mike is staring at the ground like somebody in need of their glasses, and there's a telltale tightness in his jaw.

"Mike," I whisper.

"Almost there." He slows his pace. Buying time. You can't bullshit me, Mike. I'm a professional.

"You dickhead. You don't see anything."

"It should be right *here*." He shuffles left and right, using the driftwood to align himself, but the key is simply not there. Maybe it never was. Maybe we started hallucinating after all.

"We have to go back," I say, tugging him. We're right out in the open. If queenie decides to do a scan of the beach now, there's no way she can miss us. But Mike remains stubbornly planted. I'm about to just abandon him when I see the grim look on his face.

A seagull descends from the sky and lands on the driftwood log. It slaps a dead fish to the sand and hops down, judging us with beady black eyes. Warning us to stay away from its meal.

"*Why*, bird?" I whisper. "Why right there? You have literally the entire world."

I don't speak seagull, but when it answers me, I understand perfectly. *Because fuck you, that's why.*

The bird flaps its wings and lets out a piercing cry.

18

BETH

I used to love the sound of seagulls. Their voices are so distinctly maritime. Hearing them always made me want to take long walks down grungy wharves and watch old salts haul in the day's catch. Or lie on the beach and get lost in a book.

I used to love beaches.

The gull belches another loud squawk, just to spite me, then proceeds to tear at the dead fish, ripping off chunks of flesh and swallowing them greedily. *Choke on a bone, you stupid bird—you're going to get us killed.*

Jake's face is pressed to the back window, ears cocked, eyes glued to the gull. Remember when I said he's obsessed with chasing birds? Yeah, he hasn't forgotten either. He yips excitedly, forgetting that he's supposed to be half dead from dehydration and heat. The exiled shrieker remains a lifeless lump in the shadow.

I risk making movement and point at Jake. *No! Shut up!*

He sees me, I know he does, but he cares not. His sights are locked on the gull, and all systems are prepared for launch. The end of the world is upon us, and Jake is going to chase that bird straight into oblivion, if only he can get out. He paws at the door.

And that's when, to my horror, I see that Mike, in his effort to be stealthy, didn't close it all the way. The door shudders, but it's just heavy enough not to swing open. That will change if Jake realizes how near to freedom he is.

The seagull flaps its wings and lifts into the air, clutching the rest of its prize in its beak, mocking us. *So long, suckers, too bad you can't fly like me. Enjoy dying on this sorry beach.*

None of us notice the trail of indentations approaching in the sand, or the shimmer of the air as an invisible shape cuts through it. By then, there isn't much for the gull to do but flutter spastically, right before the razor-sharp feet slice it cleanly in half.

The queen lands with a soft thud, graceful as a ballerina, bird feathers stuck to the blood dripping down one of her front legs. The jaws open, and her tongue-worm stands at attention, looking at the seagull's bottom half, webbed feet still kicking at the sand like it's trying to run away. When the feet fall still, she turns her black eyes on us.

And I swear that worm tilts just slightly, the way Jake does when confronted with something beyond his understanding. Which in Jake's case is almost everything. He's looked at me that way plenty of times, but I don't mind when Jake does it. This alien worm thing, though? Studying us like an explorer coming across some never-before-seen species? Hard pass. Can she see the terror on my face? Smell it in my sweat? Can she feel the panicked beat of my heart, the tremble of my hands sending ripples through the air?

I look down. Submitting to the monster's presence the way I always wilted under my mother's glare.

There, in the sand right at Mike's feet, is the key.

Mike glances my way, probably wondering why I haven't unloaded a clip into that worm's leering face—a damn good question—and then follows my stare. He doesn't reach for the key, though. We're in a standoff, and as soon as somebody twitches, the violence will start. But we can't stand here forever. One of us needs to make the first move.

A wave crashes behind us, rushing up and around my ankles. Oddly enough, the queen takes a step back from it. Professor Mike was right. They don't know what to make of this strange, aggressive substance. I suppose that shouldn't surprise me, many earthborn creatures are at least wary of the sea. I've watched herds of elk fleeing up the beach in thunderous terror when the surf charges them unexpectedly. It was funny then. Now it's the only advantage we have.

Jake barks ferociously, pawing at the window and door. I can hear the rattle of it from here. The queen breaks her stare to look in his direction. Almost as if that was his goal, to give us a chance to get the key and run. I wish Mike would take it. Do I have to do everything?

Jake slams the door with both paws, and it swings wide open.

My heart stops.

He stands there on the seat, head cocked in that confused way, trying to comprehend what strange wizardry he just discovered.

"Jake, *no*!" I can't help it, it just comes out. I suddenly have no fucks to give about my own health, I cannot—*will* not—watch that poor, wonderful, dumb dog end up like the seagull.

The queen whirls on me, a wet, guttural grumble building inside her, much more menacing than the chitters I've grown almost used to. She isn't fast enough. The pistol is out of the bag and aimed at the worm before it has a chance to do much more than flinch. Like the other, she instinctively senses that this pointing motion is a threat. Good. I squeeze the trigger.

Nothing happens.

The *safety*! When did I put that on? *Why, Beth?*

The queen slams her jaws closed just as I click the safety off and a bullet leaves the gun with a bang. She skitters sideways like a crab, kicking up sand and dodging the bullet, as if she can see it cutting through the air toward her.

Jake shreds the sand in similar yet less graceful fashion. Fortunately, he is smart enough not to attack. He slides to a stop, hackles raised, teeth bared, eyes huge and appearing to see right through the queen's invisibility. She darts toward him, her bloody leg swiping with startling reach. Jake bounces back, snarling like I've never heard him, drawing the queen's attention away from us.

She could be on Jake in a flash. Lop him effortlessly in two before he even realizes what is happening. But she doesn't.

She doesn't know what to make of him yet either. She and her scouts have encountered only humans with guns, elk, horses, and seagulls. She doesn't know what this fearless four-legger is capable of. Unfortunately, she'll soon find out that it isn't much.

"Mike! The key!"

That gets him moving. He grabs it and reels toward the water. "Go! *Go!*"

"Jake, get back to the car!" I scream.

The queen turns our way again, and Jake moves in, ignoring my command, strings of saliva swinging from his teeth. She spins on him and he hops away, yelping—in surprise or pain I can't tell. Rage blinds me. I fire three shots into the bitch, roaring to match the waves. Each bullet sinks into her shell, ejecting streamers of sticky black blood. It doesn't kill her, but it keeps her from pouncing on Jake. She turns on me again, that growl building into the shriek we all know and love.

Then she charges.

19

MIKE

We won't make it. The queen is too fast, and our silly human legs simply aren't made for cutting through water. It slows us down like a solid thing. I hear her back there, the cadence of all those feet tilling up the sand. Will we end up like the seagull? Will our bottom halves just keep going, like something out of a cartoon?

I brace for it, the searing snap of those jaws going right through my middle. How long do you live after something like that? Will I see the fall, see my feet blast forward ahead of me into the waves? Or will the shock of it kill me outright?

But it's the tide that saves us.

When the queen meets the water, she lets out a startled, angry screech, and quickly alters her course, flinging clumps of wet sand into the air. We're chest deep when I look back and see her prancing left and right along the shore. Her shell is coated in seawater; whatever unknowable biology allows light to bend around her, rendering her invisible, it can't fight the water beading up on its surface, bejeweling her in dazzling gems of sunlight. She looks like something made of chrome, wheeled fresh out of the wash to air-dry on the showroom floor.

"Ha ha ha!" Beth screams maniacally. "Terra not so firma after all, is it, *bitch*!"

We did it. I can't believe it. We got the key. We escaped the queen. We're going to be freed of this wretched stretch of sand. I haven't felt so alive in a year. Since Sarah walked out of our home for what would be the last time and left my life in ruins.

"Jake!" Beth pants.

My stomach plummets. The heroic, foolish dog is limping severely toward the Subaru. There's a splash of bright blood near his tail. That last swipe by the queen didn't quite miss, though I can't tell the extent of his injury from here. It's not good, by any measure.

"Come on." I swallow my anger and guide Beth into deeper water. There's no way the others didn't hear those gunshots. They'll be on their way to defend their queen soon enough, and we need to be in the car before they get here.

"But Jake—" Beth protests, as if my plan is for us to just float out to sea and leave him behind.

"We can't help him if we don't make it back," I say gently. "I don't think he can shut that door on his own."

The queen hasn't lost track of us. That's a bit of a problem. She's strafing parallel with us, matching our pace. Like she knows we're going to have to come out eventually, and she's going to be there when we do. *How?* How is she so cunning? It just isn't fair! They're the interlopers here—they shouldn't have an *advantage*!

"Stop," I say, grabbing Beth. "Try to stand still."

The queen stops too. I hear her chirping, those soundwaves bouncing off us and right back to her, building a picture of the two statues standing in the water.

It's agony. We're so close, and now we're stuck. Beth is trembling, from both the cold and from adrenaline-fueled anticipation.

"Mike," Beth whispers. "We need to do *something*."

"I *know*. How many bullets do you have?"

"Not enough. Unless I have a clear shot of that worm, I'm not wasting any more of them."

This is so stupid! Here we are, backed into a corner, in a place where corners literally do not exist. There has got to be a way out of this.

A strong wave hits us from behind, knocking me forward. Almost as if the ocean has grown tired of the standoff and is giving us a nudge. *Get on with it.* The queen takes a few steps closer, the water splashing around her feet. When she realizes that it doesn't burn, that she isn't going to melt, she takes another.

And another.

Just you wait. The ocean's deceptive. It looks harmless enough. Sings to you. Invites you in. Then it takes everything.

I grasp Beth's hand. I don't want to suggest what we do next. Sarah used to enjoy wading out until the water was above her knees, her skirt bunched up in her hands, but I always stayed behind on dry land. I've never needed a sign to tell me not to trust the ocean. "We have to go under."

"What?"

"Swim. She can't see us if we're underwater."

Beth swears, the longest continuous stream of curses I've ever heard, strung together like poetry. Then she steps back, meeting the waves.

We're in up to our chins. I feel the sand slip away beneath my feet with each pull of the tide. Out here, between the sandbars, is where the rip currents lurk.

"Ready?" I say, and then fill my lungs. "Go."

And we're under. Paddling clumsily. Battling the tug and shove of the tide in an effort to maintain our trajectory. It feels like we're under for ten minutes, and when I come up for air, I see we've progressed about six feet.

"Keep going," Beth spits, and then she's under again.

She's a much better swimmer than I am, even with her injuries, but the sight of her disappearing like that puts me into a panic. My legs stop kicking, my arms turn into noodles. The waves shove me face-first into the water like schoolyard bullies. I snap upright and search for Beth. Where is she? Why isn't she up yet?

"Beth?"

The queen is watching. Calculating. She creeps closer.

"Beth!" I shout, water rushing into my mouth as soon as I do.

"Mike! Come on!" I search for her head, but I can't find her. I hear her, but can't pinpoint her location. Did she swim even farther out? Is she lost in the waves?

Am *I*?

"Beth, help!" I manage, taking in another mouthful of water, this time swallowing it. It's so salty it tastes warm, and my stomach is clenching, trying to reject it, to force it out, but my throat is closed up. Water goes into my nose, the burn in my sinuses transporting me to last night, to that moment when I changed my mind.

But the darkness doesn't like to be cheated. It's been keeping me company for a long time, and it's not ready to let me go. Something, probably a long streamer of seaweed, wraps like cold and slimy fingers around my ankle and I want to scream, but I can't without sucking even more water into my airway. I kick wildly, my foot connecting with something soft, and those fingers loosen just enough for me to thrash away from their grasp.

The queen observes all of this. Patiently singling out the weakest of the pack to mark as her prey.

And then she strikes.

The sight of her coming gets my arms moving, at least. I paddle over the swells, very aware of the key still clutched in my hand. I cannot lose it out here. If I do, it'll be gone forever.

The queen carves her way through the waves while I feel like I'm swimming in place, except I've somehow managed to get even farther from shore.

"Stop!" I scream absurdly as the shrieker flails toward me.

Her form is sloppy but effective. She brushes against my leg. I kick again, and my heel digs into something firm and muscular. I push myself forward before she can take another swipe.

Just as I do, a monstrous wave rolls over us both, and we're under. I see the queen only briefly, tumbling through bubbles and sharp flickers of sunlight. She belts out a warped cry, and then she's gone, lost in a murky cloud.

Another wave passes before I can come up for air, pushing me even farther under. My chest feels like it's being crushed. I have to breathe soon. I won't be able to help it. My frantic heart demands oxygen, come hell or high water (*ha!*), and there's nobody to pull me out of it, no cosmic intervention to leave me gasping on the shore. We get only one second chance, and mine's going to end right where it started.

A voice reaches my ears, resonating through the waves. It isn't Beth, though. It barely sounds human at all. It's my own voice, it's Sarah's voice, it's the voice of the unseen horror on the beach, the thing with the swollen feet and the cold, blue lips. A voice from the past, from the now, and from the very near future if I don't get my ass back to the surface.

Why fight this, Mike?

For a brief moment, the water around me goes calm. I see the slope of the land, pitching gently westward before angling steeply down into impenetrable blackness. Farther out, the continental shelf drops, plummeting beyond the reach of sunlight, all the way into the deepest trenches carved into the earth's surface. The hadal zone. I'm not sure why I know that, but the name is appropriate. As far beneath the waves as jetliners fly above.

It's from down there that the voice calls out to me. From the hydrothermal vents that first spewed life into this endlessly strange, unforgiving world.

There's nothing up there for you anymore.

"Not true," I spit, bubbles carrying the words up, toward the sunlight. Something is moving out there at the edge of visibility. So massive that looking left and right, I can't even determine the full breadth of it. But this is no monster from some other world. This one has been right here all along.

Nothing but pain, the discordant voice coos. Fish corpses swirl around me in a glittering cyclone. I swear I can feel us all being pulled out, like bits of plankton into the fathomless maw of a leviathan. My head is pounding. I can't tell if it's due to that voice, from the relentless beating of the waves above, or from the starved blood surging through my veins, but I'm on the verge of losing consciousness.

"You're wrong," I insist. No bubbles rise from my lips this time.

"There's more. I've found it. I didn't think that was possible, but I did."

You'll lose her too. You'll hurt again. Let go. There is no pain in the deep.

"No!" I thrust my hand forward, displaying the key as if it's some kind of talisman for warding off evil. I have worked too hard for this. I have found something I never thought I'd find again, a reason to keep breathing, to keep fighting. And I am not letting it go this time.

It might be my imagination—hell, all of this is—but I swear the leviathan out there reels away, like a vampire from the sight of a crucifix. Its voice, which has been wrapping around my brain like some kind of parasitic worm, recoils. The pull of that darkness releases its hold, and I start to rise.

There's a crash above me, something shattering the surface of the water. I look up, and there she is. Her face, glowing like the sun emerging from behind a thunderhead. I reach for her, she finds my hand, laces her fingers through mine, and pulls.

"What are you *doing*?" Beth scolds as I take great gulps of oxygen. "You didn't drop the key, did you?" I show it to her. "Good. We need to move!"

I've never heard a better idea. Move, yes. Movement is life. Movement will get me back on solid ground, and if I never set foot in the ocean again, it will be much too soon.

The tide discards the queen, angry and hissing, on the beach, coated with dirty foam and tangles of seaweed. She skitters in a disoriented circle, jaws open, worm writhing and spitting. The grass at the top of the dunes shudders and flattens, and the sky begins to shimmer. The others. Coming to Her Majesty's aid, as if they know through some psychic connection that she's just had her ass whooped by the sea.

We run for the Subaru as they flood down the dune, a chorus of shrieks heralding their approach. The wind has blown the door shut again, and for one awful second, I imagine that we've managed to lock ourselves out. Then I remember that I have the key. The *key*.

I can feel it, radiant and pulsing, like I'm clutching a newborn star in the palm of my hand. A tiny, wild spark that will illuminate a future I never imagined seeing.

Beth flings the passenger-side door open, and I slide in behind the wheel. We're not a moment too soon; the screams are so loud, it sounds as though the shriekers are already inside the car with us.

I don't realize it's Beth screaming until I pull the door shut.

20

BETH

Jake is shoved so far into the corner of the hatch it's like he's being absorbed by the upholstery itself. I can't tell where all the blood is coming from at first. He doesn't appear mortally wounded. Red splashes on his fur, his muzzle stained from licking at his hind leg, eyes white with stress. That seems to be the source of the problem. The queen must have nicked something major.

That's when I see she took the whole leg from the knee down.

Mike says something, but I can't hear him. I can't hear anything. The sight of Jake's leg utterly eclipses the world around me. I need to help him. Need to stop the bleeding. Need to do anything but sit here screaming.

I set the pistol aside and turn to pull the door shut, but a bruised-purple shape shoots toward me, wedging its head between the door and frame. It's my buddy. I guess my sandwich didn't kill him after all, but the hellvine is certainly working at it. Deep violet cords encircle him like ratty fishnet. Every movement is a struggle against the stuff.

"Mike!" I shout, though I don't know what he can contribute to the situation. I pull as hard as I can on the door, trying to crush the shrieker's head. There is a bit of meaty give, and the creature whines in distress. More important, it keeps the thing from being able to open its jaws or get its feet in. From doing to my head what the queen did to Jake's leg.

But even in this state, the shrieker will eventually overpower me.

"Mike, *drive*!"

He fumbles with the key, like it, too, is of alien design. Then he drops it on the floor between his feet. If I wasn't busy trying to keep the shrieker out, I'd kill him myself.

The infected shrieker thrashes and shreds the side of the car with its feet. It gets its jaws open enough that I can just see the tongue-worm. The new vines are wrapped around the plump, fleshy bastard like constrictors. A few of the tongue-worm's eyes have burst like cherry tomatoes left in the sun. The others all seem to be looking in different directions at once as the worm writhes to escape the hellvine's grasp. I'm not even sure it's trying to get into the car to kill us. It might not know what it's doing at all at this point, besides going in any direction that might get it away from the things choking the life out of it.

The pistol is behind me, barrel-down in the cup holder, but I can't grab it without taking one of my hands off the door, and I really, *really* do not want to do that. I could ask Mike to do the shooting, but I've had more than my fill of that, thank you very much. No, it's better that we start moving. The shrieker won't last long being dragged down the beach.

But Mike is still trying to remember how keys work, telling me to hold on like I need telling, while staring bug-eyed at the shrieker. What's the matter with him? Did he suffer some brain damage out there in the water? He wasn't under for *that* long.

The tide comes in and rocks the Subaru. The shrieker recoils from this unexpected shock of cold. Not much, but until Mike's systems start functioning again, it's the best I'm going to get.

I let go, grab the pistol, and spin back around. Sensing a sudden lack of resistance, the shrieker's jaws stretch wide open, like curtains parting for the tongue-worm's grand arrival. Those wild eyes all focus on me, for a moment seeming to forget its nasty predicament, eager to make my acquaintance at last.

Pleasure's all mine.

I honestly don't expect the gun to fire. I don't even register the bang, the ringing ears, the pain of my bandaged wrist absorbing the kick, until that little worm explodes like a rotten pumpkin, sticky strings of black goo spraying the window. The hellvines inside flail wildly, looking for something new to grab hold of. Before they can find me, though, the shrieker's body seizes, jerks backward violently, and lands on the sand. Motionless and—*finally!*—silent.

"Aaaaah-*hahahaha*!" I bellow, then slam the door shut. I did it! I *killed* one of the miserable hellspawn sons of bitches. I can't believe it! I want to beat my fists against the ceiling and kick my feet in the air and howl until my throat bleeds.

But first we need to *go*!

"Mike!"

"Got it!" he cries victoriously, jamming the key into the ignition and giving it a twist. But our streak of luck has run dry.

Just like the battery.

≈

Maybe he just didn't turn the key fully. The instrument panel is lit up, showing us a half-full gas gauge and an outside temperature of sixty-eight degrees, while the radio spits some static. I really see no reason for the engine not to turn over. But when Mike tries again, the starter just whines and clicks pathetically.

"I don't understand," he says, dumbfounded, staring at the spread of electronic displays before him like it's all part of some vast puzzle.

"Shut it off and try again," I tell him, even though I know it's not going to work. The radio and gauges can draw enough juice from the battery to operate. The starter, on the other hand . . . But I'm not ready to accept that yet. "Turn off the radio and AC too."

I squeeze into the back seat and crawl to Jake and reach for his leg. Anything to distract myself from the whine of the engine coldly refusing to do as it's asked. Jake pulls away from me, doing his best to dissolve through the hatch and out into the wind and blow away.

"Hey, it's okay," I lie. "Let me help." I brush sand away from the wound, which does precious little except make the truth painfully clear: if he doesn't receive actual medical attention, beyond Mike and Beth's Discount Field Hospital, he is going to die.

Mike powers everything down, even takes the key completely out and wipes it on his pants, then tries again. The results do not improve.

"Why is this not working?" he asks. The defeat in his voice breaks me all over again. In his mind, we were already free, we'd hit a point where any other outcome was simply no longer tangible. But the Subaru sat in that garage for just a little too long, and then it sat on this beach a little bit longer. Just like us, it's never going to move again. Facts, cold as they come.

I tie my discarded T-shirt tightly around Jake's thigh. I have no clue how to make a tourniquet, but the blood flow does seem to slow. Maybe that's just wishful thinking.

I lift the leg as high as Jake will allow me, trying to ignore his yelps of protest. It seems like the thing to do, but I don't know. My dad taught me to drive, and a guy whose name I've long forgotten showed me how to shoot a gun, but I was never educated in caring for a dog whose leg was just bitten off by an alien monster.

Jake licks my hand, hopeful that the smart human can fix him. I've done everything else. Fed him, watered him, walked him, cuddled him. It stands to reason that when he hurts, I should be able to make him better. But I'm not magic—I don't think anything has ever been more evident, even to a dog. I might have made it back from hell, but that was a fluke at best, and really, what difference did it make? Hell just followed me, as usual. Were some of those who disappeared spared this fate? Is a universe that births such monstrosities as shriekers and cloudfish also capable of showing mercy to those it deems righteous by some unknowable standard? I suppose it's not impossible. But for those of us who didn't make the cut, we've got nobody to count on but each other. Unfortunately for Jake and Mike, that means me.

"It's the battery, Mike," I say quietly. "We didn't drive enough this morning to charge it up. It's not going to start." The last word catches in my throat, and I have to bite my lip to keep from crying. If those floodgates open now, they won't close until I'm dead.

"No," he protests, turning the key so hard I find myself waiting for it to just snap off.

I pull Jake into an embrace. He doesn't fight back, just sighs heavily against my skin, his wet nose leaving a sticky, cold trail across my neck.

I'm done. With all of it. Done with invisible monsters and creeping hellvines, done with keys and dead batteries. The sheer weight of it all is just too much to carry another inch. I want to go to sleep. I want to shut down.

"Come on!" Mike screams as another wave hits us, smashing into the front of the car and spraying clear over the roof. The dead shrieker bumps against the door.

Mike punches the steering wheel again and again, accenting each hit with a new curse and revealing an impressive repertoire. He slumps back in the seat, staring out at the ocean, and laughs. "There *has* to be something else. There has got to be another way."

If there is, I don't know it.

"How long until the car starts to fill?" I ask.

"Not long," Mike says, not meeting my eyes. There's a bleak certainty in his words. A doctor adjusting his grim prognosis from months down to mere hours. "We'll probably drift for a bit. But then . . ." He trails off, focusing on the horizon.

I scratch Jake's head gently. He lets me, giving me a big old doggy grin, even as his eyes are white and desperate. His whole body trembles like he's freezing, so I squeeze him tighter. I want to hug him until we're both safely on the other side. I made a promise to look after him. I'm going to keep it to the best of my ability.

"Do you think it hurts?" I ask. "Drowning?"

"Yes," Mike answers so confidently that I almost ask him how he knows. But he knows lots of random, weird, unhelpful things, so it doesn't come as a surprise. And it doesn't matter. There are still bullets in that pistol. I'm not going to let Jake die in agony, sucking water into his lungs, and I don't much care to go that way myself. Why should that shrieker be the only one who gets off easy?

"It's not like we ever had anything to get back to anyway," I say. The words leave a bitterness on my lips, like the juice of poisonous berries. "We were being naïve to ever believe there was something beyond this beach, Mike. It's been over since it began. We lost."

He looks at me. "At least we'll get one last sunset," he says. And I can't disagree with that.

21

MIKE

The water outside is nearly to the door handles, the floor squishy beneath my feet, puddles oozing from the saturated carpet. It seems that no matter what I do, I won't be escaping this watery fate. What a cruel trick. I can almost hear the darkness beneath the waves, laughing at me.

I finish securing the gauze pads with duct tape. It took almost all our remaining bandages to get Jake's bleeding down to a stubborn ooze, and the rest of our drinking water to clean the sand and filth from the wound. It feels a bit pointless, given none of us will be alive in an hour, one way or the other. But Beth insisted. Grasping on to whatever semblance of control she can find, here at the end.

I give Jake a deep scratch behind the ears, and he moans his approval. His injured leg twitches involuntarily toward his snout, and his tongue flips out to explore the fuzzy cast.

"No," Beth orders, and he flops over, defeated.

The queen is still on the beach. Rendered partially visible by the salt and seaweed coating her. She's not moving much. Maybe she sucked down a bunch of water and hasn't fully recovered. Maybe Beth's shots connected better than she thought. A protective entourage shimmers around her. We aren't the only ones refusing to give up without a fight. I suppose, in a strange way, I have to respect that.

Beth slips away from Jake long enough to turn the key.

"What are you doing?" I ask.

"I can't die in silence." With what little juice the battery has left, the electrical system pumps life into the radio. She scans through station after station of static, passing a few useless emergency alert tones, but there's no music. Nothing still going on auto-play. Not even an advertisement or bellowing preacher ranting about End Times to an audience of ghosts.

Then a voice crackles into clarity. But it's not a singer. It isn't a preacher, either, at least not as far as I can tell.

"—coming to you from Vernonia, Oregon," the man booms with optimistic energy that's so out of place in this new world that it startles me. "Home of the famous Friendship Jamboree and Logging Show. That could be the reason these bastards are keeping their distance. They took one look at what our lumberjacks can do to a Doug fir and decided to just keep on moving. Whatever the case, they haven't broken us yet. And they aren't gonna get a chance. We've fortified our good town. Got food, supplies, and patrols keeping watch around the clock. We should be safe until a better plan materializes. And you better believe folks are working on one. Across the pond, they even . . ." He fades out.

Is this for real? Is it some kind of horrific joke? The man's cheerfulness and faux country charm make my brain itch. I look at Beth for a second opinion. She stares dubiously at the radio.

"We're doing what we can to keep the way in clear," the voice fades back in. "We see you coming, we'll let you in. Just, if you can, try not to bring hell with you."

A wave smacks the car. The voice disappears into static, and then the electrical system zaps off. Beth turns the key a few times, but it's no use.

"Vernonia," she says. "Never been there."

"It's about sixty miles from here. Even if we could walk, it would take us a full day, and that's at a good hustle." I don't know why I feel the need to dash any hopes the radio phantom may have given her. To avoid any further heartbreak, I guess. We aren't walking anywhere. Whatever safe harbor Vernonia might promise, it's not in our future. There's nothing for us but the tide.

"Do you think that's all that's left of the entire North Coast?" Beth asks. "Or is he just the only person still broadcasting?"

"Hard to say. I can't imagine that it all fell, especially since the two of us are still alive. It isn't like people have no way to fight back. But then again, you'd think we'd have seen some sign of resistance. Helicopters, fighter jets."

"Or maybe they've just found more important places to protect than this empty, depressing stretch of nowhere," she scoffs. "We've been off the grid for so long now, Mike, there's no telling what's happening out there. People are working on a plan, you heard him say that."

"I did. I also find it mighty convenient that we turned on the radio just as he was making the announcement."

"What are you talking about?"

"I mean, that was probably a recording. Playing on a loop. It could be hours old, for all we know. Everybody there could be dead, nothing left but a generator and a radio pumping out false promises."

"Goddamn, Mike." It's all she says.

I hate making her feel that way, but I can't let hope in again. Every time I do, it turns on me, and I'm done. Maybe the darkness was right. Maybe there's nothing here but pain. I don't want to believe that again. I want to believe that magic is still out there, in some form other than a set of keys, but I simply see no evidence of it. I see only teeth, and the tide.

Beth leaves the key in the ignition and crawls back with me and Jake. I reach for her hand to give it a comforting squeeze, but she jerks it away. Not because she's mad, though. She's in pain. Her other hand falls on her bandaged wrist and scratches.

"I think I should take a look at that," I tell her. She shakes her head. "Come on. Dr. Mike is in the house. We still have a little disinfectant left."

"It's fine."

"Beth, my hands burned for hours after touching that thing. You actually got stung by the vine. Please. You shouldn't have to be in pain." I reach again, and she pulls away. What is she hiding?

"I told you no," she grunts, clamping her right hand across her bandaged wrist. Something isn't right. I can tell by the way her eyes grow and her voice goes shrill.

"Just let me look. From a distance, see?" I hold up my hands, to show I'm not going to lunge at her with medical intent. Slowly, she peels her fingers away from the dirty bandages.

They ripple.

Not much, but it's enough to elicit a gasp from me. It happens again, a small protrusion rising and falling like a pulse. There's something underneath. Something alive.

"Mike," she whispers, her eyes refusing to drop, to see for herself what she clearly already knows.

"Can you feel that?" It takes her a very long time to answer. Running every possible form of denial through her head, hoping for one that will somehow make this all go away, and coming up empty.

"Yes."

I finger one corner of the dressing, then slowly start to peel it back. Her good hand clamps around my wrist, bracing for what we're about to find.

It's like turning over a piece of fruit to find it squirming with maggots. Beth's forearm is the same bruised purple as the shrieker. The same color as the hellvines themselves. Up close, it looks like hundreds of dandelion seeds sprouting from her skin, each one blooming ugly purple and giving off the noxious odor that's been haunting us all day. Beneath this layer is an almost black protrusion, like a tree root slowly breaking through a sidewalk.

The root thing squirms lethargically as soon as it's exposed.

"Mike! Ohmygod!"

"Okay, hold on," I say, just to say something, my eyes bugging out idiotically.

"Fuck you! Get it off me!"

Yes, that is probably a smart strategy. But how? I don't want to just start ripping and tearing. There's vital plumbing in there, and we used the last of our bandages on the dog.

My eyes find the cooler. And inside is the remaining vodka. I can't help but smile at how much mileage we're getting from the little pieces of Sarah she left behind. As if she'd known I'd need the help. That thing taunting me with her voice, trying to poison her memory, got it wrong. Sarah wouldn't want to hurt me. Even after everything. I've said it before, I'll say it again: I didn't deserve her. I didn't fight to keep her, the way she fought for me. I want to change that with Beth. Even if it's just for a day.

"You already did that," Beth moans as I twist off the cap.

"Yes, well, Dr. Mike is going to do a more thorough job this time, now that he knows what he's dealing with." My T-shirt is in the footwell, now soaked with seawater. Perfect. I set it next to me in a soggy heap.

Jake stretches to sniff at Beth's arm, and she shoos him away.

"Give me your lighter," I demand.

"*What?*" She's becoming hysterical, hyperventilating, unable to rip her eyes from the thing on her arm.

"Your lighter, Beth. Give it to me." She's in too much shock to understand what's about to happen. That's probably good. She motions limply toward the cup holder, where the lighter and crumpled pack of cigarettes are still tucked, like the contents of a tinder box. I only want the lighter, but we both might need a smoke after this.

I pour vodka directly onto the black root. It curls like a salted slug. It doesn't seem to be wrapped around bone or stretched up her arm beneath the skin, so hopefully I can get it out without causing too much damage to Beth.

She groans through gritted teeth, clenching her fist.

The knife is on the seat next to the depleted medical supplies. I flick open the blade with a resounding snap, then coax a small blue flame from the lighter.

At this point, Beth understands what's coming. "Mike," she begins to protest.

"This might sting a bit," I tell her. It gets the laugh I'm hoping for. Humor, nature's great panacea. But the laugh quickly rises into a scream as I touch the flame to her skin.

The hundred-proof vodka ignites, and the purple fuzz vanishes in a flash of smoke and stink. Beth's skin sizzles and splits. She howls like I'm sawing off her arm, and soon Jake joins her, the two of them singing of all the agony in the universe. I let the baby vine burn until it's charred crisp and Beth's shrieks hit a register only Jake can detect, then I stab it with the knife. It comes out cleanly, skewered to the blade like something fresh off the grill. I shove open the door, letting in a flood of water, and fling it into the waves. I pull the door shut and slap the wet shirt over Beth's arm, smothering the flames.

The screaming stops abruptly, and her body goes limp.

22

MIKE

"Give me hope," I say. The smell of burnt flesh and hellvine has faded, but a new silence has filled the space between us. Outside, the waves mist the windshield, turning the sunset into an abstract. I took the shades out to give us a view. The car shudders like a plane in turbulence. "That's the note I'd have given the screenwriter if this had all landed on my desk. Well, one of my notes. But the biggest, I think."

"Hope?" Beth asks without much interest, still staring at her scorched arm. Nothing else is growing. Yet. I made her a fresh bandage out of tape and some lining cut from the patrol bag. I don't know why the hellvine spread so much faster in the shrieker. Different biology, or the combination of disinfectant and seawater. Or maybe it was because Beth was able to remove the actual remaining piece of vine. Starts mature faster than seeds, after all. But there's no telling if this is the end of it, or if it's going to keep returning. Which brings me back around to my point.

"Yeah. Cut off the head and the horde dies, or our gravity eventually drags them down, or all the pesticides and hormones and chemicals we pump into our world ends up poisoning them. That would be some sweet irony. But just give me *something* to make the audience believe there's even a chance of a win. Wins are good. Wins get sequels."

Beth scoffs. "Who would want a second dose of this shittery?"

"Hey, it's a good problem to have."

She looks from her arm to the windshield. To the violet and burnt-orange sky. Our last sunset. "Thank you," she says.

"For setting you on fire?" She laughs. Not much, but I'm glad she can still do that. Feels like another small victory.

"For sticking with me through the end of the world." She looks at me, no hint of a smile this time. "Nobody else would have."

"C'mon."

"I mean it, Mike." She holds my eyes for a long time.

I'm the one who breaks the silence. Not because it makes me uncomfortable but because I think she needs to hear this. "Listen. Here's the funny thing about movie producers: anybody can be one. I'm serious. It's not like you get licensed. You don't even have to know what you're doing, there are plenty of those, let me tell you. Wandering the streets of L.A. like vampires, sustaining themselves on other people's dreams."

"I was wondering why there was so little in your refrigerator," Beth quips.

"I'm not a hack," I say, ignoring that. "I'm hardly the best either. But . . . I do pride myself on knowing something special when I see it." Then, just to get back at her, I pat Jake on the head. "And I knew if he had you looking after him, you must be pretty okay too."

"You're the worst," she laughs, then scoots next to me, snagging her camera from the corner of the hatch. After fiddling with some settings, she holds it at arm's length, pulling me close, the rear passenger window to our backs. Our distorted, harrowed faces stare back from lens glass.

"Say 'doomsday'!" she sings. The shutter clicks. Beth flips the camera around to review the shot.

There we are on the little screen, holding our sadly sweet pose, the warm sunlight filling the shadows on our faces. What a story behind that shot. If by some chance humanity endures, I hope somebody finds this camera. If they clean out the sand and salt, pull the memory card, get it into a computer, I hope this is the picture that survives. This is how I want to be remembered.

I take the camera from her and start cycling through the other photos. Beth stiffens, her hands flinching toward me, to stop me, to take the camera away, but then she changes her mind. There's no more point in secrets. And what could she possibly be hiding on this, anyway?

The first picture is a standard social media profile portrait of herself in a bathroom mirror, scowling at the world. Tired eyes, messy hair, middle finger raised. This is probably the picture that will survive the apocalypse.

"Cute," I comment, and she punches my arm.

"That was my first day doing this. The picture-a-day thing."

"What gave you the idea to do that?" I ask. It takes her so long to answer I almost repeat the question, in case she didn't hear.

"My dad bought this camera for me," she says, as if confessing to murder after years on the lam. "He was going downhill pretty steadily by then. His memory, you know, his mind. I'd come around to say hi, beg for money, use the toilet, and he'd ask about boyfriends I hadn't seen since high school, jobs I'd been fired from years ago. I wasn't exactly eager to give him the latest updates. To tell him about all the cliffs I'd been throwing myself over. That I was living in my car—that's right, my crappy Toyota? Casa Beth.

"So when I started the house-sitting thing, I took pictures of the places on my phone, and showed them to him. Pretended they were *my* places. My cats, my cute apartment, my nice plants. I knew he'd forget, and next time I could be somebody else. I know, it's gross, but the truth . . . I didn't want him worrying about me. Or thinking I was in trouble. And I didn't want to disappoint him. So I lied. With pictures.

"That's the part that stuck with him. The pictures. So one day when he was particularly lucid, he got out the credit card and went on the internet and bought me a proper camera. Mom was furious. I'm sure she told him that I'd been lying. But I kind of think he already knew. He could tell I was doing my best to get back on the road, and this was his way of encouraging me."

"'Get back on the road'?"

"You know. The straight and narrow." She shrugs. "The picture-a-day bit was my own idea. Something I knew I could do, could stick with, that wasn't self-destructive. Baby steps. Mom figured I'd just sell the camera for some new way to wreck myself. I've enjoyed proving her wrong. I just wish I'd started sooner."

"Why didn't you?"

"Because for my entire childhood, she never missed a chance to point out how much of a disaster I was. To put me down. To set me up for failure. I honestly don't know why. I don't think she was always that way. My dad obviously saw something good in her. But there was something about her life that she was deeply unhappy about, and she took it out on me. I don't know, we never exactly talked it out. Eventually, it just became easier to live down to her pitifully low expectations. Messing up was the one thing even she couldn't deny I did well. After a while—I know this will surprise you—I kind of got addicted to it.

"That took me to some low places. I knew if I kept it up, it was going to get me killed, or thrown in prison. But by then, I didn't really know how to do anything else. How to *be* anybody else. I mean . . . how do you get clean from *yourself*? I've been trying, Mike. I really have. But every time I do, I just feel like a fraud. A pretender. I can hear her voice in the back of my head, counting down the seconds until I screw up again. And then I drift off the road. And crash.

"I'm no Annie Leibovitz," she says, nodding at the camera. "But I'm working at it. And I haven't missed a day. Which is more effort than I've given anything else in as long as I can remember. Just in time for the world to end."

I scroll through her pictures. A lot of selfies, interspersed with still-lifes inside other people's homes. Colorful front doors, tasteful decor, little messes of clutter and personality. Nothing that was going to win awards, but she was talented. That was obvious. And getting better with every shot. She had an eye for finding stories in things most people would glance at and forget a moment later.

I come across a picture of a shattered sand dollar in a tire track.

"That was my first day here," she says, as if remembering a moment years ago, rather than a week. There are more pictures of her stay in Strawberry Dunes: beach grass against a soft sky, fried eggs in a skillet, elk in the mist, a bald eagle perched on a telephone pole. I can still see her improving as I scroll, her subjects carefully chosen, the intent of her framing, the use of backdrop and foreground to create depth and draw the eyes.

The best photograph yet is of a man standing in his kitchen window, staring outside into the gathering darkness. The hopelessness and despair in his posture are so real, so perfectly captured, that the weight of them take my breath away. How could a human being, on a planet occupied by billions of others, possibly look so isolated? So alone?

The man, of course, is me. Beth stiffens next to me, as though she'd forgotten to clear this picture off the memory card. Is that her big secret?

"I hadn't realized anybody was living next door until I saw you that night," she confesses gently, as if this betrayal of my privacy might send me into a rage. I guess if I were her mother, it would have. On me, it has exactly the opposite effect. "I know I told you the same thing yesterday. I lied, sorry. I didn't want you thinking I was a creeper. 'Hey, I've been secretly photographing you for the last few days, wanna pour me a drink?' "

"Photographing? There are more?"

I progress through the camera roll. There's another shot of me, standing on the back deck and staring out at the waves.

A third, taken from the beach, looking in through my office window, which frames me standing at my desk. Beth's shadow is visible on the sand, her arm raised in a friendly wave I didn't even see. I was looking far past her.

This series of pictures could be shown in a gallery, if such things still existed. Masterly shots of a man wading through the ruins of his life, searching for something worth salvaging and coming up empty-handed, because he'd already let the thing he treasured most slip through his fingers.

"I'd make up stories about who you were," she says. "What you were always looking at. Or looking for. I know that's weird, I just . . . I'd never seen somebody who looked as lost as I feel. It was kind of comforting, knowing you were over there. Anytime things got heavy in my head, and I felt like I was going to lose it, I just looked for you."

The second-to-last photo was taken yesterday. Me and my stupid champagne. Minutes before we met and changed each other's lives. This evening's selfie is the first shot on the roll with another human being sharing the frame with her.

"You know," she says sourly, "it's not cool that you got to look through my pictures, but I won't get to see your new movie."

"It if makes you feel any better, nobody will."

She laughs. "Apocalypse humor is dark."

"No, what I mean is, there isn't a new movie. There never was."

"But the champagne—" she starts, as if unable to accept that she isn't the only liar in the car.

"The champagne is what Sarah and I used to do," I tell her. "It was our ritual, I was being honest about that. Whenever I'd wrap on a project, we'd come up here so I could decompress for a few days. That first evening, we'd always pop a cork, pour two glasses, and she'd look at me and say, 'So what's next?'"

"Sounds nice," Beth says.

A wave rocks us hard, splashing across the roof and streaming down the back window. Water laps against the seats.

"I thought so too."

"Then what happened? Where did it go wrong?"

"It was always wrong, that's the problem."

She studies me with narrowed eyes.

"Because I was always too busy with me. With my goals, with the things I wanted for us, the things I thought were important.

You know, with movies, you wrap, have a martini, and you go on to the next thing. Turns out, people don't work that way. They're ongoing. Always changing. I think, when Sarah asked me, 'What's next?' she was hoping I'd say *her.* Hoping I'd give some indication that I was paying attention, that I knew she was her own person, that there was a whole life behind her eyes, that she had her own ambitions, her own fears, her own pain, and that I was ready to be there for her no matter what. But I'd wrapped on that project long ago and moved on, content that it would always be great. That nothing could possibly sneak in and cut all those wonderful frames to ribbons."

I look out at the sunset.

"One year ago yesterday, she went out for a walk on the beach, and never came back."

"Oh, Mike. I thought, when you told me she left . . ." Beth trails off.

I nod. I had let her think that, because, like her, I hadn't wanted to face the truth all over again. Hadn't wanted my throat to tighten as it does now, for my mouth to contort into these ugly shapes as I try to form the words.

"She loved wading into the ocean," I force myself to say. Because I've needed to say this, to somebody other than myself, for a long time. "The feel of the water around her legs and the sand between her toes. She used to laugh at me, standing on the shore, wanting none of it. I don't mind L.A. beaches so much, but here . . ." I trail off, the words of that sign flickering across the screen of my memory. DON'T SWIM ALONE. NO LIFEGUARD. BEWARE OF RIP CURRENTS. "I didn't go with her that day, like I usually did. I had an 'important' phone call. I couldn't be bothered. So she went by herself. That was the last time I saw her, from my office window, walking down that trail to the beach."

"It was an accident," Beth says.

"If I'd been there, it might never have happened at all."

It takes me a moment to compose myself enough to keep speaking. Beth waits patiently.

"You spend so many years with a person, your love for them

begins to feel like a solid thing. Something you can count on, something buoyant you can grab hold of and hang on to for dear life when the waters get rough. I held on to Sarah plenty of times. Now that she's gone, I've just been sinking."

It's the first time I've really cried since Sarah died. You have to feel to cry, and I've just been so empty. The people closest to me advised me not to make any significant life decisions for a year. Don't sell the house, don't throw things away, don't do anything extreme, until I'd had time to process, to hurt, to bleed, and then to start healing.

Except I hadn't healed. I couldn't let myself. Not when I'd let the woman I loved down so completely.

Eventually, those people drifted away. They stopped checking in so often, stopped offering to come around, stopped inviting me back to L.A. They assumed I was just dealing with things in my own way. And I was. But in that house, with nothing to keep me company but ghosts, the darkness found me too.

I gave them the year I'd promised, and then, last night, I popped a cork. Because I knew my story had ended too. I sat by that fire, and I repeated Sarah's same anxious question, *What's next?* I don't know what answer I was expecting, nothing, I suppose, but it sure wasn't the one I got. And certainly not the one I deserved.

Hey, neighbor.

Beth holds me tight as I sob. She squeezes my hands and puts her forehead against mine, and when the shudders subside, she whispers:

"I know you feel responsible. I'm not going to try to change your mind about that. But whatever current you've been drifting on, it brought you to me. And I'm thankful for that."

"Why?" I ask with a bewildered laugh.

"Because, Mike. You don't have to spend years with somebody to know they can pull you up from the depths and keep you afloat through the worst storm."

I look at her through a blur of tears. I haven't told her what happened last night, what I set out to do, and in a way, I'm not sure I even need to. She's right. In the end, it was her face that kept me from slipping beneath the waves. Not the meteors, not fear: it was Beth. She was my fate, my lifeguard, after all. "I know."

She kisses me deeply. Every system in my body that had begun shutting down twenty-four hours ago lights up. It's absurd to be thinking about these things when we have so little time left. But we're still here, and we're going to make the most of every single moment of it.

Beth breaks off and stares at me, just for a second. She's thinking the same thing.

Her lips crash into mine once more, her hands tearing at the skin on my back. I gently tug off her shorts and guide her on top of me. We both cry out, the motion of our bodies rocking the car as much as the raging tide. I clutch her fiercely, her heartbeat rippling her skin, sending bolts of electricity through every pore and into me. We don't even try to be quiet, to avoid drawing attention. Damn them all. We're alive in the most human way possible, and there's nothing they can do to take it away from us.

We both cry out again, clinging to each other as if the slightest loosening of our grip will send the other spiraling into the void. Beth rests her forehead against mine. Sweat runs down her nose, her fingers tracing the fresh fingernail marks on my chest. I taste salt on my lips and feel the warm, trembling shape of her hips beneath my hands, and before I know it I'm ready to go again.

"What is that?" she asks, and for a moment I think she's being coy about my unexpected encore. "Listen."

I close my mouth and stop panting. I hear Beth's breathing, the ocean, the chirping of the shriekers as they try to figure out what's happening inside the Subaru. And something else. Something I never thought I'd hear again.

It's a car horn.

We both look out the window. I expect to see somebody barreling down the beach access road. A police car, maybe, or a military Humvee on a heroic rescue mission. But there's no such sight. The honking is coming from a most unexpected source.

It's coming from the Jeep.

23

NATALIA

I had to. I know it was dangerous, but I *had* to do it. It's going to be dark soon. I'm hungry and thirsty and I have to pee so bad now that it hurts.

Mom was so scared when she called. So mad at Dad for leaving me alone on the beach. I tried to tell her what happened. I tried to explain that he was signaling for help, and then disappeared, and everybody freaked out, and then a policeman went to get him and *he* disappeared too.

Mom told me to hide after that. To crawl beneath a blanket and not move until somebody came to get me. She promised somebody would, but that was so long ago. I called her back, over and over, but she won't answer the phone. I think maybe she disappeared as well. *Everybody* has.

Except for them, in the other car. I met them earlier today. They were out looking for fallen stars, for some reason. They seemed nice, and they have a dog. Jake. If anybody can help, it's them. I've heard them, shouting and shooting a gun, but I couldn't see much through the fog, so I just stayed hidden. There are other things out there. I don't *want* to see *them*. I don't want them to see me, either.

But I can't stay here any longer. I have to get home.

Dad always keeps a blanket in the car, and I covered myself with it to hide. It's scratchy and warm; I thought I was going to die when the sun came back out. I've been in the space beneath the dashboard for so long that everything hurts. My fingers tingle as I turn to the window to look through my binoculars. Well, Dad's binoculars, but he was letting me use them to watch for the boat, as long as I promised to be careful and not break them.

The *boat*. What happened to the *boat*? It was supposed to take us all up the river to get Mom. What happened to my *mom*?

The man and the woman are in the back seat still, but they aren't . . . doing what they were doing a moment ago. I don't see Jake. I'm sure he's in there. I don't know how they could do *that* right in front of him. It's a Very Private Thing, Dad says. Not something you do in your car, on a beach, in front of your dog. But nothing is happening like it should today, so whatever, I guess.

There's something outside the Jeep. It's making a creepy sound, but I can't see it. Why can't I *see* it? The fog's all gone now. I can see everything else.

It hits the windshield so hard the glass cracks. Dad would be so mad about that. He yells every time trucks on the highway kick up little rocks that smack the window, and those don't even make cracks.

Something else bangs against the door right beside me, and I scream. I hate screaming. Dad says girls don't scream, girls are Badasses, but I don't feel very badass right now, so I crawl back into the floor space and try not to move.

They're slamming against all the doors now. Are the doors locked? I'm glad Dad put the plastic top back on, instead of leaving the Jeep roofless like he does in the summer. But it has a big window on the roof. If they get up there, I won't be able to hide from them. Why did I honk that horn? Why didn't I just listen to Mom?

The Jeep bounces and rocks like it might just tip over. I bite my tongue to keep from screaming until I taste blood. I can't stop myself from crying, though.

Or peeing.

Badasses don't pee themselves, I'm sure Dad would say. But dads aren't supposed to disappear either. Aren't supposed to leave their kids alone on the beach with monsters.

It all suddenly stops, and I hear another horn honking.

It's *them*!

I raise my head just enough to look out the window. Their car is half sunk in the ocean. Why don't they move it? Why'd they stay here, and not leave with the others? I lift the binoculars.

She's the one honking the horn, or trying to. It's stopped now; she's pushing on it, but it's not making any more sound. He's still in the back seat. He says something to her, twirling his fingers. Now he's pushing on the ceiling. He's opening the sunroof! Mom's car has a sunroof. I like holding my hands up through it when we drive so I can feel the wind through my fingers. She always says it will hurt big-time if a bug hits me, but that hasn't happened yet. I think it's just one of those things moms say.

His sunroof opens a lot slower than Mom's. She reaches up and tries pushing on it. He says something to her again, and she yells back. They're arguing. He grabs something—a flashlight? It's not that dark out, the sun isn't even set. He covers his eyes and swings it at the sunroof, and glass rains down around him. Then he stands and squeezes through the roof and waves his arms.

"Hey! *Hey!* Over here!"

Is he talking to me? I *know* you're there. I honked at *you* first, don't you remember?

There are all sorts of awful screams from the invisible monsters, and marks appear in the sand, moving in his direction. He seems to be trying to get their attention, to get them away from me. They splash around in the shallows, and when the water sprays on them, they glimmer into shape like magic. One of them is farther out than the others, trying to sneak up on him the way a cat does a bird. It doesn't seem to see the big wave until it washes over it. It gets rolled onto its back like a roly-poly bug; I can see its legs kicking. When it rights itself, it runs in the wrong direction, into even deeper water, and another wave hits it. I hear it scream, I think, but I don't see it again. The others all back away from the water.

No wonder they didn't move the car—they knew they were safe out there. I wish I'd honked earlier. If I'd been with people who knew what they were doing, I might not have peed myself. I cannot believe I did that.

Other things have changed on the beach. The weird ball Dad didn't want me to go near, the thing they thought was a fallen star, has a bunch of vines growing out of it. Vines with strange flowers blooming. Some of them drift around in the water too.

There's also one monster that isn't fooled. It's bigger than the others; I can see it because it's got a lot of sand stuck to it. It's closer to me than to them. It looks like it's leaking, black stuff puddling around the monster in the sand, like the oil Dad drains from the Jeep.

It moves quickly, and I swear it's turning to look at me.

I drop out of sight. I don't think it saw me. It's not attacking. The man is yelling again, using words Dad says I should never use, even though I hear him use them all the time.

I peek again. The big monster hasn't moved any closer. The man is trying to keep the others' attention while also talking to the woman through the sunroof, both of them waving their hands around. I still don't see the dog. I really hope he's okay. I never got to pet him.

The woman looks at me through binoculars of her own. No, that's not right. It's a *camera.* A big camera with a telescope lens, like the one Dad uses to take pictures of the houses he's going to sell. I raise my hand and wave, and she puts a finger to her lips—telling me to *shhh*—then gives me a thumbs-up. Why? What does that mean? Is she asking if I'm okay?

I return the thumbs-up. She smiles and makes an A-OK sign. I'm not sure what any of this means, but I like her. She's confident. Seems Badass.

She makes another sign, pinching her fingers together and twisting her wrist. Huh? I shake my head.

He leans down to say something and she flaps a hand at him to make him be quiet, then she sets the camera down. Oh no! Why? Because I didn't understand? Don't give up on me!

Oh. She just needs to use both hands for this.

She clenches both fists and tilts them back and forth. *What?*

She drops her hands, turns, and points at the steering wheel. Oh, *steering wheel*! Got it. Is that all?

No, there's more. She grabs something and holds it up for me to see. Keys. Car keys. She points at me, at the keys, at the steering wheel.

Do I have the keys to the Jeep!

They're still hanging where Dad left them. I hold them up for her to see, and she claps her hands over her mouth. She tells him, and he fist-pumps the air and gives me a thumbs-up. Great? I don't see what's so exciting. They have keys too.

He climbs back down and they talk again. Not arguing this time, but they look very serious, like Mom and Dad used to talk before the split. They take turns pointing at the water, at the monsters, at me. She says something and he shakes his head. He says something and she rolls her eyes. I wish I could hear!

She looks around for something, and then holds it up for me to see. It's a cell phone. She read my mind! She points at the phone, then at me, and holds the phone to her ear.

Do I have a phone?

Well, I have Dad's phone. He gave it to me right before he went up into the dunes. I show it to her, and she gives me another A-OK. Then she points at me, holds her phone up to her ear, and points at herself with her thumb.

You. Call. Me.

What? How? I don't have your number!

She gives me another thumbs-up. I'm not sure she really knows what that means. Next, she holds up one hand, all her fingers out. Then she curls them together, until her fingers touch her thumb, making a circle. Then she holds up three fingers.

Um.

She does it again. Hi . . . Circle . . . Three? *Five zero three!* She's giving me her phone number!

I wake up Dad's phone and punch in the numbers, then give her a thumbs-up (which she is definitely on top of). She shows me three more numbers, then the last four. It takes so long, some of the monsters are coming back this way, the sun catching the water stuck to them and making it look like they've been sprinkled with glitter. The man climbs out the sunroof and shouts to get their attention again.

Finally, she points at me: *Call.*

I do, but it doesn't ring. There aren't any bars. Why aren't there any *bars*? There were earlier!

I end the call and hold the phone up as high as I dare. I don't want that big monster to see me. It's so much closer than the others. And I feel like it knows I'm here.

A bar appears. Then another. I hit Call again, before they can go away. This time it rings.

I stare through the binoculars, pressing the phone against my face so hard I can feel the warmth of its screen on my skin. The woman looks at her phone, but she doesn't answer. Why doesn't she answer? Is it not ringing on her end? Is this what happened when I tried calling Mom? Is the phone network broken? Did I put the number in wrong? Did I mess this up? A Badass girl would not mess this up!

She swipes her finger across her phone screen, and on my end the ringing stops. My heart stops, too, as hollow silence fills my ear.

Just when I'm about to lose all hope, she breaks the silence with two cheerful words:

"Hey, neighbor."

24

BETH

Sweet jumping Jesus, she's been over there this whole time. I just assumed the kid hitched a ride with the others. I never even imagined they'd *leave* her. I also figured her dad had the key with him went he went up into the dunes. Which means it's also been over there all along, if we'd just looked there in the first place, instead of taking that ridiculous trip up into the dunes and alerting the shriekers of our presence.

I can't even think about that. It doesn't matter now, anyway.

"I went to the bathroom," the girl on the other end of the phone says. She's two seconds from breaking into sobs. Her confession melts my heart.

"That's totally okay," I reassure her, trying not to laugh. Oh, if only some soiled shorts were our biggest problem. "What's your name?"

"Natalia."

"Natalia, right. I remember now." I zoom in until her face fills the screen. She keeps dipping her head away from the binoculars to look at something outside. The queen. The bitch isn't taking Mike's bait, still settled right between us and the Jeep. I can see from here that she's bleeding, though. So hopefully she won't be so eager to confront us again. Why they don't all just retreat back up into the dunes is the biggest mystery. Perhaps there are more hellvines out there, creeping through the grass, even more invisible than the shriekers. Or something worse, something they fear far more than us and the tide. My memory rewinds to my radio conversation with the dispatcher, to that horror on the other end of the airwaves, to my silent challenge for it to come meet me on the beach.

"Is your dog okay?" Natalia asks.

"Jake?" She perks up hopefully at the sound of his name. Unlike Jake, who didn't even twitch his ears. His eyes are glassy, his breathing slow and shallow. Blood drips from the gauze into a little puddle on the floor. I don't know how to stop it. I don't know if I even can. I made the tourniquet as tight as I could. "He's really tired, or I'd have him get up and wave. Are you okay?"

"My mom told me to stay put. To hide." That explains why she didn't reach out to us sooner. This poor girl. "She said somebody would come for me. But . . . but I don't think anybody is, and Dad's not coming back either and . . . there are *monsters* outside!"

This time she does cry, her whole body heaving violently. I need to calm her down. We've got most of the shriekers' attention, but it won't last forever if they aren't brave enough to swim out to us.

Mike taps my shoulder. "Speaker, please," he says.

I oblige. Natalia's wails crackle over the speakerphone. At this, I catch movement from the queen. A slight parting of her jaws, allowing her tongue-worm to just peer out. Is she hearing Natalia's voice in both places? Maybe, but she can't possibly understand what that means, that we're communicating with each other. Can she?

"Hey, hey, now," Mike says. "I know this is all really scary, but you've got us on the phone, and we're going to get through this together. Okay?"

Natalia nods and wipes tears off her binoculars, then pushes her red eyes to the glass. I hold the camera out so that Mike can see her face on the shaky screen.

"I'm Mike," he says cordially. "And this is Beth. Pleasure to meet you, Natalia." I give her a wave. This has got to be the most bizarre introduction of all time. Oh hey, good to meet you, you here for the end of the world too? "Do you live around here, Natalia?"

"My dad does. I'm visiting. It's his weekend. Did . . . did the monsters get him?"

Mike's lips whiten to a thin line. I'm glad she didn't ask me this. I've been telling lies my whole life, but I don't even know where I'd begin on this particular topic. He went to play in the big sandcastle in the sky? How old is she, even? What do kids her age have a grasp on?

"Yes," Mike answers, bluntly. "They did get him. I am so sorry."

Welp. I guess a straight shot of the truth works too. Might burn the whole way down, but you start feeling better sooner.

Natalia sets aside her binoculars to clutch the phone with both hands, staring at us with worried brown eyes.

"Which is why we have to get you off this beach and to someplace safe," Mike quickly adds. "That's what Beth and I are going to do." He sounds like he's trying to convince himself. We do have a plan. It sounded good when we made it, but the more it plays out in my head, the stupider it feels. What's most likely going to happen is that everything will go wrong and we'll all die spectacularly in the next ten minutes. It's a very good thing Mike took over the conversation.

Natalia stares into the middle distance, petrified as her mind tries to wrap itself around the fact that her parents are dead, monsters are real, and the closest thing she has to rescuers are two half-naked adults in a broken-down, flooded Subaru. What a mercilessly demented universe we inhabit.

Mike gives her time to find her grip on all this, but time is something we're running out of by the second. I smack him on the leg and point at the rising water.

"Natalia?" he says. She blinks, then looks at us through the binoculars again. "We're going to need your help. Our car is stuck. We can't walk over to you, for obvious reasons."

"Not anymore," I spit. I still can't believe we already ventured halfway there to get that useless, damned key.

Motion above the ridgeline of the dunes catches my eye, and my stomach plummets. It's the cloudfish—or maybe a different one, who can even say? It's a ways off yet, out above the trees, but there's no denying that it's coming this direction, drawn by the dissonant song of shriekers and car horns. Or maybe it's just making a circuit. There's no fog to hide in now, and we no longer have the luxury of time to just sit quiet and wait for it to leave again.

Natalia doesn't see it yet. That's good. We need to keep her looking this way for as long as possible. I don't want to think what the sight of the cloudfish might do to whatever courage she's managed to muster.

Mike opens his mouth to speak. Here it comes. The details of our plan. The mountain of idiocy, the monument to madness. The only chance we have left.

"Natalia, have either your mom or dad ever let you sit behind the wheel of the car as they drove?"

"No," she answers, as if nobody has ever asked a more inane question in the history of human existence.

"No," Mike repeats, his brow furrowing like she answered him with a crude hand gesture. "That's fine. Mine didn't either. But don't worry, driving is a piece of cake. Like riding a bike." He pauses to bite his lip. "You know how to ride a bike?"

"Yeah?"

Mike nods. "All right, good. Driving that Jeep will be even easier, and you don't have to worry about tipping over."

Great job, Mike. Natalia is already shaking her head, no doubt imagining the shriekers effortlessly flipping the Jeep over on its side as they drag her out and devour her alive.

"I can't," she says, panic sharpening her voice.

"Don't worry, we'll walk you through it," I intervene before Mike can further terrify her with his reassurances. If she's witnessed any of our earlier escape attempts, she's probably realized that we're the absolute worst people to be giving her vehicular advice. "I promise, it will be just fine. You'll go very slow—"

"No! The monsters will *see* me, they'll *get* me—"

"Natalia, please, just listen."

But it's a losing battle. She drops out of sight. I can still hear little whimpers from the other end of the phone, but she doesn't have it up to her ear anymore. Might have set it on the seat before disappearing into her hiding place. Damn it, kid, we don't have time for this.

And for once, it's not the tide or the monsters that are our biggest worry. "Mike."

He looks at me, hopeful that I have a grand new idea to get this plan rolling. I almost hate to break the news to him.

"The battery." I hold up the phone so he can see the little icon has turned yellow. Soon it will be red, then dead.

Just like us.

25

NATALIA

"Natalia?"

I hear his voice, but I don't want to. I don't want to hear anything. Not him, or her, or the stupid ocean. I especially don't want to hear *them.* I want to stay down here, where nothing can get me. I already peed myself, so I don't have to worry about that again. I'm still hungry, and really thirsty, but I don't care. I'll stay down here forever.

"Hey, kiddo, you there?" It's her this time.

Just like Mom and Dad. When he can't say the right things, he hands me off to her. I cannot believe what they're asking me to do. Are they crazy? I can't *drive.* I'm not even good at the racing games Dad always wants to play on his Xbox. I don't know the first thing about it. Why would I? Driving is for adults. Or at least teenagers.

"Natalia," she says. "Somebody wants to say hello." I wait, but I don't hear anything. Except what sounds like somebody breathing into the phone. Then, whispering: "*Speak. Speak, Jake. For fuck's sake. Bird!*"

Jake barks. I hear the jingle of his collar tags, too, and wet snorts as he licks the phone. I crawl up onto the seat and peer over the window frame through my binoculars. I still don't see him, though. What kind of trick is this?

"Bird," Beth says again. Another bark, more jingles, and then he sits up! She has to help him, but I see his tongue and his big eyes and his soft fur. I hear him whine, too, as she holds him steady. It's a bad sound. I pick up the phone and put it to my ear. The screen is sticky with sweat.

"What's wrong with him? Is he hurt?" She told me he was just tired, but that's exactly the sort of thing somebody would say when they don't want you to know the truth.

"Yes," Beth answers. "Unfortunately, the shriekers—the monsters—hurt him pretty bad. He saved our lives, though. He's a good boy."

"Will he be okay?" My eyes are prickling. I hate thinking about animals getting hurt, especially dogs. I can't cry again, though. Badasses don't cry.

"I don't know," Beth answers, and I can tell she means it. "Maybe. But only if we get him off this beach. Get him to somebody who knows how to fix dogs."

The man, Mike, looks at her when she says that. It's a weird look, but she ignores it.

"Can I say hi to him?"

"Of course." Beth tries to hold the phone up to Jake's ear, but he keeps angling his head to try to see what she's doing. She has to hold his head still with her free hand.

"Hi, Jake," I say, and he tilts his head at the sound of his name. He looks right at me. Does he see me? I wave anyway, and the big monster, the one I can kinda see, moves sharply. I put my hand down. "I'm sorry you got hurt," I tell him in my quietest voice.

He barks, and the big thing moves again. The others, sparkling with water droplets, make that awful screech and splash through the shallow water. They want to hurt him again, I can tell. What nasty, horrible things.

"Don't worry," I tell him. "They won't get you again. And we'll get you to a vet. Get you fixed up. Because I . . . I'm coming to help." I can't believe I'm saying this. That I'm even *thinking* it. But Jake needs me, Beth's not lying about that. They need me too. I'm their only hope. A Badass would not hide when others need them.

Beth puts the phone back into Mike's hand. As if now that she got me to agree, her job is done. Maybe it's a trick after all. Only one way to find out.

"We have to be quick," he says. "I don't know how much longer this phone battery will last. But it will be easy, I mean that. A straight shot. All you'll have to do is hold the wheel steady, push on the gas just a little, and you'll be here in thirty seconds. After that, you'll never need to drive again if you don't want to."

"Promise?"

"I'll pinkie-swear when you get here," he says, and smiles. He has a kind smile.

"Okay."

"Perfect. Now, do you see—?" He covers the phone and turns to Beth, but I can still hear them. "When she starts that engine, they'll be on her. They'll tear those tires to shreds in a second. We need a really good distraction."

"On it," Beth says. She picks up something. A glass bottle that looks half-full of water. She shakes it and grins.

I have no idea what that means, but Mike nods his approval. "Natalia?" he asks, turning to me. "Do you know where the key goes? In the ignition by the steering wheel?"

"Yes. That's where my dad left them." I try to ignore the sting of that. I need to do this right. I can't mess anything up.

"Good. Go ahead and put them back. Don't turn them on or anything, just put the key in the ignition." There are three keys on the ring, but I know which one he means. I follow his instructions and let go quickly, before I can accidentally turn them and screw something up.

"Okay. I did."

"Great. That's step one. Now I want you to sit behind the wheel. You don't have to do anything else yet, just sit there. Move slowly, and as quietly as you can. The monsters are sensitive to noise and movement, even through the car doors. We'll try not to give them any reason to focus your way."

I've never sat behind the wheel before. This is Dad's seat. Except Dad is never going to sit here again, so I guess it's my seat now.

Don't do that don't cry don't think don't

"Hey, you motherfuckers!" Her voice makes me jump. I hear her on the phone and outside. Beth. She's standing up through their sunroof, pointing at the sky with both hands. "You afraid of a little water? Come get us! We're right here!" She's got that bottle on the roof with her. There's something stuffed in it. A towel, I think?

"Not so bad, right?" Mike asks. "Can your feet reach the pedals? Down on the floor? It's okay to try, nothing will happen until we turn the car on."

I scoot to the very edge of the seat and stretch my legs. They barely reach, but I can feel the pedals down there. I don't know which is which, but I'm sure Mike will tell me.

"Yes."

"Awesome! You're tall."

"My mom says so. I think she just says that to make me feel better. All my friends are taller than me." Are my friends still out there? Did somebody come for them? Are they safe? Why didn't I try to call any of them? What if they're dead too? The thought makes my stomach turn.

"Okay, next step," Mike goes on. "You'll notice there's a pedal on the right, and one on the left. Do you see them?"

I look down at my feet.

"What?" My face burns. It always burns when I do something dumb. I must be doing something dumb now, because what I see is different than what he says I should.

"Two pedals," he repeats. "They're sort of rectangle-shaped? One is tall, the other is wide. You just said you felt them with your feet." He's stressing out. Losing his patience with me.

"Yes, I see them." My voice comes out as a squeak. He's going to get mad at what I say next. Scold me for being dumb. But it's not my fault. This is my first time driving. What does he expect?

"And?"

"There aren't just two pedals, though," I say. "There are three."

26

MIKE

My heart sinks to my feet. That energy, the feeling that somewhere a switch has been flipped and everything is about to turn around, flickers out like a faulty light bulb. Or a car with a dead battery.

"What's wrong?" Beth asks, lowering herself back in.

I cover the phone. "The Jeep is a standard transmission," I relay to her gravely.

The grim development doesn't appear to register with her. "So?"

"So *I* can't even drive one of those."

"Oh my *God,* why am I not surprised?" She rolls her eyes, tossing up her hands to illustrate how she really didn't expect more from me.

I nearly throw out how she must have got that look from her mother, then decide I'd rather come out of this with my head still attached to my shoulders. "I never had a reason to learn!" I argue, weirdly defensive over this slight. Like not knowing how to drive a standard threatens my masculinity. We're petty to the bitter end, aren't we?

"What do you call this?" Beth asks, gesturing about us. "If not a damn good reason?"

"I'll be sure to scold my parents for not adequately preparing me for the End Times when I get to hell." And what am I going to say to Natalia? Forget it, go back into hiding? It's all over, because your dad drove a stupid stick shift?

Beth holds out her hand. "Give me the phone," she huffs. I pass it over happily. "Natalia? Hi, it's Beth again. I'm taking over for Mike because clearly we can't leave these jobs to men."

"Seriously? You have to go there now?"

She waves a hand in my face, like she's shooing away an annoying bug. "This is going to be just a little more complicated than we were hoping. But I know you can do it. My dad taught me to drive a standard transmission when I was just a few years older than you, and we all know girls your age are even quicker on the uptake. Now, you see the key?"

"Yes," Natalia answers uncertainly. She sounds so tiny, so hopelessly far away.

"Go ahead and twist it away from you, toward the dashboard. Just until it catches. You'll feel it, don't turn past that." Beth watches through her camera, and a moment later, the Jeep chimes cheerfully to life through the phone.

I hold my breath until the beeping shuts up. The noise gets the attention of only a single shrieker: the queen. She whips around and opens her jaws to have a look. She's so focused on the two vehicles, I'm not sure she realizes the cloudfish is approaching.

"Don't move, Natalia," Beth says. "Don't panic. I know it's creepy as hell, but that's just how they see. Good thing is, when they do that, we can see them too."

The queen takes a tentative step in the direction of the Jeep, then closes up. She's still fairly visible, covered in sand and slime, even when she's in hiding. I can only hope that when that cloudfish gets here, it will be more attracted to her than to us, given how its first taste of automobile went.

"Mike?" Beth whispers. She holds out her lighter and pats the patrol bag. "When I start counting down, light the fuse and throw this. Make sure it lands on the beach, not in the water. Then, on 'one,' throw the bottle. And please, try to hit one of them."

"Maybe I should count down and you should throw it," I offer.

"I need to focus on Natalia. I believe in you. Just know that if you miss, it will be the last thing you ever do."

Great. So I'll die first, it seems. That's fine. I don't want to see how the rest of this goes anyway.

I check the outside pockets of the bag to make sure nothing else of any importance is tucked away, like a handheld teleportation device, or a magic wand. Unsurprisingly, there's nothing. I shove the bag out through the shattered sunroof and set it next to the Molotov cocktail I already regret having admitted to knowing how to make. And I still don't know if I did it right. My only experience with them is from watching special effects wizards at a safe distance. It might not do anything.

"Now," Beth continues, speaking to Natalia, "do you see the shifter between the seats?"

"Mhm," the girl answers.

"Is there a schematic on the shifter?"

"Huh?"

"A drawing, on the top." Beth tries to keep the stress out of her voice, but I know she's thinking about that little battery-life indicator, her eyes going back to the cloudfish. It's beginning its descent, its main body shrinking, its tendrils nearly low enough to brush the tips of the dune grass between the forest and the ridge. "Two rows of numbers and the letter *R* somewhere?"

"Oh. Yes."

"Perfect! Read me the top row."

The queen's jaws open again, the worm staring out at me. Her minions are still at the waterline, trying to figure out how to reach us without getting swept away. The dead, infected one is rolling around in the surf just past the back bumper, which is probably contributing to their reluctance. I wrap my fingers around the patrol bag's shoulder strap. I'll probably throw my arm out flinging this thing, then I won't be able to pitch the bottle. Why couldn't this all have happened when I was in my twenties and still working out?

"One. Three. Five," Natalia reads. Like a reverse countdown to the moment when she starts the engine.

"And the bottom?"

"Two. Four. Six," Natalia says, each shaky consonant bringing her closer to either doom or deliverance. "And then *R*," she finishes.

"Easy-peasy. Now, about those three pedals on the floor. Do you see the one on the far left? Push it down as far as it goes with your left foot."

I look down, over Beth's shoulder, at the camera screen. Natalia can reach the pedal, she wasn't lying about that, but it's quite a stretch, even when Beth tells her how to adjust the seat.

"Okay," she says, still straining.

"Holding it down?"

"Yeah."

"Now, grab the shifter. Keep your foot on that pedal, and push the shifter toward the dashboard until it stops. Let me know when you've done that."

"I . . . I think I got it," Natalia squeaks.

I might not be able to drive a stick to save my life, but I know enough about it to know she's got the Jeep in first gear. We're almost there. To the point of absolutely no return. My throat is dry and I can hardly hear over the drum of my heart in my ears.

"Fabulous," Beth says coolly. "You don't have to worry about that shifter anymore at all. You don't even have to touch it. But keep your foot on that pedal. Still good?"

"Yes." Something has changed in Natalia's voice. Her uncertainty is ebbing. Beth's unwavering optimism in her ability to pull this off is contagious. I wish it would spread to me.

"Put your right foot on the middle pedal and push. That's your brake. It's what stops the car. Are you pushing down on both pedals as far as they go?"

Jake senses the tension and whomps the seat with his tail, whining softly.

"Yes," Natalia confirms.

Beth looks up at me. "You're on, Mike." But before I can haul myself completely out onto the roof, she grips my hand and pulls me down for a kiss. It's not a final kiss. Not yet. She's saving that one.

And now here we are. The beginning of the end, one way or the other. The evening wind against my sweaty skin brings a chill. I flick Beth's lighter, producing a little wavering flame, then touch it to the wick we made out of strips of T-shirt. The cotton drank greedily from the remaining vodka, and ignites right away.

"Okay, Natalia," Beth says. "You're going to turn those keys the rest of the way. That will start the engine."

Hopefully, she doesn't say, but we're sharing the thought. That Jeep has been sitting here longer than we have, with the key in the ignition. Was the accessory power on? Radio low, fans running, draining its life? I know now not to trust the friendly chime of the main electrical system coming to life. It could be nothing more than an empty promise.

"When that happens," Beth adds, "keep both feet on those pedals, and be ready to do exactly as I say. Are you ready?"

No.

"I think so," Natalia says.

"You've got this," Beth reassures her, then the real countdown begins. "Three."

I give the patrol bag two healthy swings, then let go. Amazingly, rather than sending it straight behind me and into the waves, I launch it on a smooth, silent arc across the water and foam and the shimmering bodies of the shriekers to land with a soft thump in the sand, right behind them.

"Two."

As predicted, the shriekers swarm the bag like hyenas, grabbing it and tearing at it in a vicious game of tug-of-war. I pick up the bottle of vodka next, bits of flame dripping down onto my skin. I barely feel it. I'm focused like a laser on what's in my hand, and where it needs to land. And it needs to connect hard enough to shatter.

Beth reaches out and squeezes my ankle. This is it. No matter what happens next, we'll be together for it.

"One."

27

NATALIA

The engine wakes up—that's how Dad always says it—with a roar, followed by an earsplitting squeal. It's *them*! They're right outside! They were just waiting, and now they're screaming and they're going to break in and get me and—

"Let go of the keys!" Beth says.

I do, and the squealing stops. It wasn't the monsters at all, it was the Jeep. Why was it doing that? Doesn't matter, the engine is still going! Everything is working! I did it!

There's a bright flash by their car. A ball of fire, and then I *do* hear the monsters. I see them, too, burning and smoking and screaming. One of them runs straight back and up into the dune grass. Mike jumps up and down on the roof of the car, laughing and lifting his middle fingers.

"Okay, Natalia," Beth says. "We have to do this now."

"I'm ready." I have the steering wheel in both hands, squeezing tightly to be sure I don't slip. It shakes so hard it hurts my wrists.

Something lands on the roof. Something *big*.

It's that other one. The one I could just barely see until it opened its terrible mouth and stuck its tongue out at me. Its tongue had a mouth too. And teeth. That's the part that I can see now, aimed down at me through the glass.

I scream—ugh, why do I keep *doing* that?—and slide beneath

the steering wheel so it won't see me. But as soon as I do that, the Jeep shudders and the engine dies.

"No! Natalia!" Beth shouts into the phone. "Are you there?"

"Hey!" Mike shouts in the background. "Your minions are on *fire*, you ugly bitch, aren't you gonna come rip me *apart*?"

"Natalia, can you hear me? Are you okay?"

I dropped the phone. It went beneath the seat. I don't dare call out to her. The monster, it's looking right through the window above my seat. Its feet scratch at the plastic as it slinks around up there. Dad would be so mad, he took such good care of his Jeep. He called it his *baby*.

"Mike!" Beth screams. "What are you *doing*! Get out of the water!"

"Just get her going!" he shouts. Then he proceeds to hurl swears and curse words and words I've never even *heard* before.

But it works. The monster on the roof jumps off, and I hear it running across the beach. I get back up on the seat. Mike is waist-deep in the ocean, wading toward shore. He's waving and grabbing himself and making faces. Most of them aren't burning anymore, but I can see where they got burned, their shapes covered in black scorches. There's smoke rising from the dunes, from where the other one ran. Another splashes out toward Mike, then a wave knocks it over and rolls it onto the sand.

The big one stays on the dry sand. I don't know why, but it seems smarter than the others. More dangerous. I hope Mike sees it.

"Natalia!" Beth shouts, startling me. I shove my hand beneath the seat and pat around. "Please, we don't have much time! *Natalia!*"

"I'm here!" I shout, pulling the phone out and putting it to my ear. "I don't know what happened, it just stopped!"

"You have to keep your foot on that left pedal," Beth says. "I know it's a pain in the ass, but the engine will die if you don't."

"But—"

"If another monster comes, you'll just have to ignore it. They'll have trouble hanging on once you're moving. Now, push on the left and middle pedal and turn the key."

I do what she says, my hands trembling.

The engine starts up again. At the sound of it, a few of the monsters move this way. The big one doesn't. It's still watching Mike.

He waves at the others. "Nope! Look over here! Waaaaay tastier things over here!" he shouts, wading even closer to shore. The water is only up to his knees now. They can just about get him from there. He's got something in his hand.

"Got it," I tell Beth. My words catch in my throat and I cough them out.

"Good. This is the hardest part, kiddo, and it might take a few tries. That's fine. Don't get discouraged. We'll get it right. You . . ." She falls quiet.

"Hello?" I say.

She doesn't answer. A loud pop makes me jump. It's Mike. He has a gun. Dad has guns too. Usually they're in a safe at home, but he brought them with us today. They're in cases in the back seat. I don't know how to use them.

Mike's gun sounds different than they do in movies. He shoots at the monsters that come into the water, and each pop makes me jump. "Come on!" he shouts. "Gotta open wide if you wanna get me!"

Jake is barking now, too, clawing at the window behind Mike.

"Natalia? Can you hear me?" comes Beth's voice.

"Yes!"

"My phone is about to die," she says. I hate the tone of her voice. It's the same tone Mom used when she told me her and Dad were getting a divorce. The tone that means everything is about to go very wrong.

"Nooo!" I don't mean to whine. But I can't help it. I can't do this without Beth. She can't leave me. Why doesn't she have a phone charger? Why can't anything just work out!

"It'll be okay," she insists. "Just listen carefully. Because if my phone dies, you'll have to do this part on your own. To drive, take your foot off the middle pedal and push down on the right. That's your gas. It makes you move. As you push down on it, lift your foot off the clutch—the left pedal. Down on right, up on left. It'll buck like a son of a bitch, but that's okay. Give it a try."

What.

"Natalia?"

"I'm here. I . . . I just . . ."

"You can do this, girl," Beth says. "You are a badass."

I slowly lift my foot from the middle pedal—the brake—and the Jeep doesn't move. That seems fine. Beth didn't say anything about that. Then I push down on the gas. The engine gets louder, but I still don't move.

"Left pedal, Natalia," Beth reminds me.

Oh, right. I lift my other foot.

The Jeep lurches forward. The tires spin, and the entire thing goes a little sideways. It makes me feel a bit sick.

"Yes, that's it!" Beth shouts.

The monsters lose interest in Mike now, and nothing he does can get their attention. They're rushing straight for me. But Beth told me I can't worry about them. I need to drive.

"Keep going, Natalia!" Beth orders, seeing the monsters running at me, making a circle around me. "Don't take your foot off the gas!"

The tires spray sand behind me. One of the monsters grabs the front of the Jeep, and there's a sound like the screeching metal shed door in Dad's backyard, then it throws part of the shiny chrome bumper off into the sand. Dad always let me polish that bumper in the summer, before we'd go beach cruising.

Wait, why am I not moving? Why is the engine dead? I did what Beth said, I took my foot off the left pedal and pushed the right!

"It's not working, this is so dumb!" I cry.

"No, you did it!" Beth cheers. How can she sound so happy? I haven't gone anywhere! "You drove. I know it's hard, just keep at it. It's all in the timing. Don't push as hard on the gas, and lift off the clutch slower—"

"Huh?"

"Right and left pedals."

"Oh. Right. Okay." I reset my feet and start the engine. I have that part down.

I see one of the monsters in the mirror, leaping up and landing on the roof, right on the window. It stabs at it with its feet. Ohmygod it's going to break through it's going to get in it's—

"Now, Natalia!" Beth bellows.

But I can't! The monster is right above me, its mouth is open, some kind of black slime drips out onto the window.

"*Focus!* Push right, lift left!"

"There's one on the roof!"

"I don't give a shit! Drive!"

"Okay!" Down right, up left, the Jeep lurches forward, stops, then lurches again. The motion snaps my head around. I'm going to puke. The monster on the roof tumbles forward, rolls down the windshield right past me, and falls off the hood. I push harder on the right pedal, and this time the front end rises into the air as the tires roll right over it with a gross crunch.

The monster screams. Beth screams. I scream.

"I got it! I got it! *I'm driving!*"

"Yes! Now turn the wheel this way!" Beth orders, but I can barely hear her over the noise of the engine.

The back tires bump over the monster, and the others move out of my way like the little crabs I sometimes see in tide pools. Before I know it, waves are breaking against the hood, and water hits the windshield with a loud splat that makes me jump, but I keep my feet in place this time. There's a black pipe that runs up one side of the windshield. Dad said it's a snorkel, just like the ones I use when swimming, and that it helps the Jeep breathe when he drives through deep water. I always thought that was kind of strange—how do cars breathe?—but I'm glad it's there. Dad always wanted to be prepared, so if he said the Jeep would be okay in the water, it must be true. I know there are windshield wipers, too, but I don't know how to use them, and it's getting hard to see anything through all the seawater spraying the glass.

"Turn the wheel!" Beth yells. "Natalia, *turn*!"

It's too much! The wheels, left and right, wipers, waves, monsters. My stupid brain can't deal with it all at once. I turn the wheel, but in doing so, I let off the pedals.

The Jeep dies.

"I'm sorry!" I say before she can scold me.

But Beth doesn't say anything at all. She's mad. She hates me. I'm not a badass and she knows it and she's giving up. "Hello? *Hello!*"

I look down at the phone. The screen reads CALL ENDED. Either she hung up, or her phone died. Either way, I'm out here in the waves now.

And I am alone.

28

BETH

Goddammit, girl, do not make me teach you reverse.

"Are you okay? Natalia?" What's she doing? I see her flailing her arms around as the waves assault the Jeep—why isn't she saying anything?

"What is she doing out in the water?" Mike hollers.

I see flames at the ridge, licking at the deep blue sky and spitting up columns of smoke. The fire moves quickly through the grass, both along the edge of the dunes and back toward the forest. The cloudfish slows its approach, having already had its fill of smoke for the day. It inflates itself, attempting to rise above the updraft of ashy heat.

"Shut up! We're handling it!" I shout at Mike.

"Handle it faster!"

"Natalia!" I bellow into the phone. I hate to sound anxious or ragey and shatter whatever confidence she might have left, but if ever there was an opening to escape, it's right now. "Nat—!" The phone screen is black, and no amount of swiping or shaking or button-pushing wakes it back up. The battery has given up the ghost. If she wasn't listening, or forgets what I told her . . .

I learned to drive a stick on a deserted country road. I thought it would be impossible, that first time. There were so many moving parts, too many things to mind, the timing of the necessary steps too unforgiving. I can't imagine the threat of death at the teeth of monsters weighing down on me atop everything else. What I'm saying is, I'll forgive her if she screws this up. It'll be the last thing I do.

But maybe there's an alternative. The shriekers aren't attacking her anymore, she's too far out in the waves for that. We *could* swim to her.

I do a quick survey. The bowling ball is completely submerged at this point. I see the hellvines still, drifting lazily in the shallows. We would just need to get around them. Risky, but hardly impossible. The shriekers, meanwhile, look more confused than anything, seeming to realize they're caught between a quickly spreading wall of flames and the incoming tide. The cloudfish is high in the sky now, lost in the smoke, little glowing embers at the ends of a few of those retracting tentacles.

Just as I'm committing to this new plan, Mike scrambles onto the roof and drops through the opening and slams the sunshade closed. Not a full second later, something else lands up there, feet screeching against metal.

We all stare at the ceiling. A growl builds in Jake's throat. I don't even bother silencing him. They know we're in here.

The shrieker prods and pokes at the metal, searching for weakness, for the opening into which its prey escaped.

I point at the ceiling. "Mike, that is very unfortunate timing."

"What's happening?" He keeps the pistol trained on the rectangle of flimsy fabric between us and the shrieker.

"The phone's dead, and I'm not sure she'll be able to get the Jeep started again on her own."

The seawater inside the car comes up past my belly now. Jake is pressed against the hatch window, trying to get away from it, the water around him deep red. In the Jeep, Natalia stares at me through her binoculars. Waiting for me to give some guidance as to what to do next. But we've reached that point where the teacher must let the student go. I point at her, flash a thumbs-up for encouragement, then grab my camera off the dash to watch. Either she's got this, or she doesn't. I'm going to be right there with her, either way.

Natalia studies the controls in front of her, like she's in the cockpit of an unfamiliar spacecraft. She may as well be. I know the feeling. I still remember Dad methodically describing the purpose of every gauge, what each needle and number indicated, until his words bled into one another and I just wanted to cry and jump out of the car and run home.

"You can do this, kid," I whisper.

Natalia steadies herself. She mouths something, repeating it over and over. I swear she's saying *You're badass,* but most likely she's reciting my instructions. Clutch, brake, engine on.

I mentally fling the words her way: *Push gas, lift clutch. Easy-peasy lemon squeezy.*

The Jeep rumbles to life, and Natalia screams and claps her hands together. At that exact moment, the shrieker above us finds the visor and pokes curiously at the thin material. Mike's finger tightens on the trigger. Jake barks.

Natalia takes the steering wheel with both hands, repeats her mantra a few more times, and then the Jeep sputters and lurches forward into even deeper water.

I see the next few seconds clearly in my mind before they happen: five feet farther, then ten feet, and then the ocean overtakes her. The electronics short out, the Jeep dies, and this time it won't start, no matter what she does. Without a phone, I can't explain to her what's wrong. I can't tell her it isn't her fault. She watches through her binoculars as the shrieker tears its way into the car, and then its friends follow. It's like looking into a blender jar full of tomatoes as somebody hits puree, the shriekers turning me and Mike into red pulp. And then Natalia truly is on her own. Because we failed her. Failed humanity. But what did anybody expect from us? From me? Beth the human car wreck. It really couldn't have ended any other way.

But none of that happens, because this time Natalia turns the wheel. The Jeep begins a slow, labored arc in our direction. I pump my fists and squeal, even as a single razorblade foot effortlessly slides through the overhead sunshade. Mike, impressively, doesn't empty the magazine into the roof. He's waiting for just the right opportunity to introduce that ugly worm bastard to our crudely effective form of leaden death. I'm so proud of him.

Once Natalia is aimed at us, she keeps the wheel steady, not even bothering to try to steer back toward dry land. Good, that's good. Keep it simple. The engine roars, the tires spray plumes of water into the evening sky.

"She's doing it!" I scream deliriously. "Mike! *She's doing it!*"

The shrieker on the roof sees her coming, and quickly loses interest in the visor, turning its attention to this new threat.

The Jeep rolls through the drifting tangle of hellvines, the tire tread catching them and dragging them under and grinding them into the sand. The water that sprays up has a distinctively maroon tint to it.

The shrieker above us lets out an alarmed cackle, and the rest charge blindly into the waves to beat against the side of the Jeep, trying to slow it down. One of them gets on top and begins pummeling what I realize is a semi-transparent skylight panel that makes up the forward third of the roof. It must be made of strong acrylic, because it doesn't even crack or cave inward as the shrieker beats against it. Natalia ducks her head anyway, her face a mask of pure, human terror.

But she's not slowing down. Her foot is on the floor, the engine screaming at the top of first gear, steam pouring out from beneath the hood. The next wave sends the shriekers rolling back onto the beach, but the Jeep keeps closing the distance.

"You told her when to stop, right?" Mike asks.

"Hell no I didn't." I slide into the rear seat and wrap my arms around Jake, bracing for impact. Mike flattens himself against the front passenger window. Across from us, the view of the beach and water we've grown so familiar with is swallowed up by the grille of a Jeep Wrangler.

And then Natalia's world collides with ours, with all the force of a meteorite slamming into Earth.

29

MIKE

The impact lifts the Subaru's passenger-side wheels up off the sand, just as a surge of tidewater rushes in, raising the entire car until it tips sideways. Before I can take another gulp of air, Beth and I are lying on our backs, and all the water that was filling the footwells is crashing down on top of us. Jake yips and splashes frantically to reorient himself, while Beth coughs up lungfuls of salt water.

Natalia lets off the clutch, and the Jeep dies before it can roll us over onto the roof. She's screaming in there—I can barely hear it above the water chugging in through the open sunroof. She doesn't sound hurt, nor is she calling to us, she's just shrieking bloody murder. I can't really blame her, she probably didn't expect her brief drive to end with nearly killing us.

I stand and grab the door handle above me and push. The door doesn't budge. It's been dented in severely, the latch mechanism mangled in the crash. I'm not sure I'd have the strength to lift it anyway. There must be a manual release for the hatch, but I don't want to waste any time searching for it. The sunroof is looking like the best option, since it's already open.

"Beth!" I shout.

She's hunched near the hatch, staring wildly into the dark, cold, quickly rising water. Looking for the pistol, maybe. Or her camera.

The pistol might be salvageable once we're out of here and can get it dried and cleaned, but the Nikon is gone for good. There will be no more pictures of the day.

"Come on! We have to get out!"

She just gapes at me as though my words have no meaning. Blood trickles down her neck from somewhere in her hair. She must have hit her head in the rollover, and hard. Between this and that bullet graze, her poor brain must be bruised black and blue. But we don't have time for shock and trauma either. Movement is life.

"Hold Jake," I tell her. Maybe giving her a specific task will bring her back to earth. "Keep him above water. I'll try to get that window open so we can lift him out." I have no idea if the shrieker is still out there. I don't hear it, but I can't hear much at all above the waves. Which might just work in my favor.

The water level is even with the newly horizontal driver's seat. Jake's nose brushes the passenger window as he does his best to keep it in the quickly diminishing pocket of air. His eyes are huge, the water around him dark with fresh blood. The salt water must burn like live fire, but he's not issuing even a whine of complaint. Beth pulls him close and whispers into his ear, pressing her own face to the glass.

I fill my lungs and sink. The salt and cold sting my eyes, but I force them open. At first I'm blind, the world around me a claustrophobic cyclone of sand and seawater. The knife rests on the submerged window. Not as useful as the pistol, if things get ugly out there, but it's something. No sign of the gun.

I come up for air. "Beth."

This time when she looks at me, her eyes are clear.

"I'm going out. I promise I'll be right back. For you and for Jake."

"You fucking better," she says.

There's the Beth I remember. The one I need right now. I can tell she wants to smile—she knows how close we are, that we've nearly made it—but she doesn't dare. This is the point at which even an ounce of optimism will poison whatever luck you have left, and she knows we're nothing if not the luckiest people on the planet.

"You better, Mike," she says again. This time it's a warning. If I lose my shit out there, if I leave her to sink alone, she'll hunt me down from her watery grave and deliver a fate worse than the shriekers could ever have managed.

But I won't lose my shit. And I won't lose her. Not after all this.

I inhale until my lungs feel fit to burst, and go back under.

≈

I paw my way through dead fish and clouds of sand, refusing to look toward the horizon, toward that darkness into which the land plummets. I know if I do, it will start speaking to me again. I have no intention of listening. Not anymore. Not ever again. But I have no idea what other tricks it has up its sleeve. For all I know, if I look, I might see Sarah clawing her way toward me, bloated and gray, her hair swirling around like algae, mouth twisted into a toothless chasm from which tiny marine creatures dart, and I don't know if I could handle that. Hearing it on the beach last night was bad enough. A full close-up might just be enough to break me for good.

I squeeze through the sunroof, slicing open my bicep on a hidden edge of the assembly, the water clouding red around me. I don't even feel the cut as I push off the sand and burst into open air.

Natalia stops screaming as I haul myself up onto the Subaru's side. I have to do a double take. I'd forgotten how small she is. It hits me hard, how such a little thing could be our salvation. How in the face of all of this, she could be so brave. If Beth and I are evidence of the human race's will to endure, Natalia is proof that it deserves to.

The queen's minions relentlessly battle the tide in their efforts to reach the Jeep. I can feel the heat of the fire, and I'm sure they can too. I don't see the queen herself, but she's out there. They don't have many other places to go, at this point.

The window above Natalia's head looks to be made of sturdier stuff than glass, though I have no trouble believing the shriekers could get through if they put their minds to it. But they aren't going to get the opportunity.

"Hang on!" I shout, and she nods.

I pull on the Subaru's rear passenger door, and the latch catches. For a second I think it might open, and my heart leaps into my throat. I give it a great tug; it does open an inch, but won't budge any farther.

Beth stares up at me through the window. They have only a few inches of air bubble remaining.

"Cover your eyes!" I order.

She does, moving aside and pulling Jake with her as I stomp on the cracked glass. It takes a few tries, throwing all my weight into it—then the glass shatters, raining shiny pebbles into the water below. I clear out the remaining chunks with the hilt of the knife, then drop to my knees and reach both arms into the car.

"Jake!" I shout, the blade clutched between my teeth.

Beth shoves him into my arms. She pushes as I lift, my back—weak from a year of moping about my house—lights up with stabs of pain. Jake kicks and writhes and contorts impossibly, his tail tucked tightly between his quivering legs.

And then he's out.

I set him carefully on the slippery surface of the driver's door, his claws screeching against the paint as he struggles to find balance on the rocking car. I'm about to reach for Beth, but the Subaru shakes violently, nearly throwing me off. I brace, waiting for the wave to pass.

But it isn't the tide jostling us this time.

Jake's body goes rigid, his hackles rise, and he issues a short, fierce warning bark.

It's the queen. Perched on the back quarter panel, inches from my own face. And this time, there's nowhere to run.

≈

She sits there, shimmering like a mirage in the setting sun. Those massive jaws open, her rip-saw teeth part, and the ugly worm rises to stare at us like a snake on the verge of striking. I don't even try to kid myself that she's hesitating out of caution. A dying dog and a middle-aged oaf armed with what may as well be a dulled toothpick. The only reason she hasn't attacked is she can't decide which of us she wants to kill first.

"Mike! What are you doing?" Beth calls up. She grabs the window frame and starts to pull herself out, which would put her directly between me and the queen, securing her position as the first to leave the stage, permanently.

"Stay there! Don't come out here!" I say. Which is stupid. The water is rising so fast, she's not going to have a choice in a few seconds.

But she sees I mean it and heeds my advice. For the moment.

Jake keeps barking, though he's learned his lesson about those feet. He limps forward cautiously.

I grip the pathetic knife, blade pointed at the sky. Or should I hold it the opposite way, blade pointed down? That would be better for stabbing. But stabbing means I have to get *inside* those jaws first.

As if mocking me, the worm opens wide, showing me all its neat little teeth, the ring of black eyes sizing us up hungrily.

"We just want to leave." Those words come from my lips all on their own. What am I doing? "I know you're just trying to protect yourself. I know you don't want to be here any more than we do. We're trying to go. To leave you alone."

The queen is smart, I know that. She learned about water, figured out guns. But if she can identify the pleading, nonthreatening tone of my voice, she doesn't show it. We're well past the point of mutual understanding. And I don't think I can blame her. If instead Beth and I had been trapped over there, in their world, we'd have fought tooth and nail against anything that came to investigate our presence, no matter how innocuous the intentions.

Before either of us can make a move, a terrible sound reaches my ears, a sound I'd hoped dearly not to hear again once the cloudfish had disappeared behind the curtain of smoke. Instead, it simply went up and over, and now it's descending straight down toward the beach.

"Mike," Beth squeaks from inside the car.

Even the queen dares to angle herself enough to look back, and all her minions begin chittering in a panicked discord. Countless grotesquely ethereal ropes drop from the yawning black mouth. I've seen what those things can do. Seen them lift a police SUV off the beach and carry it through the air like it was an egg snatched from a bird's nest. But looking straight up into that maw is even worse. My mind rejects the sight with extreme prejudice.

The rest of the queen's brood wail in protest, their instincts of self-preservation—urging them to flee—conflicting with their need to stay and protect their queen. Some of them freeze up entirely, but they're all so caked in sand and salt at this point that their natural camouflage is useless.

The lowest tentacle gropes lazily for the first shrieker it nears, and the monster lashes out, slicing cleanly through the thorny flesh. The cloudfish barely appears to notice, another arm coiling around the shrieker from behind and yanking it straight up and flicking it into that mouth like a piece of candy, howling all the way.

Seizing on the opportunity this distraction provides, Jake attacks, issuing a volley of ferocious, short barks before clamping down on one of the queen's front legs above the bladed foot, holding it in place with his weight. Her tough exterior is no match for his teeth, and sticky black blood sprays across his muzzle, staining his golden fur.

The queen roars in protest, her other feet slashing toward him. Jake backs up, pulling her off balance, and her swings go wide. She tries jerking her leg free, but he's got an iron-trap hold, snarling and foaming, eyes white with determination, claws tearing trenches through the Subaru's paint. The rest of the shriekers raise their voices in outrage, as though they feel their queen's pain, and another one is snatched up by the living cloud.

The queen throws all her strength into a 180-degree spin, flinging Jake off into the water. He cries out in surprise, then vanishes with a small splash. Natalia screams in fury and pounds on the horn. The cloudfish rotates toward this new curiosity. Our window of opportunity is about to slam shut. But if I can keep it open, even just for a moment, enough time to allow Beth and Natalia to escape, then that's what I'm going to do.

Before the queen can turn around, I leap onto her back. The feel of her beneath me is repulsive, like squeezing a just-ripe avocado. An avocado with legs. Fighting the nearly irrepressible urge to let go, like I've grabbed on to something only to find it covered in bugs, I swing the knife.

The tip sinks through her outermost layers before coming to a sudden stop against something as hard as bone. My hand slides right down the blade, opening my palm from thumb to little finger, a river of bright red blood pouring out across the squirming body beneath me. The knife wiggles free and falls into the water.

With nothing else to fight with, I hug the monster as tightly as I can and heave myself sideways with all my body weight. Between the slippery paint and the rocking of the waves, it's easy enough to throw her off balance, and we both roll off the car and into the surf.

"Mike!" Beth screams, hauling herself out of the car just as the water goes over my head.

Please don't come after me. Please just get in the Jeep. Go, Beth. *Go!*

My back meets the soft sand, the queen's considerable heft pressing me into it. She's strong, but I'm two hundred pounds of deadweight anchoring her in place. She snaps and slashes, leaving behind swirls of black blood. Her sword-like feet peel layers off my arms and legs. There's no pain. I'm numb, from adrenaline and cold.

The worm extends from the safety of its shell, stretching desperately for the surface, for a gulp of air that doesn't belong to it. But it can't quite reach. Can't quite escape the raging black tide. I know how she must feel. I've been there. And while she's got a lot of fight left, it turns out that I do too. More than I could ever have imagined in myself last night. Because despite everything, and perhaps against all reason, I do still *want* to be here. I discovered that the hard way.

And so will the queen.

The worm goes rigid. It screams, a piercing wail that can probably be heard across the Pacific, and then the creature falls limp.

30

BETH

I spot the queen first, drifting lifelessly in the surf. I half expect the worm to jettison itself from its armored suit and flop away in search of a new home, but another wave rolls over it, and the worm disappears into the dark water. It's dead. Really dead. I wait for the invisibility to turn off, revealing the creature in all its awful glory, but it doesn't.

There's an immediate change in the others. Whatever strange telepathy connected them, it's been permanently severed, and they don't have any idea what to do. A few run in angry little circles, one even coming too close to my infected buddy. A hellvine shoots from its mouth and wraps around the other shrieker's leg in a death grip. It cries out, but the others don't come to its aid. Every monster for itself, fleeing in both directions, up and down the beach. Now that the queen is dead, getting as far as possible from the cloudfish is their primary objective.

Kinda like I should be doing.

"Mike!" I jump down into the water, mindful of those tentacles worming their way toward me. He still hasn't surfaced. Either he's drowned, and I'm going to have to drag his corpse to the Jeep with me—because there's no way I'm leaving him out here to become cloudfish food—or he's unconscious and I'll have to perform CPR, which will definitely kill him.

He saves me from both scenarios by sitting bolt upright, coughing and spitting water and gasping for fresh air. It's the best sound I've heard all day. I want to crush him in my arms, cover him with kisses, but I settle for hauling him to his feet. I can show him how happy I am that he's alive later.

"Look!" I say, pointing at the queen's dispersing horde. "We're wide open!" The only shrieker left on the beach is the poor bastard caught by the newly sprouted hellvine. It tears violently at its dead sibling, trying to kill the vine, ripping out the lifeless worm and flinging it through the air like a dog with a nightmare chew toy.

Dog. *Jake.* Where is he?

"Jake?" I ask Mike. We both look around stupidly. How do you lose a *dog*? Actually, don't ask me that.

Then I see him, dragging himself from the surf and limping onto the sand. He lies down, panting, his ears cocked attentively. The cloudfish doesn't see him; it's still drifting toward us.

I wrap my arm around Mike's waist and help him through the water. Like last night, the air smells heavily of sea spray and smoke, although this time the fire is quite a bit larger. It's spreading mostly inland and to the north, but I see flames making their way toward the access road. If only we'd managed to set the coast on fire a few hours ago, when all the shriekers were still hiding out in the dunes. Two non-native, invasive species; one Molotov cocktail. But that doesn't matter now. They're gone. There's only one thing left to do, and it's on me to do it right.

I rip open the Jeep's door and Natalia spills into my arms.

"I'm sorry!" she sobs. "I'm sorry I'm *so so* sorry!"

"Don't be!" I scold. "You did everything perfect." I plant a quick kiss on her forehead. Her skin is clammy and salty from sweat. I have to peel her away, even though I don't really want to. I'd happily let her cling to me and be carried around like a baby possum for the next year, but somebody needs to drive this thing.

Natalia doesn't protest, eyeballing the cloudfish as it whooshes to a stop directly above us. She slides into the safety of the passenger seat. Mike gets in the back without having to be told. I take my place behind the wheel, my heart hammering my ribs. I adjust the seat, force myself to breathe, to steady my hands, then reach for the keys. A quick twist, a few familiar motions of the feet, and we'll be gone. I must be dreaming. We can't really be doing this.

"Jake!" Natalia exclaims, so loud I nearly shoot straight through the skylight.

"Don't worry," I reassure her, pressing the clutch and twisting the keys. The engine chokes to life. "We're going to get him."

Jake lifts himself into a sitting position, staring at me with accusing brown eyes. *You're going? You're leaving without me?*

Not a chance.

"Hang on," I say, shifting into reverse, dropping the clutch, and punching the gas. The tires tear through the wet sand, throwing mud across the Subaru's exposed undercarriage. I slam the Jeep into first and stand on the gas, Natalia sinking back into the seat as the tires find purchase and pull us forward.

Both our heads snap as we come to a very abrupt stop.

"What happened?" Mike demands.

"I don't know!" I floor it, the engine whining in protest. The tires are spinning, spraying arcs of glittering water toward the sunset.

"Look!" Natalia squeaks. I follow her pointed finger up, just as another tentacle smacks the panel above my head, this time actually causing it to fracture, then curls around the roof rack.

"No!" I stand on the gas, intending to just pull the son of a bitch along with us, like a hellish parade balloon, but it's already lifting, the tires losing their grip on the sand, flinging water behind us.

The removable top begins to groan. I'm less afraid of being lifted into the air than I am the roof just being torn away above us. I might be able to speed away before it gets a chance to snatch one of us up. I might not. The tentacles are all around, slamming into the Jeep while the tide sprays the windows, like we're inside some kind of infernal car wash. One smacks the door next to me, those thorny grabbers piercing right through the glass. Another punches at the window above, the powerful acrylic beginning to sag along the crack. I slam the palm of my hand against it, pushing hard the other way.

I hear Mike rustling around, the zip of a bag being opened, and then a breath drawn in surprise. I look back and see a soft case lying across his lap, a shotgun clutched in his hands. He stares at it, then at me, like he's got no idea what to do next. And then his hand finds the power window button.

"Mike don't," I say.

"I need a clear shot," he insists, the tremor in his voice betraying any confidence he's trying to project. And he's right. Even if he managed to fire that thing off inside the Jeep without killing one of us, he'd be blowing out the only thing standing between us and the cloudfish. By opening the window and leaning out, he might get one good burst of buckshot into the tentacle, enough to loosen its hold, to free us—hopefully before it grabs him and pulls him out.

But before he gets a chance, another tentacle smashes into his door, the gripping spikes piercing the metal, covering the window, and the Jeep rises even higher.

"Come on!" I cry at the top of my lungs. Begging the universe to throw us a bone. We've worked so hard for this! We deserve a better ending! We *earned* it.

Jake hears me and cocks his head. I meet his eyes, and I know he recognizes the distress in my voice. Understands the terrible predicament we're in.

I watch the next few seconds play out in slow motion.

Jake musters up his last reserve of strength and charges through the waves, reaching the Jeep in less than a dozen strides, like he's running across the surface of the water. He leaps, scrambling up the hood, the windshield, and onto the roof. I watch through the cracked panel above me as he heroically bites and rends the tentacles, alien blood spraying, the cloudfish releasing the Jeep in order to retreat from this unforseen force of nature. There's just enough time for Mike to jump out and grab him and pull him in as we speed off, leaving the cloudfish in a confusing mist of sand and sea.

We suffer no other setbacks as we accelerate up the beach. For once, everything goes exactly as it should, and we make it out of there.

We're free.

That, of course, is not what happens. That's just what my masochistic brain decides to show me. A peek, perhaps, into yet another parallel universe where everything does work out in the end. But in this universe, Jake simply does what dogs do.

He barks.

The Jeep sinks back into the sand with an enormous splash. The thorny grippers pull away, leaving tiny holes in the windows through which the ocean breeze cools the sweat on my face. Looking up, I see all those tentacles swinging aside as the cloudfish reorients itself to face this new oddity, which it has already determined will be less of a pain in the ass to get at than breaking through the Jeep's shell.

Jake barks again, limping backward as he does. Just as I've seen him do on our walks together, after earning the attention of a particularly aggressive bull elk and concluding that maybe that wasn't exactly the outcome he'd envisioned.

Jake looks at me. It's almost as if he knows I'm having this memory. I also remember what he did next, after landing himself in that mean old elk's crosshairs, and I can't help but believe he's counting on that. Because he's about to do it again. I can read the message in plain English.

I'm giving you one last shot, Beth. Do not fuck this up.

With a resonant *whoooosh,* the cloudfish jets toward him, the last tentacle unwrapping from the roof rack as it goes.

Jake runs. In the opposite direction of the access road. Fighting for speed on three legs, and making impressive distance in a short amount of time. Like I said, the dog was born to run.

Natalia screams. I want to join her, but I have something more important to do.

The cloudfish doesn't react to the revving of the Jeep's engine. Even if it turned on us, it would be too late. We roar from the water as I shove the shifter into second, cranking the wheel to steer us toward the access road. I can feel the heat of the blaze through those tiny new vent holes as we rocket up the beach parallel with the fire. I turn the wheel again, racing the flames to the access road. We pick up speed as the tires hit the leveled sand, then grooved pavement. I dare to breathe again as we leave the beach and speed into the gathering dusk and smoke. There's a sob building inside me. It hurts so bad it feels like my heart is going to rupture in my chest. But I choke it down, for now. Keep my hands locked on the wheel, my eyes glued to the road ahead. I will not lose control.

I allow myself one last look up the beach before it disappears from my sight forever. I don't see Jake. The cloudfish appears to be hovering again, a short distance away. Whether it caught him or gave up the chase, I can't tell. Whether his journey ended there in the sand or he managed to flee into unburnt dunes for one final romp through the tall grass he loved so much, I'll never know. But I know which version I'll tell myself as I fall asleep on the nights to come.

If I ever sleep again.

31

NATALIA

My dad's street is quieter than I've ever seen it. All the houses are dark, and the streetlights are off. A few people left their front doors open. There's a car parked in the middle of the road that wasn't there this morning when we left. Nana used to talk about something like this when I was little. About all the good people disappearing, leaving only the bad ones behind. Back then, I thought she was calling it *the Raptor,* which never made much sense. And it scared me, when she talked about it. I'm not a bad person, but I was still scared of being left here. Dad said scaring me was the point of it, then told Nana to stop.

I don't think that's what happened today, though. My dad wasn't a bad person. I don't really know Mike or Beth, but I can tell they're good. So why are we all still here?

"Don't look," Beth says as she drives up on the sidewalk to get around the car. The windows are cracked, and one of the doors is open, but I look away before I see anything else. "I haven't heard any shriekers," she says to Mike. I really don't like that name. "Maybe they go into hiding at night."

"Or maybe something else got them. You said you heard something over the radio. When you were talking to the dispatcher."

She shudders. "Yeah. Let's not talk about that."

"Fine by me." He leans forward. "Natalia, where is your dad's house?"

"It's right there." I point, and Beth pulls into the driveway.

Dad bought this place as an investment property. He was going to rent it out to vacationers. He also said someday the house would be my inheritance? I don't really get how that was all supposed to work, but it was important to him. I guess it doesn't matter anymore. Dad moved in after he and Mom split up.

The garage door is closed. All the doors are. None of the windows are broken. Mike was worried we wouldn't be able to get inside without power—at least, not without making a racket and attracting attention. I told him about the solar panels. Dad was always talking about solar panels and the battery that could keep the electricity on even if everybody else lost power. He spent a lot of money on them.

"You're sure the battery is hooked to the garage door?" Mike asks.

"I don't know. But I think so? Dad always said he could 'weather a storm.' He keeps a lot of canned food and water too. Just in case. I'm sure he'd want to be able to open the garage door, to get the Jeep out." I look around at the other homes. It's so spooky here now. Is this the storm he was always talking about? Did he somehow know this was coming, the way Nana seemed to think the Raptor was coming? Why didn't he say anything?

Mike gets out and quietly goes to the keypad hidden on the side of the house and puts in the four numbers I told him. My birthday in reverse.

The door opens. Quiet as a whisper, as Dad said when he first used it. Mike looks around impatiently, and Beth drums her hands on the steering wheel while we wait. As soon as the door's high enough, she drives in, and quickly turns off the engine. Mike comes inside and hits the button on the wall by the back door to close up the garage again.

We stay there like that, in the pitch-darkness. I can't hear anything but my own heartbeat. They're waiting to see if anything moves around inside, but it seems like the house is empty.

There's no way to know for sure, though. Not until we go in. Mike volunteers, taking the shotgun with him, and before Beth can argue, he pushes open the mudroom door and goes inside.

≈

"It's all clear."

Mike holds the door open, but doesn't turn on any lights. Beth and I get out of the Jeep, closing the doors as softly as possible, and feel our way through the garage. It smells normal. Like car wax and lawn fertilizer and gasoline. I never really liked the smell until now. It always gave me a headache. But now it smells like home. And anything is better than the smells outside.

Mike leads the way upstairs to my bedroom, which is over the garage and looks out at the street. Dad's room is across the hall, facing the ocean, though we're not close enough to see it. But the trees are nice, and there's a small lake nearby, and in the summer you can hear the frogs. I guess it's fair that he gets the better view and his own bathroom. It's his house, after all. *Was.*

The streetlight outside used to keep me awake whenever I came to stay, unless I pulled the curtains closed. But then I couldn't have the window open, because the air blew the curtains around and woke me up and I would always think there was somebody standing in my room. It's stupid, I know. I probably won't be afraid of little things like that anymore.

Mike kneels by the window and looks out at the street.

Beth joins him. "See something?" she asks.

"No. Not that that means anything." He slides the window open just a crack and puts his ear to it.

"Mike, what is it?"

"Nothing."

She must not believe him, because she pushes him aside and looks for herself. I don't like this. I feel like I need to hide. To crawl beneath the bed and stay there until morning.

"Nothing's out there," Mike insists. "I just . . . I want to keep an eye out." He pauses, then, more quietly, like he thinks I might not be able to hear him, he asks, "What did it sound like, the thing you heard on the radio?"

"I don't know. I can't describe it."

"Beth—"

"Just trust me, Mike. If you hear it, you'll know." She pulls the curtains shut, but keeps the window cracked. They start to billow and dance right away, like two ghosts. "Let's settle in and get some rest."

They bring the rest of the guns in from the Jeep. There's a shiny silver one Beth calls a hand cannon, an older rifle with a big telescope on top, and the shotgun, along with all the bullets Dad took from the safe.

Mike insists we all take showers. There was something they call hellvines in the ocean, and he wants to make sure we wash anything off us that they might have put in the water. They take turns keeping watch. The water is cold by the time Beth takes hers, and she says a lot of nasty things to Mike about it.

It does feel good to be clean. To have the peed-in clothes off and fresh things on. It's weird seeing Mike in my dad's clothes, especially since they don't fit him very well. They really don't fit Beth, but none of my stuff is big enough. She makes do with an old pair of his shorts and a flannel shirt.

Mike finds enough food in the fridge to make us dinner, then he pushes my dresser in front of the bedroom door. We're in for the night.

"Great. Sandwiches," Beth moans. I don't know what her problem with them is. They're good. She sucks the carton of apple juice dry in one gulp. "I'll take your word for it he didn't have any beer."

Mike ignores this while he fiddles with the dials on Dad's radio, but he can only find static. He couldn't reach anybody on the cell phone, either, but he still plugged it in to charge.

"Do you know the way to Vernonia?" Beth asks him. That name sounds familiar. I think I've seen it on road signs, maybe. "Or do we need to find a map?"

"I know the way. Assuming the roads are still intact."

Something happens right then that shakes the entire house. It makes me scream, and I slap both hands over my mouth. Beth slowly sets down her sandwich and stares at Mike. I hate seeing her that way. Beth is Badass, and Badasses aren't supposed to look like that. Whatever made that sound, it scares her.

It scares all of us.

"Mike," Beth whispers. She's afraid.

He shakes his head, reaching into a pillowcase to turn off the flashlight we've been using to see by. The room is so dark without it.

Another boom rattles the pictures on the wall. Something falls and breaks downstairs. There's a long, low noise outside—a bit like a foghorn, and a bit like a giant cow. It gets into my ears and won't leave. I wish I could reach in there and pull it out.

"Is that?" he asks, and this time Beth shakes her head.

The third boom is much farther away. Whatever that thing is, it's moving its way down the coast. It passed right by us.

"Let's leave the light off for the rest of the night," Beth says.

"Good idea," Mike replies.

≈

I don't remember closing my eyes, but when I startle awake, Mike and Beth are by the window. The curtains are open, but they're sitting to the side, so that anything outside won't see them. She's holding her arm up for him to look at, and he's using the light of the moon outside to see. Beth grimaces and sucks air through her teeth as he dabs at her arm with a cotton ball. The bandage she's had on her wrist is lying on the floor.

"Still clear?" she asks.

"As far as I can tell. Looks nasty, but there's . . . nothing growing." He gently puts on a clean bandage. "I'm so sorry about Jake. If it's any comfort, he—"

"Don't say it. I know he was in bad shape. I know he wouldn't have survived anyway. But still. Please." She bites her lip. Her cheeks are wet with tears. Maybe Dad was wrong. Maybe Badasses can get scared and cry. I hope so. "We owe him our lives. Owe it to him to get as far as we can. Do whatever we can to survive for as long as we're able."

The sky outside lights up. Mike tugs back the curtain. A ball of fire rises into the night, miles away. There are other spots of orange way to the north. It's hard to tell how far, or just how big they are.

"Is that because of us?" Beth asks.

"Maybe." Mike rubs his chin thoughtfully. "It kind of looks farther away than that, though. Maybe somebody else had the same idea. Which means we haven't lost yet."

"Look who's suddenly the optimist," Beth says, and smacks him on the arm.

"You know, speaking of surviving, we have power here. There's lots of food. Water. If we keep quiet, we could weather this. Assuming the tide turns our way, that is."

"No," Beth says. Her answer seems to surprise Mike. "No, we had a plan, we should stick to it. If there are others, we need to find them. We stop here for too long, we might not get the chance to go again. The power might not run out, but the food will. And the water. Then we'll just be trapped on the beach again."

"Okay." Mike smiles at her, and she smiles back.

More and more fireballs erupt in the distance, their glows reflecting off the mountains and lighting up the night. I prop my pillow against the wall and sit there, staring out the window with them, from the comfort and warmth of my bed.

Together, the three of us watch the darkness burn.

32

MIKE

We've scavenged everything we can possibly take from the house. Natalia's father was prepared for a storm, all right. We have a cooler filled with perishable fruits, vegetables, and cheese, along with several boxes of canned soups and beans, bags of nuts, and cartons of crackers. Beth found a stockpile of camping supplies in the garage, including propane tanks, a tiny heater, a camp stove, plenty of batteries, and flashlights. I hope not to put much of it to use along the way, but it's better to be ready for anything. And there's no telling how permanent our stay in Vernonia will be, or what might come next.

Beth packs changes of clothes, all the first aid supplies she can find, and the guns, of course. The rifle and shotgun she tucks into the back seat, and the hand cannon into a strap that fits snugly around her shoulder. Someday I might ask where her experience with firearms comes from. I might not. But I like feeling as if I have that choice. I like feeling that *someday* is a possibility again.

I strap a red plastic gas can to the Jeep's rear bumper, and Beth patches up the cracks in the windows with duct tape. It's tempting to just secure plywood over the cracked roof panel, but neither of us particularly want to lose sight of the sky. Natalia acts as lookout while we do all this, bouncing between her bedroom and her father's with those binoculars, but reports nothing suspicious outside. There are fallen trees and massive craters carved out of the landscape where the giant walked past us in the night, but it's far enough away now that we can no longer see it. I'm glad for that, but there's no telling what new horrors we'll meet as we head inland.

"I think we're ready," Beth announces after we've buckled Natalia in and triple-checked our list.

I put my ear to the garage door. I don't hear anything out there. "Go ahead and start it up," I tell Beth, making my way to the garage door button.

The only thing Natalia's father doesn't seem to have, for whatever reason, is an opener in his Jeep. Natalia insisted he always got out and punched the code in by hand. A minor inconvenience, but those extra seconds could be deadly if something is lying in wait out there.

"Be quick, Mike," Beth warns. "If something is outside, I'm running it over, and your butt better be in that seat next to me when I do."

"Yes, ma'am," I say with a salute. She isn't amused.

The moment the engine comes to life, I slap the button, and dawn light spills into the garage.

≈

The highway is surprisingly clear. The few cars we do pass are just far enough apart that Beth is able to steer around them. A truck is split in half on a power pole, the pole itself splintered at the base and lying in the trees. The lines caused a fire that has long since burned itself out. I hope that's not all we were seeing last night. The fireballs and explosions sure seemed like counterattacks of some sort. Guerrilla warfare. But I could have been wrong. They could just have been the dying breaths of our civilization.

There's the pessimist again. Stop that.

Beth doesn't dare drive above forty miles per hour. She's determined not to lose control of the Jeep under any circumstances. I have no complaints. As we drive by a passenger bus, lying on its side, the windows blessedly pointing toward the morning sky, I'm tempted to tell her thirty might even be fine.

Natalia stares at the bus with bulging eyes.

"It's all right," I try to reassure her. "This all happened yesterday. The monsters aren't here now." Which, as far as I can tell, is true enough.

"Where did they go?" she asks, and I honestly can't answer.

I don't know where they've gone any more than I know where they came from to begin with. Maybe they dissolved back into that other place over the course of the night. That's how they came to be here, it stands to reason they'll leave the same way. Could we really be that lucky?

"Turn here," I tell Beth as we approach a private road marked by Strawberry Dunes' weathered welcome sign. The gate is open, and there's a deer carcass lying in the road, little left but bones and fur.

"Why?" she asks. "You leave the stove on?"

"Actually, that isn't a bad idea."

She gives me an impatient look, but I don't elaborate. If I tell her what I plan to do, she'll keep right on driving. I know she doesn't want to make any pit stops if we can help it, but I need this one. And I promise her it will be quick.

≈≈

Beth pulls into my driveway, next to her beat-up old Toyota. I barely recognize my house. Not only because it feels like a lifetime has passed since I was here last but also because it's completely covered in hellvines. That answers the question of whether or not the alien life was taken back to where it belonged during the night. Unfortunately.

Fleshy ivy creeps up the cedar siding and across the shingled roof. The flower buds have blossomed into what appear to be Venus flytrap mouths full of spindly teeth. One of them is closed around a seagull, the bird's black, lifeless eyes staring out at us in surprise.

The HOA would have a fit if they saw this.

The hellvines, which undoubtedly sprouted from the bowling ball I hauled off the beach in the red bucket, have reached across the fence where Beth and I had our first conversation, creeping up the side of the house she was supposed to be looking after. I imagine she'll be forgiven for shirking her duties.

The grass and shrubbery, so meticulously maintained, is dead and withering, whether from the pollutants the vines pump into the air or by sheer proximity, I don't know. If their spread keeps up, entire forests could turn brown and collapse, hungry alien foliage rising from the ruins to claw at a sky that, by then, might barely be recognizable as our own. If we let it get that far.

"Oh wow," Beth gasps. "In a couple days, this whole street will be gone. Are you sure you have to go inside?"

"Yes."

"I really think I should go with you."

"Beth, it's okay," I tell her, taking the shotgun with me. "I've got this."

≈

The front door is the only way in. Fortunately, I left it unlocked. My key is still in the Subaru, and who even knows where that is by now. Maybe the cloudfish went back and ate it. Good riddance.

The view out the sliding door onto the back porch is completely obscured by purplish-brown vines. Thousands of tiny hairs squirm on their undersides, ready to stick into anything the vine grabs hold of. The glass is cracking. They'll be spilling into the house soon enough. There aren't any shriekers, though; that's a plus.

I make my way to the freezer. The smell in the kitchen is overwhelming. Like being in a closed garage with the car running. I'm already dizzy, my thoughts watery. I need to move faster, before I collapse.

Inside the freezer is Sarah's remaining fifth of vodka.

The cap comes off with a snap, and I wave the bottle around, showering the room. I splash the window, the icy liquid seeping through the cracks in the glass. The hellvines curl away angrily. If they don't like that, they're really going to hate what comes next.

At Beth's unintentional suggestion, I turn on all four gas stove burners. They hiss appreciatively. I don't turn on the flame, though. The flame will come soon. But there's one more thing I need. Well, a few things.

First I go to the bedroom and fill an overnight bag for Beth. Some clothes that might actually fit, underwear, a box of tampons. I'm sure there's more I'm not thinking of, but she'll probably at least be amused by my attempts.

Next, I go into the office.

Through the window, I see the trail into the dunes. The path I walked the night before last, Jake barking at me from next door. The path Sarah walked a year and one day ago, for the last time. She's looking back at me from the window. From inside that picture frame. I took that picture the first time we ever came to this beach. When we were young, and the future stretched as far as our imaginations.

I hear her coming up behind me again. Just as she did last night. Dragging her wet, bloated feet across the floor. I had a feeling she'd come. She's been here all along.

"You aren't her," I say. She stops in the doorway, water dripping onto the floor. "You're just the part they found in the tide that day. The part I chose to remember, to keep me company here, because I didn't think I deserved anything more."

I stay focused on the picture. On the way she was before I let her sink. Before I resurrected her to haunt me for what I'd let happen. I think it's the way she'd want me to remember her too. Not as some monster bent on torturing me into the same fate but as the person I fell in love with. Radiant and complicated and full of dreams.

"Please forgive me," I whisper. "I'm sorry it took me so long to ask."

She shuffles forward. When she speaks, it's in a voice that slices my heart in two. "I forgive you."

I wait for more. Because I know what's coming. This time I'm listening. This time I have an answer.

"So what's next?"

"I have no idea," I say. "And that scares the hell out of me. But I trust her. She'll get us wherever we need to be. I'm sorry for all the promises I never kept. I'm sorry for all the times I wasn't there. I won't make those mistakes again. I won't let either of them go. I hope that counts for something."

The room behind me is empty. For the first time in as long as I can remember, the house doesn't feel thick with her presence. I know now that I can leave, and I won't be abandoning her all over again. The picture folded into my pocket is a kindness more than anything. That last trace of her deserves better than what I'm going to give the hellvines. Her face will always be in my mind, though. Maybe not at the front, but that's okay. We have to keep moving forward. I think she knows that better than anybody.

I light a single match on the way out, and flick it into the kitchen. The vodka ignites with a *whoomf,* and I walk out of the house and into whatever's next.

≈≈

"You should hear this," Beth says, not seeming to notice the house going up in flames behind me. She turns up the volume of the radio.

A man's voice rises through the static. I recognize it instantly, and my heart sinks. "This is Jared Jessup, coming to you from Vernonia, Oregon, home of the famous Friendship Jamboree and Logging Show. That could be the reason these bastards are keeping their distance. They took one look at what our lumberjacks can do to a Doug fir and decided to just keep moving—"

I turn it down. "So it is just playing on a loop," I say, hoping the disappointment isn't obvious in my voice.

"Maybe he just needed a bathroom break," Beth says. I can't even pretend to laugh. "Or, yeah, maybe they're all gone, and it's just playing on a loop. Both options are equally possible."

"I don't know if I'd say 'equally.'"

The flames devour the inside of my house. The roof begins to steam. It's downright cold outside this morning, yesterday's heat wave a thing of the past. There's a familiar dampness in the air. It's going to rain today. Fall is finally upon us.

"Hey," Beth says, taking my hand and squeezing hard, like she's never planning on letting go. "I don't want to hear any downer shit from you."

"I'm not," I say, squeezing back, looking into her eyes. Once again, I feel that swell lift me up off the seat, and this time I let myself drift with it, my hand still locked safely with hers, secure in the knowledge that wherever it takes me, we'll be there together. "Honestly, looped message or not, Vernonia still feels like the place to go. If you and me survived, then I think the human race has a pretty decent chance."

"Good." Beth turns the Jeep around and drives away from my house, her car, and Strawberry Dunes—forever.

"If there's nobody there, where do we go next?" Natalia asks. "Portland?"

"Sure," Beth answers, turning onto Highway 101 and punching the gas and speeding into the dawn. "We're alive. And we have hope. I say, no matter what, we're heading in the right direction."

ACKNOWLEDGMENTS

I have to thank Amanda Jain and Kristin Temple, my wonderful agent and editor respectively, for taking a chance on me and this story. From a one-sentence Twitter pitch to the pages I'm looking at now, your keen eyes, expert guidance, and endless patience, during a global pandemic no less, made publishing *Black Tide* not only possible, but a true joy for me. You saw exactly which edges to file down and which others to sharpen to give this book just the bite it needed. Thank you.

Likewise, thank you to the rest of the Tor Nightfire team: Andrew King, Alexis Saarela, Dakota Griffin, Esther Kim, Jordan Hanley, Sarah Pannenberg, Emily Hughes, and Michael Dudding. It has been an absolute honor to have so many talented and passionate people working to make this a real thing.

I also want to thank Erik Howell and Matt Misetich for helping me shape the screenplay (and so many others) that would eventually become this book and for keeping me propped up and hammering at the keyboard through my darkest and most insufferable times. Twelve years and too many drafts to count is a lot to give, and I owe you for every word. Seriously, I love you guys.

And speaking of support, I owe a lifetime of gratitude to my family. Mom, Heidi, Bill, Don, Sue, and of course, my amazing wife, Kendra. Thank you all for your brutally honest feedback, the time and energy you've sacrificed so that I could pursue this dream, and your stubborn refusal to let me give up.

Also, Dad, thank you for your unwavering faith that someday this would happen in some medium or another, even though you never got to see it.

And lastly, I want to thank my readers, the real reason any of us do this. I hope this story lingers with you for as long as it's haunted me.

KCJ

ABOUT THE AUTHOR

After graduating from the University of Nevada, Las Vegas with a degree in film production, KC JONES returned to the Pacific Northwest to focus on a career in screenwriting before making the leap to novels. When not writing, he can usually be found cooking, playing video and board games, or exploring the local wilderness with his wife. *Black Tide* is his debut novel.

kcjonespnw.com
Twitter: @PNWScribe